Lost American Fiction

Edited by Matthew J. Bruccoli

The title for this series, "Lost American Fiction," is unsatisfactory. A more accurate series title would be "Forgotten Works of American Fiction That Deserve a New Public"—which states the rationale for reprinting these titles. No claim is made that we are resuscitating lost masterpieces, although a couple of the titles may well qualify. We are reprinting works that merit re-reading because they are now social or literary documents—or just because they are good writing. It isn't that simple, of course, for Southern Illinois University Press is a scholarly publisher; and we have serious ambitions for the series. We expect that "Lost American Fiction" will revive some books and authors from undeserved obscurity and that the series will therefore plug some of the holes in American literary history. Of course, we hope to find an occasional lost masterpiece.

Twelve titles have been published in the series, with four more in production. The response has been encouraging. We are gratified that many readers share our conviction that one of the proper functions of a university press is to rescue good writing from oblivion.

M. J. B.

Continued from front flap

A quiet masterpiece by a member of the group of writers who emerged in the 30s, one of the group of notable women who are the precursors of today's feminists, *The Wedding* is both an affirmation of the continuing vitality of the storyteller's art and a finely-wrought novel of Southern life at the turn of the century.

The Wedding is the third of Grace Lumpkin's novels. In spite of excellent reviews, it had only one printing in 1939, and soon dropped from sight. Her first novel, *To Make My Bread,* won the Maxim Gorky prize for the best labor novel of the year in 1932; but her second novel, *A Sign for Cain* (1935) was flawed by leftist didacticism. Along with many other writers during the depression years Miss Lumpkin was touched and troubled by the Communist influence. Though not a member of the party, she wrote for it under pressure, and was a friend of Wittaker Chambers, to whom she loaned all her savings at the time he was preparing his dramatic break from the party.

Like other writers of the Great Depression, whose reputations now are being given a rehabilitative new look, Miss Lumpkin has remained known only to serious students of American literature and has been underappreciated until now.

The Wedding is a significant addition to the small shelf of the American novel of manners. It is permanently valuable as social history, but it is also a perfectly controlled work of literary art in which Miss Lumpkin compels the reader to share the characters' concerns.

As in the novels of Jane Austen, nothing exciting happens in the most convincing way. The story is literally nothing but an account of the marriage of Jennie Middleton, the eldest living daughter of a ruined aristocratic family who live by the code of the Confederacy, and Dr. Gregg, a tough, earthy mountain man, from their quarrel the night before the wedding to the description of the ceremony going off on schedule despite it.

However, the novel recounts with great fidelity the period of the South when there was little money but considerable compensatory pride. In Miss Lumpkin's handling of details, the Southern town of 1909 comes to life visibly—the minister showing his authority by refusing to let the Bishop replace him; the old Confederate veterans confusing the Middle-

Continued on back flap

lthier branch of the family; n which traditions are all the and the bridesmaids reflect- be if they could be widows eing wives; and the pathetic, amily, trotting about obedi-

dding is low keyed, its tone on of romantic comedy; the all its spiraling human rela- es in a happy outcome, ful- tation that the lover's quarrel d and that the wedding will ot, involving the children, ll suspense.

n Gilkes writes in her After- n, "has given us to date two to be considered classics, a d short stories and one long he finest examples of Ameri- e. For these Grace Lumpkin llege literature courses, along peers: Eudora Welty, Kath- on McCullers, [and] Flannery

GILKES has taught creative niversity and elsewhere and writer and a book reviewer. a Crane: A Biography of Mrs. es in Tryon, North Carolina.

he Lost American Fiction 976)

Kelley—$7.95
Turns to Love by John Thomas

ka by Harold Loeb—$7.95
h Summers Kelley—$8.95
t Flanner—$8.95
French Whitman—$8.95
Robert M. Coates—$7.95
by James Ross—$8.95
al Romance by Lincoln Kirstein

oad by Donald Ogden Stewart—

oyd Phillip Gibbons—$9.85
umpkin—$8.95

The Wedding

By Grace Lumpkin

With an Afterword by Lillian Barnard Gilkes
And A Postscript by Grace Lumpkin

SOUTHERN ILLINOIS UNIVERSITY PRESS
Carbondale and Edwardsville

Feffer & Simons, Inc.
London and Amsterdam

Library of Congress Cataloging in Publication Data
Lumpkin, Grace.
   The wedding.
   (Lost American fiction)
   Reprint of the ed. published by L. Furman, New York.
   I.   Title.
PZ3.L9712We5   [PS3523.U54]   813'.5'2   75-28481
ISBN 0-8093-0767-7

THE WEDDING

I

THE year before Jennie Middleton's marriage Lexington was a town of thirty thousand people. Twelve months later the population was increased by thirty thousand souls. Citizens, especially business men, coughed apologetically when they gave the old census by mistake and proudly changed the figure to sixty thousand. The Superintendent of Schools sent out a memorandum to his teachers telling them to emphasize the new census in their classes. Strangers wondered at the curious and miraculous growth in population.

But there was a simple explanation. That year for the first time two outlying sections of the community were included in the city limits. One of these was to the northeast of town between the original city and the state asylum for the insane. Most of the colored people lived in this section. The other part of the community which the city fathers voted to include was the factory district. The mills, which spread over a large acreage of ground, were some distance beyond the Union Station, but near enough so that early in the morning, at midday, and at evening the sound of the factory whistles mingled with the sounds that came from the engines in the yard of the station.

The city fathers also tried to include in the new census a town just on the other side of the sluggish yellow Santee River. This small town was reached by a steel bridge. The people who lived there were descendants of Germans who arrived there about 1850 and established a prosperous farming community. These farmers did not wish to have the town they had built lose its identity in that of a larger city. And since their prosperity made them independent they were able to vote to keep Beckersville intact. This was done not because they had any quarrel with Lexington. They were peaceful folk. The only quarrel they ever had was with the state officials over the State Prison. It was too near to Beckersville for their comfort. The Penitentiary was built in a curve of the Santee River only three miles below the bridge which connected Beckersville with Lexington. The record of the prison showed that no inmate even if he managed to climb the wall had ever succeeded in getting beyond the treacherous muddy bank of the river. But the people of Beckersville always felt anxious about escaped convicts, and to this day they embarrass politicians during a campaign with demands for the removal of the penitentiary.

The Penitentiary was just outside the city limits, but it was not included in the new census. Its inmates did not find any deprivation in this, because they were not citizens and had no property whose value might be increased.

The value of property did increase in Lexington. In fact the sudden attention to population was caused by the wish to increase the value of property. Some of the wealthier citizens wished to attract new and prosperous business concerns to the city. And they knew that a large population would impress those they wished to attract. They were right. Lexington began to wake from a long slumber in which it had rested since the march of Sherman to the sea. Sherman had been like the wicked fairy who put the princess to sleep. For years the city had been like the sleeping beauty drowsily quiet. But just at the time of the Middleton wedding a new factory was built by people from Massachusetts. Other enterprises were started. The magic kiss of business was beginning to wake the town. She yawned, stretched and held out her arms in welcome to the newcomers.

Probably most inhabitants of Lexington knew nothing about Jennie Middleton. But in certain groups her wedding caused almost as much talk as the shooting of the editor and owner of the largest newspaper in the state some years before. The crowd that collected in front of the Episcopal church the evening of the wedding reminded people of the crowd which had come there when the editor was shot and killed in broad daylight by a political opponent. From behind the walls of this church the murderer walked out on the street to meet his unsuspecting victim.

A monument was raised to the editor's memory. The monument stood in the middle of Lady Street under a large oak tree. Along the whole length of this street, stretching east for many blocks great trees like this oak grew at regular intervals along the sidewalks.

The Middletons lived on one of these blocks. Their home was a nine-room house with a wide lawn. In summer the shrubbery and trees on the lawn concealed the shabbiness of the house, but in winter only two pine trees remained green and the house, which had not been painted for years spread out drab and dilapidated behind the two green trees. But in spite of its shabby winter aspect the house managed to give an appearance of festivity in December, 1909, because it was filled to overflowing with guests for the wedding. All the guests were young people and for several days before the wedding their voices, sounding all over the house on the verandah and on the lawn, because the weather was clear and the sun warm outside, seemed by their very cheerfulness and joy to predict a happy life for the bride and groom.

But unexpectedly on the very evening before the wedding, the bride and groom had a bitter quarrel.

II

THAT night the bride lay uneasy and sleepless in her bed. In his hotel room far uptown the groom slept. He was a doctor and accustomed to getting what rest he could under the most trying circumstances.

Dr. Gregg was born in a great log house at the side of a beautiful valley on Black Creek high up in the mountains. There were seven children, six of them boys. The father was a stern old man with a long beard, whose shoulders never bent unless at work and whose will was not known to bend to anyone. He felt that his first duty to society and to himself was to break the wills of his children and he did this thoroughly just as he broke the wills of the colts that ran wild on the mountains until it was time for them to be made gentle. His sons inherited determination and energy from both the father and mother, but in some of them the will was gone. The mother had been a plump, rosy-cheeked mountain girl and remained plump and rosy-cheeked even in her old age. She liked a joke and was romantic. There was a book of poems her mother had owned which she liked to read and when her oldest son was born she named him for the poet, Percy Bysshe Shelley. He was the son who became a doctor.

The old man owned many fertile valleys and mountain peaks around Black Creek. He was careful with money and knew how to save and how to work hard and make his family work. When he had accumulated enough money the great two-storied log cabin his ancestors had built was torn down and another house put up. The new house was very ugly. In that valley between the high mountains leaning up to the sky and sloping gently from the meadows where the cows grazed the new house was a blemish. It was square with an el and covered with plaster on which many small rocks were dashed before the plaster hardened. Inside the house there was new furniture ordered by mail from pictures in a catalogue. A spool bed of old maple, left over from the old house, stood in the same room with a sofa upholstered in bright red and green velvet. An old walnut secretary stood against the wall in a corner and beside it was a row of bright varnished oak chairs.

This home was built after Doctor Shelley Gregg had already gone through college and medical school, supported partly by the money which came from the fertile valley his father cultivated and partly by his own earnings. In the summers he worked hard on the farm. He was accustomed to work. When he was seven his father woke him at daybreak and told him to go out and milk the cows. He had never milked them, but he did not say this to his father. He went out and learned. From that time on, except when he was in school he worked steadily on the farm. There was no cheap colored labor in the mountains and old Mr. Gregg hired men only at harvest time. In later years friends of the doctor wondered at his pleasure in dawdling. But they did not understand about his father. No one ever dawdled when the old man was near. His wife might be sitting with friends talking and laughing, but when the tall gray-bearded silent old man came in she became uneasy and said there was work to do in the kitchen. Even visitors felt in his presence that they should be at some kind of work and those who were less controlled felt their hands fluttering uneasily.

Young Gregg disliked his name and was glad when friends began to call him Doc. They did this when he was still a boy because he took care of the animals that were hurt and helped to deliver the colts and calves that were born on the place. Also people noticed that he took a special interest in slaughtering. He could cut the pork and beef better than anyone on the farm. Once, to show his brothers and the hired men during the harvest season that he was not squeamish he caught a live robin and bit its head off. He spit the head out and stood triumphantly before them with the still quivering body of the red-breasted bird in his hand. But he was very tender with the sick animals.

His first experience with a woman was at the age of sixteen. Drusilla McCabe had gone down from Black Creek to Mountain City and had become a prostitute

used by the tuberculous patients who swarmed there.
She came back to the mountains sick with the disease,
but more beautiful than ever with the flush that many
people in the last stages of the sickness have on their
cheeks. The illness made her thinner than she had been
and this thinness only added to her beauty. It made her
dainty and fragile. She was eighteen, two years older
than Gregg. They slipped away in the evening after his
work was done and lay together on the open face of a
mountain. The daisies that grew there were crushed beneath them. She told him about Mountain City and how
she had stayed for two nights in one of the fine hotels
where the rich tourists came. He did not talk, only listened and watched her and when it was necessary to
him he touched her. She died early that fall before all
the flowers had disappeared from the mountains.

When he was thirty-two and already had a good
practice in Mountain City the doctor met Jennie Middleton in a rustic hotel. Most of his remunerative practice came from the tourists, people who stayed in the
expensive hotels or took large houses for the season to
escape the mosquitoes and heat of the lowlands. There
were others who came from the north and west because
Mountain City was a fashionable resort. But the Doctor still kept his old patients, some of whom lived far
out in the country. When these patients could not pay
he was indifferent, but with the others who could he
demanded what he felt was just. He was close with
money just as his father had been and was able to save
and invest in property and bonds. He fell in love with

Jennie at once. She was dainty and fragile with olive skin, a pointed face, brown wavy hair and brilliant dark brown eyes. The brilliant dark eyes said that this girl who appeared so reserved, so different in culture and knowledge of another sort of life from that he had experienced, was nevertheless a girl like Drusilla. He was afraid of her and yet deep in himself he laughed at her tenderly. When he was a young boy at school his teacher was a revered being to him. She knew so much more than any of them knew. And there was one thing that made him especially reverent. She had a clean handkerchief every day. At that time he thought that kings and queens and princesses who were mentioned in the history books did not have the same needs as everyday folk. And in his mind he put his teacher in the same category with a princess, not quite so high, but almost as remote. All of this foolishness had been left far behind when he met Jennie Middleton. But some of the admiration for fragility remained in him.

At the time he met Jennie everyone called him Doctor. Some of his older friends from the mountains called him Doc, but his nickname did not represent any lack of respect. It seemed natural for people to call him Doctor, not because he had the manner of a doctor or put on any special dignity. But in his manner there was a suggestion that he had always been mature with mature thoughts. He talked very little and yet everyone after talking with him seemed to feel that he had understood them. He was never especially polite to his patients and did not like them to confide in him.

At thirty-two he was prematurely bald in a spot exactly on the top of his head, like a monk. The rest of his head was covered with fine curling hair. His eyes were deep blue with the long lashes that people from the mountains often have. They were almost girlish. But the rest of his face was exceedingly masculine, broad and ugly with a thick nose and a large ugly kind mouth. He was not tall like his father, but was tall enough, and his body was thick-set with large bones and broad shoulders. Above his mouth was a silky moustache lighter than his hair. He was ugly and yet people were heard to say that he was a very handsome man. He never tried to make himself agreeable and everyone found him agreeable and liked and trusted him. He wore his well-tailored and expensive clothes carelessly, using and not showing them.

This was the way he appeared to Jennie Middleton when she was introduced to him in the lobby of the hotel. She had never met anyone like him. She came from the lowlands and her people had always lived in the lowlands.

Her first ancestor on her father's side came from England and settled in Virginia in the seventeenth century. He was loyal to the Stuarts and hated William and Mary, the monarchs who had stolen the throne from the Stuarts. He disliked the Governor they sent to Virginia. In September of the year 1690 he was summoned to a court to answer to charges of "seditious, unlawful and dangerous words expressed against their Majestyes and their present Governour." A witness said that when in a company of people who were drinking to their "Majestyes" this ancestor of Jennie's "sleighted itt and refused to put off his hat," and afterward "mounting his horse swore he was as good a man as ye Govenr and swore God dam him if he were there he would fight him."

The ancestor refused to be tried and the matter was dropped. But the account of the swearing ancestor can still be found in the court records.

In 1780 two of this ancestor's grandsons migrated further south carrying their slaves with them. The caravan of one brother consisted of a coach and four white horses, two large wagons with five mules, a two-horse wagon, a Desbon wagon and a sulky, besides fourteen horses and mules. The land in Virginia had been made unproductive by repetitions of the same crop and these men were delighted with the fertile new soil. The two brothers settled in different parts of the same county and prospered. As children grew up in the two families one side developed more ability than the other. The direct ancestors of Jennie Middleton were content to live a quiet country life, farming, hunting and taking part in the county life as justices of the peace. At that time these county offices did not pay any salary and only those men who were called gentlemen, that is, those who were planters with slaves, were able to accept such positions. They considered it their duty to do so.

The other branch of the family became more distinguished. They were chosen for high political offices

in the state and in Washington. They prospered finan-
cially and built one of the old-fashioned mansions in
the low-country on a rice plantation, in addition to the
great brick house they had built in the city.

Robert Middleton, Jennie's father, was fourteen years
old when the Civil War ended. He had fought during
the last eight months of the war. During Reconstruction
he ploughed the land over which he had expected to rule
as a master of slaves. Later when the radicals who had
wished to give each head of a family of ex-slaves forty
acres and a mule had been driven out of the South and
the Negroes had been forced to go back into the fields
as day-laborers, Robert Middleton became a lawyer.
When he began to practice law people predicted that
he would become as brilliant as the lawyers on the other
side of the family. He married and he and his wife
struggled to keep him at his law practice. But at that
time there were many lawyers in the South and few
clients with money. He kept his office for eight years.
Then the five children died during an epidemic of
diphtheria and the expenses of their illness forced
Robert to give up his law practice. He loosened the
reins of his ambition just as a man who cannot hold
them any longer might let the reins drop when he has
given up the struggle with a run-a-way horse. Robert
gave up his law office and took a small salaried position
in another state.

He became one of that large group of Southerners
who had many traditions behind them, but no promise
for the future. Some of these men accepted their life

and enjoyed it in a quiet simple manner. Others were continually disturbed by the contrast between their traditions of comparative grandeur and the present reality. Robert Middleton felt the bitterness of his meagre salary and his lost independence. Though he tried to reconcile himself he was never actually reconciled to the loss of past glory. He always promised himself and his wife that he would go back to practicing law and even kept his license framed on the wall of his small office. But in his heart he knew that this would never happen. From the day he began to work as a salaried employee of a railroad Robert began to project his lost ambitions and tireless energy into the lives of his children.

Jennie was his favorite child and she clung to him with passionate loyalty. When she was a child some man during a heated political discussion threatened her father's life. He told the story at home. Robert Middleton did not take the threat seriously. But for almost a year Jennie remembered it. If her father sat near a window she imagined the assassin was just outside waiting in the darkness with a revolver. She would suddenly go to the window behind her father and pull down the shade or close the blinds. Or she would beg her father to change to another chair. No one knew what was disturbing the little girl. They had forgotten the threat long ago.

As she grew into young womanhood Jennie's father watched her jealously. Eventually it became necessary for her to leave home to earn her own living. But even when she was away from him Jennie felt her father's watchful eyes on her. She was oppressed by a consciousness of his opinion and the feeling that his eyes were watching whatever she did.

Just as she had imagined the eyes of the assassin watching her father through the window when she was a child, in the same way, when she was older, she felt her father's presence. If a young man was with her alone and tried to touch her except in the most formal manner she drew back from him filled with a sense of guilt and fear.

III

AT school Jennie was a brilliant student and before her twentieth year was teaching dramatic expression in a college for women. Just after her graduation Mr. Middleton borrowed some money and took her to New York for a six months' course at a school for actors. This study helped to prepare Jennie for the teaching position and in the summers she attended a dramatic school in Mountain City. The first summer Jennie went to Mountain City with friends of her father's and stayed with them in a hotel until they found a suitable boarding house kept by people from her own state and one that did not take tuberculous patients. She was still watched carefully by her father as if he distrusted her and all mankind. But the responsibility for her weighed on him so that without realizing that he did so Mr. Middleton looked forward to the time when he might transfer his responsibility for Jennie to a husband.

It was in the hotel where she was chaperoned by Mr. and Mrs. Bell that Jennie met Dr. Gregg. From the very evening when he met her in the hotel lobby Dr. Gregg saw Jennie as much as possible. A year later in

the month of June, just after she returned to her home
for the vacation, he visited her in Lexington.

One evening he and Jennie came in from a small
party at a neighbor's. It was late. The wide street was
silent. As they mounted the steps to the venandah there
was no sound in the house though the downstairs lights
were on. The moonflowers that grew on the trellis of
the verandah were open and appeared startlingly white
against the dark background of the vines. The weather
was warm and Jennie and the Doctor remained on the
porch hardly speaking but kept together by that mutual
attraction which has such a peculiar charm and delight
when it is secretly felt and unacknowledged. And then
with an exclamation of pleasure Jennie saw that the
night-blooming cereus which grew in a tub on the
verandah had opened. They bent over the tub in which
the cereus was planted. The brilliant white petals and
the yellow pistils still quivered from the amazing energy
that had accumulated in the stem and produced this one
flower after so many years. The flower was not fully
open and each petal quivered and shook with the force
that came into it from the plant as the flower opened
wider before their eyes.

As they leaned over the tub the Doctor let his arm
slip gently across Jennie's shoulders as if that were the
most natural position for him to take. His hand closed
over her shoulder with a strong pressure and he pulled
her closer to him. Suddenly she could not see the flower
any longer. Her eyes blurred. Her body trembled just
as the flower was trembling. With his other arm the

Doctor pulled her up to him and kissed her on the mouth. She returned the kiss. And then without a word of explanation he let her go and ran down the steps and across the lawn and on to the street as if he were trying to run away not only from her but from himself. She heard his heavy footsteps on the sidewalk as he went down the deserted street.

Those steps taking him away were to remain in her memory to torture her, because the Doctor did not return the next day or the next or for many days. During that time Jennie was consumed by a strong anger and impatience against him.

She longed to go to her father and tell him to bring this man back to her. But knowing her father's strict, his almost fanatical attitude about a girl's behavior with men, she did not dare to admit that she had kissed the Doctor. And she knew that her mother shared the stern attitude, only with her mother it was reinforced by a religious authority. So Jennie felt that her mother and father were enemies because they could never understand that kiss and would be opposed to it unless it were presented to them along with a promise of marriage. She even felt that everyone was her enemy because neighbors, relatives, friends, even those residents of the city whom she did not know, would also be opposed to that kiss and any others which might follow unless they were sanctified by a promise of marriage. And because she felt this pressure she hated the Doctor because he had not immediately put the kiss on the proper basis. It seemed that he had robbed her of the natural right of a woman. He should have put her in the position not of one who waited anxiously for some word, but of the person who was given an opportunity to make a choice.

At times it gave her pleasure to plan how she would humiliate him before other people if he did return. At other moments, if she heard a voice in the hall or on the street that reminded her of his deep pleasing voice she forgot her plans and only knew that it was necessary for her to see him again and have his arms around her again.

And all her plans for his humiliation vanished when she actually did hear his voice in the hall one evening while they were at supper. Her brother, Hugh, went to answer the door and when he came in and said the Doctor was in the living-room she could not rise from her chair. All the members of the family, sitting there at the table, stared at her as if she were a stranger. Finally she roused herself and went into the living-room.

At once, looking ashamed and with a strained smile the Doctor asked her to marry him. He asked her quickly, sharply, almost angrily as if he did this against his will. As soon as she saw him Jennie's only impulse was to reach out and touch him again. When they were in each other's embrace, very close as they had been that other evening, the Doctor seemed to be relieved of a burden so that he was no longer rather ashamed and angry but became himself again, good-natured and self-contained. And he remained so even when it was neces-

sary for him to ask Mr. Middleton if he and Jennie had
the parents' consent to the engagement.

When Jennie appeared at the dramatic school in
Mountain City that summer she was wearing a large
diamond on her left hand and everyone understood that
she was engaged. The date for the wedding was not
fixed. People at the dramatic school became accustomed
to seeing the Doctor's expensive and luxurious buggy
and his team of black horses outside the school where
he often waited for Jennie when the afternoon sessions
were over.

One evening Jennie promised to go to a concert with
the Doctor. A well-known symphony orchestra came to
Mountain City from the North for two weeks every
summer and the Doctor had season tickets. This was
the evening of the first concert. But that very evening
the Doctor received a call from an old friend out in the
mountains. The son had broken his leg. There were
clouds over the mountains that surrounded the city
and even the air smelt of rain when the Doctor drove
by Jennie's boarding house to tell her that he could not
go to the concert. He offered her the tickets. But when
she heard that he was driving out into the mountains
Jennie insisted on going with him. He hesitated to take
her because of the storm. Yet he wanted her. And she
insisted so fearlessly and was so lovable in her insistence the Doctor could not refuse.

His buggy was large and roomy and had a deep
spring-cushioned seat. He put up the storm curtains be-

fore they left, only leaving the front curtain a little way down on his side so he could see better to drive.

Before they were out of town the rain began to spatter on the curtains. They left the lights of the town behind and followed a road that curved sharply around the bulging sides of the mountains. On one side of the road there was a steep ravine and on the other the side of the mountain. Lightning began to come in sharp flashes and thunder followed it. But within the shelter of the storm curtains with the Doctor beside her Jennie had no feeling of danger. The lightning showed her the face of her companion. It was calm as he leaned slightly forward. There was a smile on his lips under the moustache as if he felt a sort of joy in the concentration needed for keeping the horses on the road. By leaning toward him Jennie was able to see what was ahead. The rain spattering on her face was pleasant to her. She saw the dark forms of the horses as they dragged the buggy up a steep hill or as they reared back as the wheels slipped in the mud going down a slope. At the front of the buggy she saw the puny lights of the carriage lamps. When a flash of lightning came she saw the great trees on the left standing like ghost trees in the greenish light of the electrical storm. And just in front the polished nickel of the harness gleamed on the backs of the horses. She saw their long manes flying upward.

When they slid around a sharp curve and she felt the deep and black threat of the ravine below them she held to the bars at her side. But she was not afraid. As they began to descend the wheels slid more often in the mud. The darkness became thicker and there were trees on both sides of the road sheltering them from the sharper flashes of lightning. But the thunder was like a giant whip that cracked the side of the mountain just beside them and then cracked the range far off beyond the ravine.

As they descended Jennie heard another sound which was different from the thunder. It was a sound that continued. At first it was like the heavy beating of a heart that has been strained by running. And then the sound became louder. It was in front of them, a heavy pounding rushing sound. The wheels of the buggy left the mud and grated over rocks and pebbles. A flash of lightning showed her what was ahead. It was a body of water rushing down from the mountains. A whole mound of foam was pushed up on the surface of the water. She saw the Doctor turn his head slightly toward her. He opened his mouth and his lips moved. But she could not hear what he shouted. She clung to the back of the seat. The trees that had been overhanging the road disappeared. The lightning came sharp and clear and the thunder sounded nearer. But along with the thunder was the boiling sound of the river. With the shelter of the trees gone the rain pelted their faces. The Doctor tore down his side of the storm curtain. He leaned forward tensely and his hands gripped the reins tighter. Jennie saw the horses pause for an instant and then their heads disappeared and appeared again with the water flowing around them. The buggy teetered at

the edge of the steep ford and rolled down into the boiling mass of water. The horses struggled. Their heads
bent and lifted. Their hoofs slipped on the rocks of the
ford. In the center of the stream they swam for a little
way. The torrent pushed them always toward the left
and as it did so the Doctor continually pulled them
toward the right. A lightning flash showed the horse at
the right with its head twisted that way. Its mouth was
open, resisting the bit, and the teeth gleamed. The round
haunches of the animals went down under the water as
they struggled up the opposite bank. The buggy slanted
from one side to the other so that it seemed it would
overturn. Jennie felt the Doctor's body press against
her heavily and then she was leaning on him clinging
desperately to the edge of the buggy.

Finally they were upright on land again and under
overhanging trees that protected them from the rain.
The water had reached the seat of the buggy and they
were drenched from the torrent and from the rain.
Suddenly as they drove along the road, almost peaceful
in contrast to the flood, the Doctor put his arm out
and drew Jennie close to him. He said nothing but she
knew by that caress that he approved of her and loved
her. She was exalted by the excitement of the ride, by
the lightning and thunder which still sounded about
them and the dull far-off roar of the flood which was
behind. The caress added to her excitement. She knew
that she loved her Doctor exaltedly and that their love
was different from that of all other beings.

This feeling continued in her after they reached the

Calhouns' farmhouse, though there was a moment when she felt lost and insecure and resentful. That moment was when the Doctor forgot her. He followed the mother and father to the bed where the boy was covered with a quilt. The Doctor wrenched off his raincoat, pulled back the covers and bent over the boy. There was low talk that Jennie could not hear. All of them had forgotten that she was there. The woman bent over the bed with a lamp in her hand holding it close and then further away as the Doctor's hands went over the boy. The child groaned.

The Doctor took off his coat and rolled back his sleeves. They pulled up a table and the woman set the lamp on it and hurried into the other room and brought back a kettle of steaming water and a pan. While she was gone the Doctor remembered Jennie. He spoke to Mr. Calhoun, who beckoned to Jennie and led her into another room. This was the parlor of the house. Mr. Calhoun lighted a fire in the wide old chimney and returned to the other room. There was no lamp in the parlor but the light from the log in the fireplace showed up the furniture. There was a bed in one corner with a heavy counterpane and embroidered pillow covers, a table with a crocheted cover, two chairs and an organ. Jennie sat down in a low chair by the fire and took off her shoes and stockings which were soaked with water from the flood. Her skirt began to steam as the fire dried it out. She had recovered from the moment of resentment at being forgotten and thought of her future husband in the next room with an immense pride in him. She remembered how Mr. and Mrs. Calhoun looked on him as if he were some god who had come out of the storm to help them. He gave short clear orders which the parents hurried to obey and then they waited breathlessly for him to speak again. Jennie felt that this man who was to be her husband held the power of life over death. He was life. This was what he meant to people. He was a triumphant being.

She heard a scream in the next room. After the scream the child continued to moan. There was a sharp order from the Doctor. Then heavy significant footsteps. And then quiet. There were more footsteps. The moaning became lower and then quieted. The Doctor laughed cheerfully and hopefully. The man and woman talked in voices that sounded cheerful like the Doctor's voice.

The door between the two rooms opened and the Doctor came in pulling down his sleeves. He sat opposite Jennie in a large hickory arm-chair. Mrs. Calhoun brought in two cups of coffee in heavy thick cups. Her husband, a tall stooping man, came behind her. He had a jug in his hand and the weight of the jug seemed to make him stoop more.

"Have another, Doc?" he asked. The Doctor drank his coffee down and held out his cup. The whiskey gurgled from the mouth of the jug into the cup. He drank it at one swallow.

"Have some?" Mr. Calhoun asked Jennie in his slow, quiet voice. "It'll keep you from catching cold, won't it, Doc?"

Jennie held out her cup. "Only a little," she begged.
Both men laughed. Jennie sipped the whiskey. It was
the first she had ever tasted. It burned her throat un-
pleasantly. But after it was down she felt warm and
comfortable. The effect did not wear off at once. All
the details of the room and the people before her appeared clearer than before. She saw Mrs. Calhoun's
leathery face and all the wrinkles in it and the soft tender curve of her mouth that was different from the
harsh wrinkles. Mrs. Calhoun spoke to her. She spoke
in a voice that was almost without sound. She said, "If
you get sleepy there's the bed." And Jennie understood
that it was impossible for them to return that night.

The Calhouns left them to go to the other room and
presently the whole house was quiet. Outside the wind
was still making the trees bend, but the thunder came
at longer intervals. The Doctor put some wood on the
fire and the flame crackled up into the chimney. Jennie
did not look at the Doctor but she felt that he was
looking at her bare feet and drew her feet under her
skirt.

"You can lie down," the Doctor said. She looked at
him. He was smiling in a way that she had not seen
before. Jennie stood up in her bare feet. The bare floor-
ing was rough to her feet. She said, "goodnight," shyly.
As she went toward the bed the Doctor leaned forward,
put out his hand and drew her to him. She stood within
his arm and a rapture she had not felt before took hold
of her as she leaned against him. He pulled her down
to his knees.

"Are your feet cold?" he asked. There was excitement in his voice. It was rough and tender. He put his large square hand over one of her feet and held it toward the fire in the same way that a mother holds the foot of her child to warm it. He said nothing. Her arm was about his shoulder. As she had felt when she was close to him in the buggy out in the storm Jennie had a sense of protection and security. But there was an additional feeling of lassitude and pleasure in surrender. This was new and strange and yet not strange at all. It seemed natural and right. It seemed right not to think of anyone or anything beyond the man who held her so closely to him. As he spread his hands over her, feeling her shoulders and her face she was still. His spread-out hand covered her breast. A vague uneasiness stirred in her at this touch. But it remained dim and unreal like a voice that shouts far off on the side of a mountain and can not be heard distinctly because of the distance. At the same time she was overwhelmed by an ecstatic joy. For the first time in her life her whole being, her body and her mind, her thoughts and dissatisfactions, her joy were completely fused into one self so that there was not any division in her. Only a complete acceptance and joy.

Her lover moved. His spread fingers went to her thigh. They moved softly, but this further caress startled her. It waked her from the ecstasy like a pitcher of cold water wakes a person who has been in a deep slumber. She struggled out of his arms. Now she was terrified and angry. Her mind became alive and vigorous and critical. She felt weak and exposed. And she saw how strong he was and that he could take something from her. And that he had no right to take what he wished. She felt as a person does who finds that another is trying to cheat him out of a great and valuable possession. And she was weak like a person who has nothing with which to defend his possession. She was being cheated and hated him for trying to cheat her. This man whom she had trusted was a cheater and swindler.

She stood far on the other side of the fireplace hating him. And at the same time she was frustrated. It seemed that life also had cheated her.

The Doctor looked at her. His face was blank and unresponsive. She was very lovely with the firelight on her. Her dark brilliant eyes showed plainly what was happening in her and the indignation that she was feeling. Her chin was lifted. The firelight shone on her olive skin and dark hair which she had loosened so that it could dry. But he did not look on her with approval. There was a light contemptuous smile on his face. He drew back into himself ashamed like a boy who has been accused unjustly. And he was proud and contemptuous.

Jennie did not go to the bed. She was afraid. They sat across from each other for the rest of the night with the fire between them, hating each other with a dry resentful hate. As soon as possible in the morning they drove back. The stream was swollen but in the night it had gone down and by daylight did not seem nearly so dangerous.

Jennie shut herself against the Doctor. She wished to punish him because he had tried to cheat her. And she succeeded. He was very unhappy until the quarrel was made up a week later. Only there was left in each of them a feeling of obscure resentment against the other. This feeling like all strong emotions left a residue which remained in them just as the trash washed from the banks of a swollen torrent becomes part of the bed of a stream when it has once again become quiet and still.

Later another difference developed between them. As the engagement continued Jennie put off the wedding date. Perhaps she was thinking of the future she had dreamed for herself as an actress, because she had wished to be a great actress and had gone to New York to study that profession. Perhaps she merely dreaded to give up her independence.

One day a year after they had become engaged the Doctor said to her, "If you can't tell me that we will be married on a certain day then I am through."

At that time the first discoveries of love, the first excitement of kisses that had been forbidden before were left behind. They saw each other in a clearer light than at first. Their love could not breathe. It neither lived nor died but was near to death. And it was necessary for their love to go on breathing freely and naturally if it lived. The Doctor understood this and so he spoke to Jennie about the marriage date. He left her on that visit without an answer from her. But he did not return and did not write to her. Perhaps he also was willing to allow their love to die. But Jennie at last made her decision. When she did not see him and when he did not write she found it impossible to do without him. She wrote him a letter and set a date for the wedding and resigned her position. The date she set was for the following December.

IV

ROBERT MIDDLETON was fond of telling people that his children learned Confederate history along with their prayers at their mother's knee. He taught them to revere the gray uniform and the Veterans who had worn it and to feel a tender loyalty for the stars and bars, the Confederate flag. As a Confederate Veteran he attended reunions and when it was possible took Jennie with him. She went not only as a spectator but as a Sponsor or Maid-of-honor from the state. And often she made passionate speeches to the Veterans, recalling their past glory and their suffering during the Civil War. They loved her for it. At one of the reunions they elected her "Daughter of the United Confederate Veterans" and voted unanimously that she was to be the only person ever to have that distinction.

It seemed natural as a result of all this that Jennie Middleton should have a Confederate wedding with Confederate officers in their uniforms as groomsmen. No one knew who had first proposed such a plan for the wedding. But there it was, fully developed, with every detail carefully worked out. On a shelf in the bride's closet next to her new travelling hat was a white box which contained seven expensive and made to order Confederate flags. The bridesmaids were to carry these small silk flags instead of flowers.

These very flags, of heavy red silk with white stars set on crossed bars of blue, inoffensive in themselves, caused the first outward manifestation of a division that had secretly developed in the church over the new minister, Dr. Grant. He had come to the parish a year and a half before from the North.

Dr. Grant was a great beefy man with a red face but the most cajoling and delightful voice and manner. At first he charmed everyone and then, very slyly, rumors began to circulate about him. It was said by those who did not like him that he drank and though he had a wife and children that he made love to some of the women of the congregation.

Robert Middleton was one of the members of the congregation who had never liked Dr. Grant. Perhaps his dislike sprang from an obscure prejudice against Northerners. Yet Mr. Middleton would have denied this because he thought that he had no sectional hatred. He kept a biography of Lincoln on the same bookshelf with a life of Robert E. Lee. And though he insisted to his children that the Southern planters were right to secede he taught them also that the nation was one and indivisible.

Therefore when he visited Dr. Grant on the day before his daughter's wedding he did so without any par-

ticular feeling of prejudice. He went to the minister's
home to ask him not to take part in the wedding ceremony. But he explained the reason. He told Dr. Grant
that he had talked the matter over with the Bishop who
had been a Captain in the Confederate army and they
had both agreed that for sentimental reasons, since the
whole wedding was to be Southern, it would be more
appropriate if the Northern minister did not take part
in the ceremony at the church. He did this as a matter
of courtesy because usually when the Bishop performed
a marriage ceremony the minister of the church assisted
him. Robert Middleton urged Dr. Grant to come to his
home for the wedding reception.

Dr. Grant, who had a hearty manner, seemed to think
this arrangement fair enough, so Robert Middleton
went to sleep the night before the wedding-day feeling
that everything was arranged satisfactorily with the
minister. As he went off to sleep he felt a warm glow
of friendship for Dr. Grant and decided that he had
been unjust in his unfavorable opinion. He even
planned a little speech for the reception in which he
would propose a toast to Dr. Grant and say that the
Confederate wedding with a Northerner as an honored
guest only proved that there was no longer any sectional hatred.

When the young people returned from a reception
given that evening by a neighbor to the bridal party
Mr. and Mrs. Middleton were already asleep. They had
left the reception early with the two youngest children.

Jennie and her Doctor came back together. The

bridesmaids and the two ushers who were staying in
the house as guests and the bride's two brothers returned almost at the same time. But they did not remain on the first floor. Yet before they went upstairs
the bridesmaids could not resist the impulse to tease the
bride and groom. They halted outside the folding doors
and laughing among themselves at the couple in the
living room and laughing also because the young men
were watching from the stairs, they peeped back into
the room where the Doctor and Jennie were standing.
They ostentatiously closed the doors on the couple and
left them alone, standing in the midst of a tangled mass
of smilax and gray moss which lay all over the floor.

That afternoon Christopher, Jennie's brother, had
brought the smilax and moss from the country and left
part of it at the house and part at the church for decorations. Christopher had seen to most of the details of the
wedding. In his hands everything became organized and
was done simply and easily. He hired two wagons
driven by Negroes and went out to the swamps for the
smilax and moss. On the way back into town as they
drove through the streets the bright green vines trailed
off the backs of the wagons and swung over the sides.
Hanging from the vines were wisps of gray moss like
sparse beards of old men. Christopher sat on the front
seat of the first wagon dressed in an old suit. A vine
was slung around his neck and part of it waved over his
forehead. Even in the old clothes he was handsome.
Girls came to their windows as he passed and sighed
to think that he would never notice them. Some of them

remembered a kiss or a pressure from his hand at a
dance and their sighs had more pleasure of remembrance and hope in them. Some people seeing Christopher on the wagon drew down their mouths and said
he was making an outrageous exhibition of himself and
his family. At that time it was the custom among people whose families had been wealthy before the Civil
War to pretend that they still had wealth. No matter
how poor a family might be nor how hard its members
worked in private, it was considered beneath their dignity to do any menial work in public. No one dared
carry a bundle on the streets if he did not wish to lose
caste in the eyes of the others. A Negro servant must
walk just behind him with the bundle in his hands.

Robert Middleton said to his children, "I won't have
any false pride in my family." He reminded them that
during Reconstruction he had ploughed the fields that
his father's and grandfather's slaves had worked and
that it had not hurt him to do so. When the family lived
in the country he made his sons work in the fields, and
in the city if the roof must be mended or some other
work on the house was necessary, his sons put on old
clothes and did this work in broad daylight before the
astonished and disapproving neighbors. The mother
and Hugh, the oldest son, suffered from this. But Christopher enjoyed it. So he felt no self-consciousness when
he drove down the residence street beside the Negro
driver on the broken-down dray with the graceful vines
hanging about his shoulders.

To his mother's dismay Christopher dumped all the

smilax and moss in a corner of the large living-room where it would be at hand for decorating the house the next morning. There were sharp little feelers on the stems of the smilax and they caught on the women's skirts so that the vines were dragged into all parts of the room.

When the bridesmaids closed the folding doors on them Jennie and the Doctor were standing in the midst of these trailing vines. The Doctor looked at Jennie admiringly. She was dressed in a yellow brocade evening gown trimmed with black velvet. The low-cut bodice revealed her shoulders, and small puffed sleeves stood out from her round arms. The skirt trailed on the floor in a handsome and graceful train. Some of the smilax fell across the end of the train and made a pattern of delicate green leaves across the yellow silk. The color of the dress set off Jennie's dark eyes and hair and her olive cheeks that were flushed with excitement. She was radiant and joyful with all the attention she had received. That evening it was not the Doctor who was looked up to with admiration, but herself. Toasts were drunk to her. The older men made flowery speeches in her honor. One of the Generals called her the fairest ornament of the South. Another veteran said, "To Jennie Middleton, a true woman of the South. Sweet as her roses, holy as her tears."

The Doctor saw all the radiance in Jennie's face. It gave him a sense of joy to know that he was to have this joyful and radiant being near him, and at the same time he found it hard to realize that he was to have this

joy for the rest of his life. Jennie did not see his broad
happy smile. She did not know it was there on his face.
At that moment he was not her lover, nor even a separate and individual person to her. He was another man
from whom she was receiving the admiration which
had stimulated her and made the whole evening pleasant and delightful.

It was the first time since the Doctor had come that
they had been alone together. And the Doctor thought,
"Now I will tell her." The day before he left Mountain
City he had performed a most delicate operation. He
wished to be a surgeon, and he was confident that this
operation had started him fully on that career. The
patient had been wounded by a bullet which penetrated
his skull and entered the brain. The Doctor opened the
skull. He saw the brain pulsing and felt it pulsing beneath his fingers. He removed the bullet and all the
fragments of bone and trepanned the skull with a
silver plate. The man was whole again. The Doctor
knew that he had done well. And a telegram that morning had told him that the patient was stronger. He felt
a pride in his work, and he wished to tell Jennie and
have her feel that pride. But even as he stood before
her and told himself, "Now I will tell her" his natural
reserve and modesty prevented him. And Jennie was
talking. She spoke in a high clear voice, but he did not
hear what she said. She was talking rapidly and excitedly, glancing at him with bright excited eyes and ges-
turing with her hands. He watched her with the broad
kindly smile on his face and waited. She leaned toward

him and looked up into his face. Her head was almost against his shoulder. He felt her nearness. And as her hands reached out in another gesture he took them softly in his and pulled her closer to him. His arms went about her bare shoulders. He held her closer and felt her young excited heart pounding against him. With one hand he raised her chin upward and bent toward her.

But she did not respond as he had expected. She struggled against him. Her chin wrenched itself from his large hand. At first he held her with both arms trying to keep her, trying to make her see him, for as he looked into her eyes he saw that they were not conscious of him. He wished to make her see that he was there, an important being. But she struggled fiercely. He could not understand, but he let her go. And as she stood away with the smilax tangled in the train of her dress it seemed to him that she looked at him with a sort of hatred in her eyes and on her face.

She said, "You didn't even hear what I was telling you." And it was true. He had not heard.

He shook his head. He was bewildered, and at the same time he felt an unreasoning impatience with her because she had not known that he wished to tell her about his triumph, so that his triumph would be included in her joy. Instead of the kindly smile on his lips there was a grin of shame because she had drawn away from him and of irony, as if he said to himself, "This is the way life turns out each time. I must remember, nothing is as you hope it will be. I must remember not to expect or hope."

Jennie did not understand his shame or his disappointment. She only saw that he looked at her and it seemed to her that his eyes were critical and hard.

She said defensively, "I was planning our life. But you don't care. I can see that you don't."

"What were you planning?" he asked with a cold politeness.

"Only—nothing . . . but it was important and so I will tell you. I was saying that I will have an afternoon at home. It can be put on my visiting cards . . . I think it should be Thursdays . . . don't you, or perhaps Sundays, when you could be there? We can serve tea. I have Mother's service, only the sugar bowl is missing, and we'll have your friends . . ." she was enthusiastic again, "a meeting of people like a salon."

"My friends don't like tea," the Doctor said stubbornly.

"But they could learn to like it, couldn't they?" Jennie asked sharply.

"They feel more at home in a Greek restaurant."

"Yes, I know, I know. But why can't they feel at home in your house? Why can't they?" And as she said this something that had disturbed her before, a vague feeling of resentment that she had not before felt consciously came up in her. "You have selected and bought the house we are to live in," she told him resentfully, "you have furnished it. Why shouldn't you and they feel at home in it. It's a man's house," she said spitefully.

He saw that she was hurt and could not understand the hurt. He had selected the house and prepared it lovingly for her, like a gift. And she was angry because it was all prepared and ready for her. Every room was done, even a guest room for members of her family was ready. He felt a great anger at her and at the wedding and at the house which was waiting for them. A hopelessness came over him again. He moved impatiently and one of the vines caught at his ankle. The sharp feelers pricked him. He leaned down and pulled the vine away and threw it to the other side of the room.

"Damn the house," he said angrily. As he lifted his head again it was reddened and his usually good-natured and tender mouth was stretched in a grin of anger. "God damn the whole wedding. What's the use of it. A heap of debts on your father's shoulders. No, we won't have any goddamn teas in my house."

"You are narrow and provincial, and all you think of is saving a nickel," Jennie's eyes flashed at him. She lifted her head angrily. "I tell you we will have the teas. My father doesn't mind spending a little money . . ."

"Even if he hasn't got it," the Doctor said dryly.

"Yes, even if he hasn't got it. He's generous at least. And I want a husband who is generous."

"Not with teas."

"We're going to have them. I've made up my mind."

"Don't tell me what we will do," he said furiously.

"I will, I will tell you. Because I know what is good for you. I know, I know. A woman knows."

"You know about as much as a child of six," he said. He spoke in a low voice and yet his anger showed through the low tone in a stronger and more compelling way than when he had shouted.

"Then if I am no more than a six-year-old child I shouldn't get married," Jennie said in a clear and cold voice, "I shouldn't. So I won't marry you." She looked at him and hated him, hated his hard face that was red with anger, and his strong fine mouth and his eyes that had so often looked at her with a kindly amused glint in them. His words burned in her. "Go on," she said childishly, but at the same time that she spoke childishly her voice was clear and cold and wilful. "Go back to Mountain City. And don't come back here. I won't ever marry you. I am glad. I am glad this happened in time. I am glad I found out what you are. I am glad," she repeated.

The Doctor stumbled through the smilax toward the folding doors. Once he turned and looked at Jennie and for a moment a strange feeling of pity for her came in him. He saw her standing in the vines, small and so concentrated on herself. He was older than she, and he felt many years older. She was a child and would never grow up in her emotions. This knowledge that she would never grow up gave him again that feeling of hopelessness, and at the same time he had the feeling of pity for her and that too took hope away from him because he felt that the pity would often betray him. Even

now he pitied her and because of the pity was almost
ready to give in to her.

The pity on his face as he turned to look at her
angered Jennie. She did not want pity, not the pity
that said, "I am stronger than you." She did not know
what she wanted, but she could not endure the look on
his face and the compassion in his eyes. She ran past
him to the folding doors. Her fingers were not strong
enough to pull the heavy doors apart. He was close to
her as she fumbled at them. Another surge of anger
went through her. She wished to do something that
would take the look of pity from his face, put it out,
obliterate it forever. He was close to her. She lifted her
face impudently to his and said as if she dared him,
but in a high screaming voice, "I am a child then. I am
a child. Then why don't you slap me for doing wrong?
Because you think I am doing wrong. Why don't you
slap me? I know you want to. You want to."

And curiously as she said the words, although he had
not wished to before, when she spoke of it and defied
him, he did wish to slap her, to beat her. The feeling of
strength came up in his arms, the feeling of heated
anger went into his arms and fists. But he held his
hands tightly at his sides and stared at her.

"Why don't you?" she demanded.

He lifted his hands. But his hands did not go to her.
They swung the folding doors apart so that they
slammed against the lintels. His hat and coat were on
the rack in the hall and he lifted them unconsciously.
There was a blurred and confused singing in his ears.

It continued all the way through the streets until he reached the hotel. In the lobby the night clerk looked at him curiously. He had come in from the cold night with his overcoat slung over his arm. And he was shivering. The singing was still in his ears.

When the Doctor left her Jennie walked drearily up the stairs and down the silent hall to her room and slowly removed the brocaded dress and the dainty new underwear. In her bed, after the light was out, she pitied herself and thought that her life was ruined.

As she lay awake she heard rain-drops begin to fall outside her open window on the roof of the verandah. Then a whole shower came down and after that a pouring rain. The sound of the rain on the shingles was not cheerful as it sometimes is when people are sitting cozily before a fire with door and windows shut. The sound added to Jennie's misery. At one time she thought, "It will be raining for the wedding tomorrow," and this made her feel sad. Then she remembered and said, "It doesn't matter. There will be no wedding," and this also made her feel desperate and lonely. Toward morning she went to sleep, burying herself far under the bedclothes because the air in the room became distressingly cold.

While she slept, outside in the quiet world there was happening one of the sudden changes that appear almost miraculous and that occur only once in several years in the South. Before the rain had dropped from the bushes, roofs and trees a slight breeze came up. This breeze became a wind that carried an icy current from the North. The icy current blew on the bushes and trees, on the water-covered roofs and turned the water to ice. By daylight everything was coated with ice. Trees and bushes crackled each time the wind came against them. Their limbs drooped heavily and gracefully with the weight of the ice. Occasionally a twig, too heavily burdened, broke off and dropped to the ground.

V

THE first member of the family to wake on the morning of the wedding was the Middletons' youngest child, Susan, who had slept in a small store-room on an old trundle bed brought down from the attic.

She did not know that the weather had changed and that all the world outside—the world that she knew—was covered with ice. Even the cold that had penetrated to the unwarmed trunk room did not disturb her. She was in a state of bliss where neither cold nor heat made her uncomfortable. As a rule she was a quiet little girl going about her studies and play and taking part in the home life quietly and unostentatiously so that people did not pay much attention to her. But since the first guest had arrived at the house a week before all the outward circumstances of her life had changed. The door-bell was constantly ringing and every ring meant that a surprise waited at the front door. The presents that came in mysterious bundles, the bride's new trunk and bags, the different articles of the trousseau, each gave Susan a fresh sensation of delight. Even the door-bell itself seemed to ring in a new and significant way as if it too shared in the general joy and bustle of preparation.

The cousins who were staying in the house praised and petted her. One of the young men cousins would slip his arm around her while he was talking or lift her to his knee. The other said out loud before everyone, "After the wedding you will be Miss Middleton, Susan. It's your turn next." And Cousin John, the one who liked her to sit on his knee, said. "You can marry me then." Everyone laughed when he said this and Susan ducked her head shyly. But she did not forget. The word love, this especial and significant love connected with marriage, had become a word of the greatest interest. She listened to all the talk and from this talk and the mysterious allusions to this love and to marriage she was constantly absorbing fresh ideas. The girl cousins let her sit in their rooms while they dressed and chattered about men and love, and they also paid her special attention, admiring her long thick hair or exclaiming over her drawings which had won a prize in her class at school.

Mr. and Mrs. Middleton did not believe in praising their children, so the unusual attention gave Susan an exaggerated notion of her own importance. It was like a match to a skyrocket. Susan felt as she did on Christmas night around a bonfire when she watched the skyrockets, after a match had been put to them, go straight upward into the darkness. Then, although the rocket itself could not be seen, the colored balls of fire spurted out and broke into lovely sparks that obliterated the quiet stars which had been so clear and brilliant only a moment before.

As she woke on the morning of the wedding day in the darkness of the trunk room all Susan's expectations for the day flashed and spurted in her like the colored balls of a rocket. She thought with a shock of delight, "Another day of pleasure." Her life was full and there was nothing else to be asked but that it should continue just as it was.

For the past week Susan's mother and father had relaxed their usual discipline and this was another reason for pleasure, and it gave Susan the courage to rush to her parents' room as soon as she was dressed. She knocked on their door which was at the end of the long hall next to the bath-room, and without waiting for an answer put her head inside. Her heavy plaits of blond hair, dishevelled from the night's sleep, swung inside the door as she looked joyfully into the dark room.

"It's morning," she said just as she did on Christmas day when the usual formalities had been suspended.

Carrie Middleton raised her head from the pillow and said in a loud whisper, "Go away, Susan. Your father is asleep. Oh my soul and body!" she exclaimed under her breath.

Mr. Middleton groaned and turned over in the bed, lifting the bedclothes around his shoulders.

"You see," Mrs. Middleton whispered reproachfully to her daughter.

With a frightened and apologetic expression as if afraid of what she was doing and yet urged on by the excitement over which she had no control, Susan tiptoed with long steps into the room and even to the foot of the great walnut bed. She peered over the high footboard at her mother's head lifted from the pillow and her father's, half-hidden by the comfort.

"But they're going to serenade the bride at seven. That will wake everybody." Susan spoke in a loud whisper, secretly hoping it would wake her father. She was successful. Suddenly he sat bolt upright against his pillow. This sudden awakening was so unexpected Susan sprang backward and struck her leg against a chair. She held her knee with both hands and moaned.

"What is it? What time is it?" Mr. Middleton demanded in his quick clear enunciation that was quicker now because it had the startled sound that is in the voice of a person waked suddenly from a deep slumber.

"I told her not to disturb you," his wife said.

"Who is it?" His eyes blinked as he tried to get them fully open and see in the dark early morning light that came in the window. "Is it Susan? What do you want Susan?"

Susan had gone to her parents' room because her clothes and other personal belongings were being kept there, but also because after waking it was necessary for her to do something active and because she wished to hear a human voice. But she did not understand this and so could not tell her father why she had come.

"Go back to sleep," Mrs. Middleton said to her husband.

"No," he answered, "there's too much to be done," and he began to lift the covers.

"Wait outside," Mrs. Middleton told the little girl, "I'll call you."

When Susan was called in the windows were down and the electric light on. Her father had on his shirt and trousers and with his legs over the side of the bed was putting on his socks. Her mother was also out of bed and had slipped on the faded blue dressing gown with which Susan was so familiar. The parents were discussing the ice which had formed outside and Susan heard about it for the first time. She ran to the window to see the wonder that had happened during the night.

"It must have been nine years ago," Robert Middleton said, "when it happened before."

"Ten," his wife told him, "because," she lowered her voice, "it was the year before Susan was born. We were living in the country and you know how careful I had to be in walking down the steps.

"Give me the brush and comb, Susan," she said aloud, and when Susan had come from the window and was standing before Mrs. Middleton who had seated herself on the bed, Mrs. Middleton asked, "Did you wash?"

"Yes'm," Susan answered. Down in the folds of her short dress where her hand rested she crossed her fingers because it was not a sin to tell a white lie if one's fingers were crossed. "I'll take a bath this afternoon," she added, speaking to her mother and to her conscience.

"You must take it early because your sister and the bridesmaids will need the tub later."

"Yes'm. Do you think any more presents will come today? Jennie said I could have her old red crepe dress. It isn't really old. You could make it over for me, couldn't you? General Iredale has a scar right across his cheek. He told me it is a sabre cut. He is the only veteran without a beard except father. Oh, Mother, that hurts!"

"Hold your head still, then. Don't jerk it forward. Your father fought only eight months. But you had eight great-uncles in the Civil War. Four were killed in battle. And your grandfather on my side . . ."

"Is it true that Cousin Lucy has hooked General Stephens?"

"Susannah! Oh, my soul!"

Mrs. Middleton laughed silently. At the same time she cautiously held her daughter's hair so that Susan could not turn and see that she was laughing. But Susan knew that her mother was amused by what she had said and a self-conscious smile came on her face and spread over it so that her nose and mouth puckered into a queer little grin of pleasure.

"Well, is he in love with her, is he?" Susan demanded.

"How can we tell?" Mrs. Middleton exclaimed. "You mustn't ask such questions. Love is not a . . ."

"I know what love is," Susan giggled, "it is dizziness . . ." she was about to quote a rhyme she had learned from the children at school, but her mother came to a knot in the hair and took up the dreaded comb, so that Susan became entirely concerned with the pain caused by the jerks at her scalp.

Robert Middleton had put on his shoes and was at the walnut chest of drawers between the windows searching for his collar button. "Do you think I can have breakfast by half past eight?" he asked his wife. "I must get down to the Bank."

Carrie Middleton held the comb suspended over Susan's head as if she were playing a game of forfeits and stared at her husband. "Again?" she gasped.

"Well, Mother, a daughter doesn't get married every day."

"Oh, Robert!"

"Yes, Mother, but what can we do?" He struggled with his stiff collar and the button. His tense knuckles were against his throat and he spoke in a choked voice, "There's no use worrying. We've gone through worse things than this. I have borrowed a little money, yes . . ."

"Little!" Carrie exclaimed.

"But we can pay it back. We've had debts before."

Susan looked at her parents impatiently. She moved impatiently and her mother parted her hair and began to plait it. "I can hear them in the hall. They're getting ready," Susan told her mother.

Mr. Middleton went to the closet and took down his coat. As he struggled into the coat he halted before Susan and spoke directly to her.

"So they're going to sing love songs to your sister," he said.

Susan looked up into his face and her own face became sober as if she expected a reproof. Mrs. Middleton also looked up at him and her face took on the same expression of anxiety that was on the little girl's.

"You think all this hurly burly and fol-de-rol is romantic," Mr. Middleton said to Susan, "and soon you will be looking forward to your own wedding day, thinking it is the entrance to paradise. Instead of love songs they ought to shoot off a cannon like the one that started the war at Fort Sumter. Because marriage is a struggle . . ."

"Is this necessary?" Mrs. Middleton whispered.

Her husband did not hear her. He was looking down into the sober and frightened face of his little daughter. Evidently she did not understand or did not wish to understand what he said, but the forlorn expression on her face made him regret that he had spoken so harshly. He bent his tall spare body and took her cheeks between the palms of his hands.

"Your old Daddy loves you a world full," he told her in a sentimental voice, "he only wants to spare you disillusionment and pain. That's all he wants."

He saw that she resented his serious words, that she almost hated him for disturbing her joy and that she wished more than anything else to get away. He took his hands from her face. "Run along, then," he said roughly, "go along and serenade the bride."

Mrs. Middleton tied the last bow and Susan ran out

of the room. When the door had closed behind her Carrie Middleton spoke to Robert. "I know you don't like to look through rose-colored glasses . . . it is nothing new . . . but why did you say that—because I thought our marriage . . ."

"Yes," he said, "our marriage. But young people think it is one long picnic," his well-formed and sensitive mouth twisted at one corner into a familiar ironic smile, "and it ain't no picnic."

"No, but then . . ." Carrie stammered.

He interrupted her, speaking some thought that had been in his mind, "Do you think Daughter loves this man enough?" he asked abruptly.

Mrs. Middleton laughed, and the very laughter, thin and forced, so different from her laughter at Susan, showed that the question frightened her.

"What a question to ask on the very day of the wedding," she said. "Every girl dreads . . . you know . . . it is not easy for the woman . . . But why do you ask? Did she say anything?"

Her husband did not answer because at that moment the noises in the hall became louder. Mr. Middleton went to the door of the bedroom, opened it and looked out. "They are at her door," he said and unconsciously he lowered his voice and whispered just as those in the hall were whispering. He left the door partly open.

The laughing, whispering voices were now concentrated in one place. There was some scuffling, more laughter, and the young voices began to sing:

> "Faithful and true
> We lead thee forth
> Where love triumphant
> Shall crown thee with joy . . ."

Most of the voices did not sing the words, but the three Middleton boys, who had sung this chorus for a number of weddings because they were in the church choir, sang all the words correctly.

The music burst out triumphantly and then softened to a gentle harmony. Mrs. Middleton heard her sons' voices above all the others, Hugh's bass voice and Christopher's tenor. But the voice that really shook her was Bobby's soprano. His voice had not yet changed. She could feel her body in a spot on her left side under her heart vibrating to his clear notes.

> " 'Tis thy wedding morning
> Dawning in the skies,
> Bridal bells are ringing,
> Bridal songs arise,
> Opening the portals
> Of thy paradise."

"Isn't Bobby's voice like . . . like heaven," she whispered. Her husband was at the window. He had pulled back the curtain and was staring out of the window. Mrs. Middleton sat with her hands relaxed in her lap, though one of them still held the comb she had used on Susan's hair.

There was quiet after this song. They were waiting for Jennie to come out of her room. But she did not come and the silence became embarrassing until Bobby's voice began another song:

"Drink to me only with thine eyes . . .

As his voice took up the lead on a higher key, tears came into Carrie's large gray eyes. She remembered that Dr. Grant had told her that Bobby's voice was as good if not better than any he had heard in the boy-choirs in the North. "At least," she told herself, "we can be proud of our children. And we have been happy," she emphasized the word have in her mind, "only the lack of money, and sometimes when I have rebelled, and Robert's temper. But he tries to control it. And that period of a year or two after he gave up his law practice and the little ones died. Then he drank and there was that woman. But it was so long ago. There hasn't been another woman. I am sure of that."

The song was finished. There was the strange silence again as they waited for Jennie to come out of her room. Mrs. Middleton felt impatient with Jennie because she did not come out and speak to the singers.

Christopher called out, "Jennie." Then Susan's voice shrieked at her sister and Mrs. Middleton told herself that Susan was too exuberant and something must be done about her after the wedding. But these voices that broke the uncomfortable silence relieved her.

One of the bridesmaids, it was Lucy, giggled in an embarrassed way and said, "Doesn't she know it's her wedding day?" Then Christopher's manly voice wheedled, "Doctor is here, Sis. He wants to see you."

Nancy DuPre, the maid of honor, laughed. "Foolish Chris, she knows the bridegroom isn't allowed to see the bride on her wedding day."

Then Jennie's door did open. Carrie, listening intently, heard it. There were exclamations and the sound of someone rushing along the hall.

"Is that Susan again?" Mrs. Middleton asked herself. But on the other side of her door she heard Jennie speaking imperiously to the young people. "No," Jennie's voice said, "no, let me go. I must see Father. Yes, I am much obliged for the song. It was pretty. Thank you. Now I must see Father. Please go away."

The door opened and slammed shut. Mrs. Middleton said, "Why, Jennie, you weren't very gracious." Her back was toward the door but at the silence which followed she became uneasy and looked to see what had happened. Jennie had not moved from the door. She was leaning against it with a look of despair on her face.

Mr. Middleton did not turn from the window when he heard his daughter come in. He hated sentimentality, or thought he hated it and was ashamed of the emotion which had come over him as he listened to the songs. There were tears in his eyes and he did not wish the others to see them. So without looking at Jennie he spoke to her with an affected heartiness.

"Well, daughter, so this is your wedding day."

"Father . . . Mother," Jennie said and could not go on. Her voice choked in her throat and her face became contorted with the effort for control. Carrie Middleton saw the misery in Jennie's face and all the pleasure she had felt in the songs left her. She was weak and could not rise from the bed.

Jennie said to her, "I know I wasn't gracious, but it was because . . . because I have broken the engagement. There won't be any wedding tonight," she said dramatically.

She ran to the bed and flung herself on it and sobbed. Mrs. Middleton leaned toward Jennie and stroked her hair that spread out over the pillow. "Why, Daughter," she said in a bewildered, questioning voice, "why, Daughter."

She continued to stroke Jennie's hair as Jennie sobbed loudly. "This is a very sudden decision," Carrie said and laughed in the same thin and frightened manner in which she had laughed when her husband asked if Jennie loved the Doctor.

Jennie raised herself from the pillow, shook her hair from her face and clasped both her mother's hands. "I have been awake all night," she said, "I can't marry him!"

"I know," Mrs. Middleton told her soothingly, "but all girls feel this way. The feeling will pass and then . . ."

"No, it isn't the same. I quarrelled with him, don't you understand? He swore at all of us, Father," she looked up at her father who had come to stand by the bed, "I won't marry a man like that. I told him I would never marry him and that it was final. And it is final." She pressed her mother's hand. "You must tell him, make Father tell him," she begged, "tell everyone it is over . . . that I can't . . . I will never marry him."

Mrs. Middleton tried to go back into her own life and remember so that she could understand her daughter's behavior. And she did remember the night before her wedding when she had packed the small leather trunk, brass bound and studded with brass, which was now in the attic. And she remembered how it had seemed that marriage was like dying and waking up into a new life. It was painful to die in the old life, but there was the new ahead. She spoke to Jennie, trying to tell her of this feeling. "No," Jennie kept saying, "no, this is different. He hates us all. He does," her voice rose defiantly, "he despises us. He despises me."

"You are hysterical, Jennie," her father said. His voice sounded cruel and unfeeling. Jennie lifted her head and stared at him in surprise. She had depended on his sympathy.

"Hysterical!" she gasped.

"You are making us all unhappy," Mrs. Middleton told her, "when we are trying our best," she remembered the heavy debts and added, "and sacrificing everything for you."

Jennie sprang from the bed. Her whole body quivered with feeling. She looked at her father and then at her mother. "Sacrifice," she cried, "it is you who want to sacrifice me. I never wished to get married. You forced me . . . you, Father, you did. You want to get rid of me, both of you. And I can't understand it," she said pitifully, "because I have been supporting myself. I am not dependent on you. I have given you no trouble. I have even loaned Father money," she said cruelly. Her lids came down over her eyes and she looked at her father from the corners of her eyes. She saw that he was hurt and was afraid because of the stern expression that came on his face. "I didn't mean that. You were welcome, but I . . ."

"That will do, Jennie," her father said harshly, "go to your room." When she hesitated his voice became louder and more irritated. "I won't have hysterical women about. I won't have it. I can't stand it. Go to your room," he ordered again.

A look of self-pity came on Jennie's face. She became quiet and still, like a little girl who feels that she has been punished unjustly, but can do nothing about it because the others are stronger. She did not speak again but went quietly to the door. But before she went out she looked at her father reproachfully as if she wished to say, "You are callous and indifferent to my suffering and I worship you and depended on you. But I can see you don't care."

"I know," Robert said to his wife when the door had closed behind Jennie. "I know I insisted once when she was thinking of breaking the engagement that she keep on with it. But it was necessary. It was necessary," he said in a loud voice.

"There are people in the hall," Mrs. Middleton whispered.

He lowered his voice to an agitated whisper. "I told you," he said, "I told you that I saw him kiss her passionately and she returned . . . you may talk about innocence being its own protection . . . I know . . . I know what you believe. But she has a passionate nature even if it has not been aroused. But it was aroused. And she has a reckless streak in her somewhere . . . reckless. I was afraid for her. No, Mother, I was right to make her go on. I was right. She needs the safety of marriage."

"I know. But what are we to do now?" Carrie asked miserably. "You must go and talk to her," she said. "We don't understand each other, though I try. But she has always loved you best . . ."

"Nonsense," Robert interrupted.

"No," she insisted, "she does. You and Jennie understand each other."

"All nonsense," Robert repeated. "Jennie is not partial to me. It is you who should talk to her. It is a mother's duty on a girl's wedding day." A warning gesture from his wife made him lower his voice again. "You yourself said all girls dread marriage and this quarrel may be just an excuse that you could explain away. Why don't you learn to talk to your daughter when it is your duty to do so?" he demanded irritably. "I tell you it is your duty. Your daughter knows nothing. She is not prepared for . . . for life. You have neglected your duty and now you try . . ."

"Please, Robert, please," Carrie whispered. "Then don't go," she said, "don't. Leave her. I know I have failed. But this is different. They did have a quarrel. She loves you and respects you and will listen to you.

But don't go if you feel it isn't best. Leave her. But Lord have mercy on us. I don't know what to do. I don't know what will become of us."

Carrie's voice always took on this tone of mournful despair when there was an argument and she was especially anxious for him to agree with her. Robert knew that this was so, but her sorrow always affected him. And he knew that Jennie loved him and that in some ways they understood each other. She was his favorite companion, bright and quick and responsive. And her loving, passionate admiration had become necessary to him. He lifted his shoulders in a gesture that said "You have won."

"I'll talk to her then . . . but later . . . after breakfast, if you insist."

He left his wife alone in the bedroom. Carrie heard his steps going down the stairs to the dining-room. She had won a victory, but it did not make her happy.

VI

BECAUSE she was the bride everything had been
planned for Jennie's comfort and privacy. She was the
only person in the crowded house who had a room
alone. After leaving her father and mother she returned
to her own room and slipped under the covers of the
bed. The bed was warm because she had been out of it
for such a little time, but in spite of the warmth her
body shook with a nervous chill.

"I am not hysterical," she told herself in an agitated
whisper and for the first time thought of her father as
an unjust and cruel person and wondered if her mother
had borne injustice like this all the years of her marriage. Jennie and her father always had a little conspiracy to spare the mother any worry. Mr. Middleton
would say, "We won't tell Mother. It might worry
her." This little conspiracy had made Jennie feel that
she and her father were in some way superior to the
mother, or at least that they were more sensible and had
a more complete understanding of the world outside the
home. But in the other room that morning the parents
were together. They were the sensible ones and Jennie

was the hysterical person who worried without any
cause. Her father had made her feel that this was so,
and her mother had supported him.

Jennie angrily put her father and sweetheart together. They were both unjust men who did not understand and never could understand a woman's delicacy
and sensitiveness. Jennie hoped that her father would
come in to see her. She expected him to come and imagined what would happen when he did. She thought he
might put his arms around her and say, "I am a man
and can never hope to understand you. I can only stand
apart and worship because what you are is so far above
me that I can never understand it nor comprehend it. I
can only wonder at you and your bravery and the
beauty of your soul." The thought that her father
might come in and say something like this made her
happier. If once he took this attitude she could be
happy. Because then she knew he would go to the Doctor and say, "You see, Doctor, you and I are only men.
We are miserable and coarse and unworthy. Women
are so much finer. And we must acknowledge this truth
and try to make them happy in our blundering way. We
belong on our knees."

The mere thought of her father saying this and the
Doctor accepting it and acknowledging her in this way
calmed Jennie so that the nervous chill did not shake
her body and her muscles lost their tenseness. If they
would only do this, how she could love them. What a
splendid unselfish love she could give them. It was only
necessary for them to say, "You are far superior to us

and we acknowledge it," to loosen all her splendid unselfish love.

Jennie imagined this very thing happening and when
she heard steps along the hall thought they must belong
to her father. But the next second she knew this was
not so. Her father's step was too familiar for her to
mistake it. There was a soft knock at the door. Jennie
did not answer but pulled the bed-clothes closer around
her throat. Ed, the Negro boy who had been hired for
that week, opened the door slowly and came into the
room on tiptoe with kindling and a scuttle of coal. He
had come to make Jennie's fire.

As the fat kindling rolled from his arm to the hearth
the smell of pine and rosin was let loose in the room.
The fresh clean odor reached Jennie and reminded her
of the balsam smell when she had driven or walked with
the doctor in the mountains. The boy moved quietly
and carefully because he thought Jennie was asleep. As
she looked over the covers Jennie could just see his
brown hand setting each stick of kindling carefully in
the grate. His hand moved rhythmically building up
the kindling into a framework. Jennie heard the crack
of the match and then flames shot up into the chimney. The sound of the fire was cheerful and comforting. Again she saw the boy's dark hand as it laid pieces
of coal one by one on the flames, jerking back to escape
the fire as soon as a lump had been placed in the right
position.

Ed picked up the rest of the kindling, and again the
resinous odor came into the room. The scuttle handle

creaked as he lifted the coal and tiptoed out of the
room and closed the door gently behind him.

As soon as this human presence was gone Jennie's
thoughts returned to herself. She tried to put her mind
on other objects in the room, on pieces of her trousseau
that lay across the new bags, at her old trunk in one
corner, but there was no movement to hold her attention and thoughts returned. They crackled in a lively
way in her head like the fire had crackled when the
kindling began to burn high in the dark chimney.

She was angry and hurt because her father had not
understood her terror and distaste at the Doctor's
swearing. It was more terrible because she had prepared herself for the wedding not only materially with
the trousseau, but spiritually. But neither of them could
understand that sort of preparation, she told herself
bitterly. They could never understand the significant
and beautiful experience of the Sunday before at the
steps of the chapel and within the chapel itself.

Though Susan had not yet been confirmed Jennie
took her little sister with her to early communion. This
special distinction had delighted Susan. Jennie knew
that Susan thought it an honor to be selected to go and
it gave her pleasure to know that Susan felt this and
that she had made Susan happy.

They left the house in the early dawn, because in
winter the light came much later than in summer, and
walked down Lady Street to the church. The service
was not held in the large church with the stained glass
windows and high columns, because this building was

temporarily closed while a reredos was being set up above the altar. The reredos was of pure white marble, carved in Italy and shipped from that country. Dr. Grant had raised the money for it and for the new jewelled communion set by asking the women of the church to give their old jewels and silver and gold. Dr. Grant was also building a parish house and club rooms at the left of the church buildings and connected with the church by a passage like those seen in pictures of old monasteries. The church was to be cleaned out for Jennie's wedding, but on the Sunday before the chancel was still cluttered by the scaffolding and pieces of timber around the new reredos.

Early communion was therefore celebrated in an improvised chapel in the wooden Sunday School room. And the fact that she went to communion in the humble chapel held some significance for Jennie, though she was not sure why, except that it was necessary for her to feel humble and to know that she was humble and the wooden chapel helped her to feel so.

At the steps of this humble chapel Jennie and Susan came face to face with a bent old woman. She was not anyone Jennie had seen before, and for some reason this fact was also significant to Jennie. She knew the people in the congregation at least by sight, but the old lady was a stranger. She wore a slouch felt hat which might have belonged to a man, and at the back it sloped down over her hunched shoulders, over which there was an old black shawl. With all the energy that the early morning air had given her Susan was rushing up the

steps, but Jennie quickly held her back so that the old
lady could go first. But the old woman hesitated at the
foot of the steps, gathering up her strength to climb
them. Jennie saw the hesitation and understood the
cause of it. She took the old lady's arm and helped her
as she slowly mounted the steps one at a time like a
child.

Everything about the old lady, the way she hobbled
up the steps, her faded clothes, the fact that she was a
stranger, stimulated a superstitious awe in Jennie. She
remembered stories of people who had entertained a
beggar who turned out to be a visitant from heaven.
Even while such a story came into her mind and she
felt the superstitious awe that went with it, Jennie
smiled at herself for entertaining such a thought. And
yet the feeling of superstitious awe remained in her.
At the door of the chapel the old lady looked up into
Jennie's face with a surprisingly sweet glance of appreciation. Jennie returned the smile and a joyful feeling
of ecstasy came up in her.

In the chapel when she left Susan and went to the
altar to receive the symbolic body and blood of Christ
Jennie bowed her head over the railing as Dr. Grant's
hands placed the wafer in her outstretched hand and
gave her the silver goblet studded with gems, and promised God that she would dedicate her life to helping her
future husband in his holy work. As she knelt there in
the early morning, the incident at the door fresh in her
mind, and the taste of wine on her tongue, and the soft
unctuous, cajoling voice of the minister in her ears, the

wine suggested to Jennie, not only the blood and suffering of Christ, but suffering humanity to whom she and
her husband would dedicate their lives. . . . In her
imagination she pictured her future husband, a sort of
shadowy being, very different from the reality.

This shadowy person her thoughts had conjured out
of the morning and the service became more real to her
as the days went by. And this shadowy being, not the
actual person, was the man she was going to marry. The
Doctor had arrived the day before, and the actual person, not the imaged one, had stood before her and
cursed heartily at the wedding and all her plans.

"He is a stranger," Jennie told herself miserably,
"who doesn't care about my thoughts, only about my
body. All he ever wanted was my body. . . . How did
I ever make this terrible mistake and promise to marry
him?" she asked herself, and as she did so remembered
the first kiss they had exchanged as they bent over the
night-blooming cereus on the verandah. "Yes, it was
that kiss," she told herself, "it began everything. And
that is all he ever wanted. . . . But why should they
make me go on if I do not love him?" she asked herself
and asked the others, her father and mother, the friends
and neighbors. "I will not let them force me to go on,"
she told herself rebelliously. "I will not. They do not
understand what a splendid life I have had. I was independent. I had money of my own. I could go where I
pleased. I want that life back again. Not this one. Not
this one."

Out in the hall she heard people opening doors and

talking softly and laughing quietly. They were the
voices of the bridesmaids and the ushers and her two
brothers. The voices sounded happy. The cheerful soft
voices of the guests showed that they did not know
anything about the quarrel and Jennie wished to go out
and tell them. It gave her satisfaction to think of their
faces if she suddenly opened the door and said, "There
won't be any wedding. You can all pack your things
and go home." They would be disappointed. But it
seemed to Jennie that they should be so, that they
should all be suffering as she was suffering.

Soon after the guests had gone down the stairs the
maid who had been hired for that week came up with
a tray of breakfast for Jennie. Annie May looked well-
contented, and she was. She was delighted with the
wedding festivities and with the two dollars earned
that week. In the bosom of her dress there was a fifty-
cent tip done up in a handkerchief. And Jennie had
given her a number of pieces of clothing, discarded
because of the trousseau.

Jennie sat up in the bed but she did not answer when
Annie May said "Good-morning, Miss Jennie." Annie
May moved a table to the fireplace and arranged the
tray on it. She glanced at Jennie. She had expected to
find a happy bride, and was repelled and puzzled by
Jennie's sullen air of defiance. It made her uncomfortable to see the bride so thoughtful, looking inward on
herself.

"Your breakfast is ready," she said. When Jennie
did not answer she went closer to the bed. "You better

get up an' eat," she told Jennie, "your Mama said to eat well. This is yo' weddin' day."

"Annie May, why do people get married?" Jennie said in a despairing voice.

Annie May giggled in an embarrassed manner. "Lord, Miss Jennie, ain't you know why?"

Jennie heard the giggle and the inflection in the Negro girl's voice. And this answer was disgusting to her and made her feel more dissatisfied.

"What are you standing there for? Why don't you go down and help Mother?" she asked irritably.

"Yes'm," Annie May answered. She hung her head and looked sad. "Yes'm. I'm going."

But before Annie May was out of the door Jennie was sorry for what she had said. "Look in the closet," she told Annie May, "and get that blue dress. You can have it."

Annie May went out of the room with the dress. Her face had become cheerful again and Jennie was glad that she had made the girl happy. It took so little to make her happy.

The door closed. Jennie got slowly out of the bed, put on her dressing gown and went to the fireplace. She drank the coffee but did not eat. Her fingers rested on the handle of the cup and she stared out of the window without seeing the branches of the pine tree and the ice-covered needles that swayed a little in the wind.

But when she heard her father's steps coming along the hall she sprang up from the table with a joyful and eager expression. All the things she had imagined he

might say had become almost real to her so that she
expected them to come from his mouth as soon as she
heard and recognized his step in the hall.

As the door opened she put her arms softly around
her father's neck and laid her head against his shoulder.
Robert Middleton looked down at her tenderly. He had
an impulse to give up and accept everything that Jennie
wished him to accept. She was so warm and loving and
he longed to go back to their old companionship when
she admired him passionately and did not look at him
reproachfully and critically. But he reminded himself
that if he became emotional then she would be able to
control him, "because," he told himself, "women are
more at home in emotion. They know instinctively what
to do in that sphere while I am lost . . . lost. Emotion
is a tyrant if it isn't controlled by reason." He understood that his wife had won a victory over him. He
still felt that he was right and that it was her duty to
have this talk with Jennie, but her emotion had con-
quered him. And especially because of this victory of
his wife's he distrusted himself, and because of this dis-
trust he did not allow himself to respond to Jennie. He
lifted her hands gently from about his neck and kissed
her cheek lightly. He told himself that he must behave
as if nothing had happened to disturb the wedding
plans. He must ignore everything Jennie had said in
the bedroom and go on as if she had never come to
them there and said the engagement was broken.

But it was hard to think of anything casual to say
when Jennie was standing before him waiting eagerly,

quivering with expectation of his sympathy. He saw
the open suitcases on the chairs and the folded dainty
silk and linen underwear that had been packed loosely
so that some of the lacy garments hung over the edges.

"Well," he said, avoiding Jennie's eyes and going
past her into the room, "are you satisfied with all your
finery?"

To Jennie his voice sounded affectedly cheerful. She
looked at him reproachfully. "You know I don't care
about all this," she said.

He lifted his eyebrows and said in an amused tol-
erant voice, "Not the trousseau, not anything? You and
your mother have talked about nothing else for the
past three months."

"No, but it meant nothing to me. It means nothing.
I only want to be good and do good and be happy . . .
a little," Jennie said pitifully.

She lifted her chin in a gesture that he knew and
understood. There was a sort of nobility in this gesture
and yet he knew, because he shared it, that there was a
dramatic instinct in Jennie which made her conscious
that the gesture and the words were noble. When this
thought came he felt ashamed of it because her face
was so pitiful in its misery. And he had to acknowledge
that the misery was genuine.

"I want you to be happy," he said quietly, "that is
most important . . . your mother also. But we must
be sensible."

"I don't want to be sensible," Jennie said angrily.

"Then what do you want?" he asked. His voice was

irritated. He walked to the window and looked out. He understood that Jennie was waiting for some nobler and more emotional words that would rouse her. She wished him to meet her on that plane, the emotional one, and he could not do so, or would not.

"Your mother and I have been happy," he said from the window and still in the quiet tone as if he tried with difficulty to say only that which he could actually mean. "But there is one thing I have wished. Your mother has never made a single loving advance toward me. She always waited for me."

He hesitated and there was a silence. But as he spoke of her mother, not complainingly, but confidentially, Jennie's face changed. His back was toward her but she leaned to him from the place on the bed where she sat. A triumphant look came into her face. This was what she had been waiting for. This brought her father back into the relationship where he said, "We mustn't worry Mother." It was a step in the direction Jennie unconsciously wished to go. Her father was recognizing their special relationship and in another moment he would also acknowledge that she was right and that he must go to the Doctor and tell him that Jennie was right and that he must respect and love her and respect and love whatever she did. She listened eagerly for what her father would say next.

He was fingering the cord of the window shade. "You see," he continued, "any man appreciates love and active affection from the woman he loves. You can make us all happy if you will be sensible. Your Doctor is . . . stubborn. I know that. But just one loving word from you would bring him to you in a moment . . . in a second . . . I am sure of this . . . and he will be sorry. But you must be sensible, Daughter."

As he said these words Jennie's face changed again. The eager look left her face. Her shoulders drooped. When Robert looked to see what effect his words had he saw that they had had no good effect.

"You must brace up," he said irritably and then knew that it was a mistake to become irritable. He must remain calm so that he could help her and help them all. He stared out of the window again.

Jennie said, "You want me to be sensible so you can be happy. I must sacrifice myself so that everyone else can be happy. But no one cares about me or my happiness. You want me to marry a . . ." she hesitated and then said spitefully, "countryman. You want me to marry a brute so you can all be happy. Is that it?"

"I didn't know you were a snob," her father said.

"I am not, only that is true . . . You want me . . ."

"As for family, it is true you have traditions of good family behind you. The women of our family have been good wives and mothers and the men . . . but this behavior of yours . . . I can see you are not interested," he said coldly and the irritation came back into his voice.

"No, of course I am interested," Jennie said in a voice that was cold like his, and then she spoke in a loud voice without control, "You come and talk to me about my 'finery' when you know I am suffering. You

want me to be like mother, sacrificing myself like her.
You are old and think in an old-fashioned way. You
don't understand. I don't want to be timid and just
. . . just . . . a mother. Of course I want to be a
mother, but not that only . . . I want to be a person.
But you want me to be a slave . . . to a man who is
coarse . . . and . . . and . . . that   is   what   you
want. . . ."

"On the contrary . . . you misunderstand me completely . . . completely . . . I may be 'old,' but I understand . . ."

"No, it is true. You want me to marry him so that
you can get rid of me. I must make him happy and you
and the others. But what of me? You don't care what
becomes of me." She began to sob just as she had
earlier in the morning.

Robert went to the bed and laid his hand on her
shoulder. He pressed his fingers into her shoulder.
"You must brace up," he said miserably, "you must
brace up."

He sat on the bed beside her. But as she continued to
sob he rose and stood before her again.

"I can't stand it," he said, "you must do better than
this. You must control yourself. You misunderstood me
completely." He spoke loudly and emphatically. "What
I wished to say was this. The reason I spoke of your
ancestors, and you know I don't often speak of them—
what I wanted to impress on you is this . . . this. Let
these ancestors rest in you. They are yours by accident
of birth and they are part of your blood. But this is no

reason for self-congratulation or contempt of others, calling the man you love a 'countryman.' For that matter I am a 'countryman.' You were born with this gift. It is like the parable of the ten talents. What you do with your talents is the thing that counts. You are brilliant and sweet . . ."

Jennie raised her head and the eager look came back on her face. It said, "Now you are saying the right thing. Now you make me happy. Go on, go on."

Robert saw this look and it seemed to him that Jennie was thinking that at last she had made him say what she wished and that she had done this by crying and that her tears had won and that she was proud and satisfied because she had won. The look of triumph and satisfaction on her face irritated him. He controlled his voice and made it completely matter-of-fact as he continued to speak.

"What you have made of yourself is the thing that counts, just as what the Doctor has made of himself is what counts . . . in . . . character. And you have done much of it alone. You have made yourself a fine woman. Your mother and I could not give you all the advantages we wished. I would have been so glad to give you everything you needed or ought to have in material ways. We could not do much, but we have tried to give you something else. We have prepared you for life the best we know or could know. We have made mistakes. But try, Daughter, lift up your head and listen to me. Try to hear, not the words, but the meaning of what I am saying. This Doctor of yours is a

fine man. You chose him and should not be ashamed of
your choice. Never be ashamed to stand up for what
you think is right. You remember our ancestor who
would not drink to the King and Queen although everyone else did so.—And let me remind you that this ancestor you are proud of—because I know you are proud
of him—swore at the whole assembled company and at
the Governor, it is down in the records. He was not
afraid to swear and he was not afraid to say what he
believed in the face of those who disagreed with him.
Never be ashamed. If you must be snobbish and hold
yourself above other people, do so, and for God's sake
don't be ashamed of it. But I would like you to have a
bigger view of the world than that. Your mother and I
have tried to give you a bigger view. We would like
you to be so sure of yourself you will never be ashamed
to call anyone you love your friend, no matter how
despised by others for his place in life or his opinions.
No," he repeated, "never be ashamed before anyone.
The main thing is to love wholeheartedly and to respect,
and that is all, and to respect yourself . . . that is all
of life.

"Now," Robert said, and the familiar ironic smile
came on his lips, "my little philosophical sermon is
finished. You did not look interested and I imagine you
were not interested. The thing for you to do," he said
briskly, "is to get on your clothes and come downstairs
and help with the decorations. You are going to marry
a fine man, remember that." He leaned down and kissed
her forehead.

"No," Jennie said, "I am not going to marry him. I told you so and I mean it," she insisted stubbornly and looked at him. She did not look at him frankly, but tilted her head and glanced from the corners of her eyes.

Robert flung up his hands. "Then I don't know what to do or what to say. I have done everything in my power to bring you to reason. But you won't behave like a sensible girl. You refuse . . . there's nothing I can do."

He left the room and closed the door sharply. Jennie sat very still. The sound of his feet going down the hall and the stairs seemed to represent the steps of her old life going away leaving her alone stranded in a middle place where she had neither the old life nor the new, but some indeterminate position which was empty of all joy and hope. And it was intolerable to her to be in this neutral position.

VII

W HAT was the use of all that. Why did I let Caroline persuade me," Robert Middleton asked himself after he had left his daughter's room. As usual when he resented something his wife had done he called her by her name. He tried to calm himself by thinking about the practical things that must be done and took from his pocket a yellow sheet of paper on which there was written a list of things to be done that day. He and Christopher had made it out the morning before. The first item on the list was "Go to the bank." But even while he wondered if the hundred dollars he intended to borrow that morning would be enough the irritation at Jennie returned and pushed the more practical matters away. He thought, "Trying to persuade someone who doesn't understand what you say and does not wish to understand—because Jennie did not wish to understand, I could see that plainly—is like shouting from a cliff and hearing your own echo come back from the unlistening hills."

As he felt more despondent the thought of the future, tomorrow, bore down on him. Because in that future, that tomorrow, he must ask his oldest son, who was already engaged and planning his own marriage, to give up the plans and help pay the debts. Not only that, Christopher must leave college for a year or longer until the debts were paid.

Wherever his thoughts turned, to Jennie, to his sons, to the present, to the future, there seemed no place where he could take a confident step. He looked into a void as he had once looked from a cliff in the mountains. He remembered how Jennie, laughing excitedly, had foolishly stepped out on a little promontory of rock, scarcely two feet wide, to look far down into the valley below. He followed to pull her back to safety. There he retraced his steps and went back the way he had come. Here he knew he must go forward. It was impossible to retrace any of the steps that had led up to this moment. And a sort of dizziness and nausea came over him, very much like that which had come on him when he went out on the rocky promontory to bring Jennie back and looked straight down at tiny figures like ants moving in the yard of a cabin far below in the valley.

As he reached the landing of the stairs he saw that his two older sons were standing together by the fireplace. Their faces were anxious and they whispered together. When they heard him they separated quickly. Christopher came and stood at the foot of the stairs. As he looked up at his father his face took on a consciously cheerful expression, different from that it had worn when he was talking to Hugh. Robert understood that this cheerful expression was for him and wondered if they knew about Jennie.

Hugh remained by the fireplace. He had a cigarette in his hand. There was a look of aloofness about him as if he did not quite enter into all the things that happened around him. Robert thought of Hugh's last year at the University when the boy had taken a leading part in an old Greek comedy. The play was given in Greek and though most people did not understand the words they leaned forward to listen when Hugh came on the stage. Because Hugh's voice was rich and full of meaning it held their attention. And not only that, his appearance was enough to make people applaud. He did not look foolish and out of place in his Greek costume, but as if he had actually, just at that moment, come from a banquet with Socrates and Agathon. Or so Robert felt. Perhaps he only imagined that others had the same feeling.

Robert looked at this son and as he looked a deep pride took possession of him. Yet when he was with Hugh he felt uneasily that he was being judged with critical eyes. This made him uncomfortable so that he turned instinctively to his younger son, Christopher, when he was in need of sympathy or help.

Christopher was looking up at his father with intelligent and brilliant eyes in which there was no trace of critical reserve. He appeared alert and attentive and confident like a runner who only waits for the sound of the starting signal to give him a chance to outdistance all the others. He took the yellow sheet of paper from his father's hand and said, "Let's get down to work." He led his father to the table. There they bent over the list. "I will check the church decorations," he said and put a mark beside that item. "I promised Doctor to see about the license . . ."

Hugh continued to stand by the fireplace smoking his cigarette, a small frown between his brows. He envied his brother the easy demonstrativeness that made people like and trust him at once. And yet he could not change. He must show his love in more subtle ways. Sometimes, as he had just now, he felt that Christopher was too showy, too demonstrative, and that he was not entirely sincere, and criticized his brother for this fault. He listened while his father and Christopher went over again all the details of the wedding.

"I ordered the carriages for seven, though the wedding isn't until eight," Christopher said and smiled at his father, "because the girls will be on time if the carriages are waiting for them." His smile was so gracious and understanding and so full of confidence Mr. Middleton felt a return of confidence in himself. He felt that tomorrow when he revealed to his sons the full extent of the debts perhaps Christopher would say, "It's all right. We won't worry," or "You couldn't help it, father. We'll stand by you."

While they were bending over the table Susan came into the room and went to her father. Her mother, who was busy in the kitchen and dining-room, wished to see him before he left. Robert Middleton, checking off an item, answered Susan in an absent manner that he must hurry and get to the bank. Susan took this message to her mother. Then, believing that serious matters were being considered in the hall, she returned there to listen to her father and brothers. She went to the furthest corner and stood behind a large wicker chair. There in the dark corner she could see everything without being noticed. It was possible to hear her father's voice and Christopher's cheerful words and at the same time there were other interesting sounds coming from all over the house. She listened to these, also.

Far away toward the back of the house she heard Louisa, the cook, singing. This sound made her remember the evenings when she had sat on the verandah of their home in the country and heard the Negroes singing along the road when they had finished a day's work in the fields and were returning to their cabins. It was sundown. The singing retreated and became softer with distance and presently the sound was like a faint echo. Then she gave up straining to hear and leaned back on the steps and let the sounds of the country come into her. Now, just as she had in the country, Susan drowsily listened to the sounds in the house without an effort to hear them. And it was possible to hear everything, even the slap of the polishing cloth in the back hall where Ed was cleaning the men's shoes.

When Bobby, her youngest brother, came into the hall, Susan was glad. He did not go to her, but gave her an almost imperceptible nod and went to stand on the other side of the fireplace from Hugh. He stood there and leaned against the fireplace almost in the same position as Hugh. The forefinger and middle finger of his right hand curved as if he felt between them the cigarette which was forbidden because he was too young. He slowly raised this hand toward his mouth just as if he also held a real cigarette.

In the country Bobby was much more friendly with Susan than in the city. There he taught her how to make cigarettes out of the gray leaves of rabbit tobacco which grew in the fields. When they quarrelled there was a ceremony which they performed with great solemnity. After a quarrel they made cigarettes from rabbit tobacco and sitting on an Indian mound or what they had decided was an Indian mound out in the pasture they smoked the peace pipe. With this ceremony their differences were made up until they quarrelled again.

Christopher said, "And that is all." He made a long-triumphant flourish at the end of the list with his pencil, folded the list and gave it to his father.

"Won't you need a list of your own?" his father asked.

"No, sir," Christopher said confidently. "I can remember."

Mr. Middleton sighed with relief. He knew that Christopher would see to everything just as he promised, and that he was capable of doing so. He would have liked to ask Christopher's advice about Jennie, but the younger children were in the room, and it was best to ignore the quarrel as long as possible. He thought that his sons knew, but decided not to bring that dark subject into the open. One of the items on his own list, one of the things they had put down the day before, was a visit to the groom and his best man. It was a matter of courtesy. He wished that he might give this duty over to Christopher but felt that it was his.

He put the folded yellow paper in his pocket. "I am glad," he said, looking at Hugh and smiling, "that the next wedding in this family will be yours, Hugh. Then all I'll have to do is put on my best clothes and enjoy myself. Natalie's father will have all the responsibility then, eh?"

"That's right, Dad," Hugh smiled. His smile was intimate and showed the deep tenderness of his nature. Encouraged by this attention from his father, he moved from the fireplace closer to the others.

Mr. Middleton continued. "I tell you, Christopher, love is a splendid thing, a good thing. Love makes the world go round. But if you could just manage," he smiled, and in his eyes came the familiar look of ironic humor, "if you could just manage to love a rich girl! I told Hugh the same thing. But he got himself a poverty-stricken aristocrat . . ."

All the tenderness went out of Hugh's face. "I am contented with Natalie. I have nothing to regret," he said stiffly. Robert put his hand impulsively on Hugh's arm.

"Don't mind my poor little joke, Son."

"I don't mind, except . . ."

Mr. Middleton interrupted. "We all love Natalie. How well she rides. My father used to say that he could tell a gentlewoman by the way she sits a horse. I am glad you and Natalie care for each other because such love will last through trouble and even if your marriage is . . ." he had thought to say, "even if your marriage is postponed" but caught himself remembering that he must not speak of that postponed wedding until the vague tomorrow which had nothing to do with the present, the today that stretched ahead so endlessly.

Christopher saw that his father hesitated and was uncertain how to continue. And with the tact and genuine good feeling that was natural to him said, "But I will have plenty to do at Hugh's wedding. It won't be a holiday for me. The best man is always busy. I am to have the honor, am I not, Hugh?" he asked.

"Yes," Hugh said, but there was a note of doubt in his voice. He recognized this and said again in a more cordial tone, "Yes, of course."

"Then shake," Christopher said. The brothers smiled into each other's eyes as they shook hands. After that they stood closer together, as if those few words and the cordial touch of their hands had healed a misunderstanding between them.

Mr. Middleton fumbled with a button on his coat. "Perhaps you had better see the bridegroom, Christopher," he said. "No," he contradicted himself, "it is best for me to go, I know that." The smile came again to his mouth. The wrinkles at the corners of his eyes deepened as the smile spread over his face. "The bridegroom must have some attention. You know," he lowered his voice confidentially, "we men should make the bridegroom feel that he is important. Because at a wedding the bridegroom is not considered important unless he does not appear at the church. Then he becomes a scandal. It's only in the New Testament that the bridegroom shines. You remember there they don't say, 'here comes the bride,' but they shout, 'the Bridegroom cometh.' No, men are not important at a wedding. But we must do out part. And, after all, the women can't do without us."

"Yes, sir," Christopher said. He smiled at his brother as if he said, "We understand these philosophical flights of Dad's. They are queer. But what can we do. We love him."

"There is one thing," Hugh said, "we—er—that is," he looked at Christopher.

"The fact is we haven't any cash," Christopher explained.

"Yes, yes, of course." Robert took out his wallet and a bill from the wallet. "That is all I have for the present," he said, "but later, after I've gone to the bank, I'll have plenty, plenty."

Hugh lifted his hand to receive the bill, but his father, not knowing he did so, gave the bill to Christopher. Then he turned to Hugh.

"Son, I want you to stop by the florist and have him make up a bouquet for your mother. One of those things women wear . . . here," he pointed to a spot at his waist.

"A corsage," Christopher interrupted.

"Yes, that's it. Not too elaborate. Your mother likes

simple things. Something very fine but simple. You'll
know what to get, Hugh. You have so much taste. Your
mother often speaks of it. Charge the bouquet to me,"
he said quickly because he saw through the folding
door that his wife was coming towards them through
the living room. "Thank the Lord I won't have another
daughter getting married for a long time, eh, Susan?
When you grow up, Susan, just remember a license
costs two dollars, and the Bishop lives around the
corner."

They all looked at her amused. Susan stared at them
tongue-tied. She had thought no one but Bobby knew
she was in the room.

Mrs. Middleton stood between the folding doors. She
wore a black dress with a soft white ruching at her
throat and down the front of the waist. Since the death
of her other children long ago, she had always worn
black. She looked at her husband and her lips formed
a question. He understood that she was silently asking
him about Jennie. He shook his head sadly and she
hurried to him.

Hugh and Christopher went to the closet under the
stairs and took out their overcoats and hats. Mrs. Middleton said to Susan, "Go up and ask your sister if she
isn't ready to come down."

Susan lingered on the stairs and her mother said
"Hurry and tell your sister."

But Susan hated to leave them. She looked down
from the stairs on these members of her family and
felt that her arms had grown very long so that she

touched each one of them softly and lovingly. This feeling of love was mixed with dread. That morning when she was in the kitchen while the servants ate their breakfast Louisa had told her and Annie May and Ed about the death of her brother. Louisa described the corpse. She told how someone had neglected to put the pennies on the eyes of the dead in time and how the eyelids of the corpse kept lifting so that the pennies fell off. When Louisa told this Susan trembled with a feeling of dread and despair and horror.

Now she looked at her family and prayed, "Oh God, please don't let any of us die. Let us all live forever." But a desperate and terrible conviction came over her that they must die, just as Louisa's brother had died. "But if we must," she prayed, "let me die first." She did not wish to die, but it would be better to be dead herself than to see any one of these people she loved lying stiff and cold with pennies closing their dead eyes. She went slowly up the stairs, weakened by the feeling of dread.

Hugh and Christopher with their coats on and hats in their hands kissed their mother. She waited until they were gone and then faced her husband anxiously.

"What did Jennie say, how did she seem?" she asked.

"I talked to her, Caroline, but nothing I said made an impression on her, nothing." There was a slight note of triumph in his voice because what she had insisted upon had not accomplished anything. But his anxiety did not leave much room for triumph. "I tried everything, but she still insists that she will not be married," he said.

"The only thing I can think to do is talk to Doctor. I was going there anyway, and perhaps something can be done at that end. I doubt it, and dread . . ."

"Why not talk to Dr. Greve," his wife asked, "he seems to be a nice little man. And he is a close friend of Doctor's and the best man. Why not talk to him . . ."

"That's the idea," he said more cheerfully. "Mother, you're a genius. Doctor Greve is sensible and friendly and . . . but I am sure that is the thing to do. Now I must go. I am late," he went to the closet for his own coat and hat.

Mrs. Middleton stood at the front door watching her husband and saw as he went down the walk to the street that his shoulders were lifted nervously. The bent shoulders sent a pang through her because it meant that he was disturbed and because they made him appear old. She did not want him to be old. He was so straight and young and walked so swiftly always. She was thinking of him and when Susan touched her she was surprised and startled. Susan leaned against her.

"Is your sister coming down?" Mrs. Middleton asked.

"No'm," Susan told her mother, "she said, 'go away. I want to be alone.' "

"So Robert was right, and his visit did no good," Mrs. Middleton thought. She put her hand on Susan's shoulder and did not notice that Susan winced from the pressure of her fingers.

"I am afraid for your sister," she said, speaking more to herself than to Susan, "she is so headstrong.

And in marriage she must subdue her will . . . She wants to be loved . . . she demands love and it can only be given . . . My poor child! What will become of her. Lord help us."

Susan looked up at her mother and saw that she was praying. Her eyes were closed and there was the same trembling note in her voice that came in it when they were in church and her mother was saying, "We have erred and strayed from thy ways like lost sheep."

VIII

Bobby was next door playing with his friend Jack with whom he was staying at night since the guests had come. Susan wandered about the front yard. She touched the branches of the bridal-wreath bush. The branches always curved gracefully but with the ice on them they drooped a little. It was hard to imagine them with the soft clusters of little white flowers that came early in the spring. While Susan was in the yard the sun came out. It shone on the ice-covered bushes and trees and made them glitter. The pine trees were especially bright in the sunshine because they had color beneath the ice. The needles hung downwards and shook a little in a breeze. When they shook they glittered more than ever, sending out sparks of greenish light. The brown pine bark of the tree trunk was mysterious under its ice-covering.

All of Susan's enjoyment in this new world of ice was disturbed when she saw a carriage draw up at the front and her cousin, Saint John Middleton, step out of it. Saint John had come to Lexington with his mother who had married into the wealthy branch of the

Middleton family. They were staying with an old friend of his mother's who had no small children. Susan knew that Saint John's mother had sent him to play with her and Bobby. But the day before Bobby had refused to play with Saint John.

Susan had been told by her mother to be polite to Saint John because he was a guest. She met him at the steps, invited him into the house, asked him to sit down, and feeling that her duty was done, left him. She went out of the front door and around the side of the house to the kitchen.

Ed was at the table in the kitchen eating a second breakfast. He had an enormous appetite and could always clean up whatever was left over on the plates or in the dishes. Ed had worked for the Middletons before at Christmas or when they had company. He was about seventeen and said little except "Yes, sir" and "Yes'm" in his soft voice. Some people might have thought him surly, but he was always good-natured, at least Susan knew him to be so. And because she liked to stay in the kitchen she knew him quite well. She knew he had no father, but a mother and seven younger brothers and sisters. One sister was in bed, sick most of the time. His oldest sister worked for some white people in another part of town and his mother did washing. His mother, whose name was Big-Foot Mary, did the washing for the Middletons and that was how they knew about Ed.

For the past two years he had come with a wagon made out of some junk and on every Monday took the washing, done up in a sheet, back to the Negro section of town, and on Saturday returned the nicely laundered clothes folded neatly in a large basket. When he was working Big-Foot Mary came for the washing herself, balancing it on top of her head. She would never use the wagon. This was beneath her dignity.

Susan always helped her mother count the soiled clothes when they went out. Each piece of clothing was put down in a note book and the number checked on Saturday when the clean ones arrived. Susan liked the clean smell of the clothes and the fresh crackle the starched pieces gave out. She helped her mother search for bed-bugs in these clean clothes. The counting was always done in the kitchen so that if there were any bugs they would not get further than the pantry where they would die because there they had no beds to sleep in. This was the way Susan understood it. At times Susan was embarrassed by the search for bugs because Big-Foot Mary or Ed, when he brought the clothes, stood over at one side of the kitchen waiting for the counting to be finished so they could have the money. At other times she forgot all about Mary or Ed and enjoyed looking into the creases of the nicely folded sheets and dresses and other pieces of clothing for the brown dot that meant a bug. And if she found one her Mother would say, "There, I told you," in a voice that made Susan feel that something very fine had been accomplished.

Occasionally if they had to wait for Mrs. Middleton to come down to the kitchen and Ed had brought the clothes, he gave Susan a ride in the yard in his wagon. But she was getting too old for such childish amusements. Ed had made her a sort of musical instrument out of willow bark. It was a whistle and yet more than a whistle because there were three holes in the stem and if a person put his fingers one at a time on these holes he could play Dixie and Yankee Doodle. Both tunes sounded alike, but there was no doubt that four distinct sounds came out of the whistle. Susan kept it as one of her treasures. Only Bobby was allowed to handle it.

That morning, after he had made the fires, Ed had slipped off to the pressing club with some change he had received for tips to get his suit from the pressing club. He did not get the suit, and for the first time since she had known him Susan found Ed in a bad humor. He was sitting at the table in the kitchen sopping up some gravy with a piece of bread. There was a deep frown between his eyes and his kindly soft voice was agitated.

Louisa was also angry. "You got to do something about that man, Ed," she told him. "It ain't right him stealin' your only and best suit. Right after the wedding you got to get Mr. Hugh to put the law on him. Mr. Hugh's a lawyer and he'll do it."

"I do' know," Ed mumbled. "I just know I need my suit. I wanted it for today, for the wedding. And next week I was going to take my two dollars and visit my Granma. She's particular how I clothe myself, and I wanted the suit for going to see her. My Granma always give me bacon and other victuals to bring back if she's pleased with me. She lives on a farm."

Susan went to the sink, pulled down a towel and
began to wipe dishes that Louisa was washing. Louisa
slapped the cloth on the dishes as if she would like to
use it on the man they were talking about.

"What did he do?" Susan asked them.

Louisa told her. Ed had given his only and best suit
to a colored man who had a pressing club, so the man
could clean and press it. But when Ed went to get the
suit the colored man, looking so innocent, said that the
suit was gone. He said, "Somebody stole it."

"Somebody!" Louisa snorted. "I know very well who
that somebody is. That somebody is him."

"I don' know. Maybe it was stole," Ed told Louisa.
It made Louisa angry to see how easy Ed was on
people, how he seemed to think the best of everybody.

"It's probably right now in the back of that sto',"
Louisa said. "You can't tell me. Unless he already sold
it."

"I was going out with Annie May tomorrow eve-
nin'," Ed told them sadly. "Now I ain't got no suit."

He sopped up the last of the gravy with his biscuit,
put the biscuit in his big mouth, took a last swallow of
coffee and went into the house to help Annie May with
the cleaning.

Susan wiped the large hominy dish, holding it carefully, because once she had broken the willow-ware
soup tureen which was one of her mother's treasures.

"Is Ed sweet on Annie May?" she asked Louisa.

"Don't ask me," Louisa said superciliously. "I know

she ain' sweet on him. She's jus' usin' him for her own ends."

"What ends?" Susan asked.

"Don' ask me," Louisa said. "She's got something up her sleeve. I don't trust her, way she snickers and puts on airs and wears highfalutin' shoes when she works. She's a stand-up nigger."

"What's a stand-up?"

"She jes' works when she feels like it. She goes out where the white folks live and stands around on the street corners and a lady comes by and says 'you working' and Annie May says, 'no'm, I ain't working' and the white lady says 'come with me.' And then Annie May works 'til she got money enough to buy her a new dress and get some cast-off clothing and then she stops. And when the money give out she goes out on the street again and stands up. Ask your Mamma, ask her if she didn't get Annie May like that."

For some reason, perhaps because she loved Louisa, and did not know Annie May very well, Susan did not like Annie May as she did Louisa and Ed. And it was true that Annie May wore high-heeled shoes at work and Louisa said "nobody can't work good unless they got their feet solid on the ground."

Louisa was fat and her small feet hurt because they had to carry so much weight. So she wore some old felt slippers that had belonged to one of Susan's brothers. Susan could not have told anyone exactly what Louisa was or about her appearance. But she knew that from Louisa's mouth came good stories and laughing and wisdom, and from her eyes which saw clearly when Susan did anything the wrong way, there came also a feeling of friendliness. And her hands were capable and strong.

This morning Louisa was not sparing her feet, because so much depended on her. Two extra chickens must be fried for dinner. The chickens were scratching and feeding in a wired box on the back porch outside the kitchen. There was an agreement made between Louisa and Susan and Bobby that when Louisa killed a chicken she would call the children to witness the executions. And in return they picked the chickens for Louisa. So this morning Louisa had told Susan that she and Bobby might come down after breakfast and watch. Bobby was not there and Susan knew that so long as the cousin Saint John was nearby he would keep away.

Louisa and Susan finished the dishes and then it was time for the executions. They went on the porch and Louisa reached in the box for the chickens. As she tried to get hold of the legs of the chickens they ran from her and flapped their wings so that the feathers flew out. They squawked loudly. Louisa talked to them in no uncertain language and at last pulled the first one out by a leg. Then came the moment for which Susan had been waiting. Louisa stalked majestically into the yard. She clasped her right hand firmly about the chicken's neck and whirled it around her. The body came off and flapped on the ground. Usually when this happened and the body flapped without a head Susan and Bobby jumped around it and flapped their arms as if they were wings. They shrieked with excitement. But this morning, perhaps because Bobby was not there, Susan could not do this. She looked on, seeing the blood come out of the chicken's neck and felt distressed and afraid. Something was wrong. She could not enjoy this as she had before. When Louisa brought the other chicken out to the yard she turned the other way.

"I'm ready," Louisa said, "you ain't looking."

"I thought I saw a mole track," Susan answered. She kept her eyes on the mud and ice at her feet until it was evident by the sounds behind her that the second execution was finished.

"I'll have it back here in a minute," Louisa said and went into the kitchen. There she dipped the first chicken in a pan of boiling water and brought it out to Susan along with a pan for the feathers so they would not scatter in the yard.

As Susan began to pick the chicken, lifting her fingers quickly because the feathers were still scalding hot, Saint John came around the side of the house. He was looking for her. She knew he was staring at her with his brown eyes that at times seemed to be popping out of his head, but she did not raise her eyes from the chicken. She thought of him as a bull-frog like those she had seen along the edge of the pond out in the country. He had an innocent, inquiring and agreeable look like that of a bull-frog as it puts its head out of the water to see if it is safe to come out on land for a little time. His mouth was large and words rushed out of it in a breathless manner. Susan's dislike was very unreasonable, because Saint John had tried to make himself very agreeable to all of them. He was exceedingly polite.

"What are you doing?" he asked Susan.

"Picking a chicken," Susan answered.

"Let me do it," Saint John said.

Susan considered in herself whether it was necessary for her to do this because Saint John was a guest. She did not come to any conclusion about it because Saint John reached out and pulled the chicken from her hand. He was strong for such a small boy. The feathers that were in Susan's hand where she had kept them as a squirrel keeps food stuffed into his cheek until he is ready to swallow, fell out of her hand and scattered away into the yard.

Saint John set himself down opposite Susan on the steps and held the legs of the chicken toward her. "You can hold it while I do the picking," he said.

He was so confident that she would obey him, Susan reached out and held the legs of the chicken, but she whispered "Old Papa bull-frog."

"What did you say?" Saint John asked.

"I said bull-frog," Susan told him and jerked the chicken's legs.

"Hold still," Saint John ordered in an irritated voice.

"Now I've done," he said finally. But Susan saw that there were feathers left on the chicken. She told him, but he ignored her and ran into the kitchen. She followed him to the door thinking, "Now Louisa will give him down the country." She felt smug and self-satisfied thinking of what Louisa would say to him.

And Louisa did begin. She said, "What kind of picking is this . . . all the pin-feathers still on . . ." but Saint John interrupted. He spoke in his confiding, slightly breathless voice, "I know it isn't done well. But Susan wanted it done that way, Louisa. She said the pin-feathers give it a better flavor. And she said I could do the next one. You'll let me, won't you, Louisa? Because I know how to do it."

And Louisa gave the other chicken to him. He came back on the porch with the other chicken smoking in his hands.

"Louisa says you must pick all those pin-feathers off," he told Susan. "She says I must do all of this, but if I leave any pin-feathers you can pick them."

As she watched him Susan thought bitterly that even Louisa had believed him. "He is mealy-mouthed," she said to herself, "a little mealy-mouthed nothing." But this did not help. Her indignation mounted.

Saint John said, "You don't know anything about picking a chicken," and he added, "but I do. I know all about it."

But Louisa was not satisfied with his work. And it was necessary for Susan to go in the kitchen and pick out all the pin-feathers he had left, because Mrs. Middleton thought it a disgrace to the household if a chicken came on the table with even one little pin-feather left in the skin.

Louisa said to Susan when the chickens were ready,

"You better go up and change your dress. Your Mama
will be mad if she sees you covered with water and
feathers." And Susan was just going up the back stairs
when Saint John came to the back door and called her
out in a mysterious voice. She went to the back porch.
He said in a whisper, "The Yankees are coming. General Sherman is coming."

"Where?" Susan asked.

"Yonder," he said and pointed. She looked. He was
pointing to the other house. In the back yard of that
house Bobby and Jack were playing with Jack's collie.

"We must hide the silver," Saint John said mysteriously, "so the Yankees can't find it."

"What silver?" Susan asked in a harsh voice. She
did not wish to enter into any play with him.

"Wait," he told her. He went tip-toeing into the
house.

Presently he came out with a large bundle in his
arms. It was done up in an old greenish torn coat of
Ed's that had been hanging in the pantry. Over the
coat he had wrapped a newspaper. He opened the newspaper and coat and let Susan see that there was a silver
object underneath them.

"This is our silver," he whispered. "Where can we
bury it so the Yankees can't find it." He looked toward
the other yard, but Bobby and Jack were not there.
"They are hiding in ambush to creep up on us," Saint
John told her, "we must hurry."

In spite of herself, in spite of the fact that she did
not wish to play with him, the mysterious words and

manner entered into Susan and suddenly she began to feel that it was true that the Yankees were coming and that they must hurry or the silver would be lost. She followed Saint John into the yard.

At that moment Ed came out and emptied a scuttle of ashes into the garbage can. The ashes came up into his face and he sputtered and gasped and fanned them away with his shovel. But his face was covered with the finest ash and it looked as if he had suddenly become very pale.

"Wait," Saint John said to Susan. He went to Ed and spoke to him. "You come with us," he said to the Negro boy. "Come," he ordered. It was curious that no one seemed to think of disobeying Saint John. After only the slightest hesitation Ed obeyed him.

"Take your shovel," Saint John said to him, "and go over under that bush, no, under the fig tree and dig a hole. Go on," he said because Ed was staring at him. "I said go on and dig that hole," he repeated.

Ed walked to the tree, looked up at the spreading limbs where the sun shone hotly on the ice. He looked back at the house and there was a doubtful expression on his face. But Saint John made a lordly motion with his hand and Ed knelt down on the wet grass and began digging.

"It is night and Ed is our faithful slave," Saint John whispered to Susan. "The enemy is almost here. Hide under the branches," he added.

As he spoke Susan felt that the enemy was surely

hiding somewhere near them and that Ed was actually the slave who was burying the silver in the dark night.

"I know," she whispered, "my grandfather hid ours in a hollow tree with dead leaves over it, at night, so they couldn't see."

"My grandfather buried ours," Saint John said and the manner in which he said it made it seem a very superior thing to bury silver rather than hide it in a hollow tree. "At least his faithful slave buried it," Saint John whispered.

They crept under the limbs of the fig tree to watch. The sun made the ice on the limbs of the fig tree melt, and the water dripped on their faces. It dripped on Ed's face and streaked the gray ash that covered it. It seemed as if the streaks of water that passed through the fine ash on Ed's face were tears.

When Ed had finished digging, when Saint John had told him it was enough, Saint John put the wrapped-up bundle in the hole. Then he told Ed to cover it with the dirt heaped up at the side. Ed looked at Susan enquiringly, but she was intent on getting the bundle safely buried. Ed shovelled on the dirt and patted it down.

"Now you can go," Saint John said to him. As they straightened up after bending over the hiding place, he said, "You mustn't tell even if the Yankees torture you. Because you are my faithful slave and faithful slaves don't tell their master's secrets."

Ed did not answer and it was plain that he did not understand this foolishness and only wished to be done with it. He went off with a relieved expression on his face, wiping it with his elbow, for he had begun to feel uncomfortable with the water and ashes mixing there.

Saint John turned on Susan. "And don't you tell either," he warned her. "If you do I'll wring your neck like . . . like a chicken. And I'll tell your Mother you said a bad word."

"A bad word!" Susan repeated. She was still living in the darkness of night when they had buried the silver and the enemy was still hidden out in the night ready to attack them. Then she understood what he had said. "I did not say a bad word to you," she told Saint John.

"Yes, you did. You called me a son of the devil."

"I did not call you a son of the devil," Susan protested. But she thought to herself that perhaps she would like to. Only she had forgotten for a little while that she disliked him.

"Yes, you see," Saint John told her derisively. "You did, you just did. And now if you tell . . ."

Susan ran into the kitchen. Louisa called out, "Ain't you changed that dress yet?" But she did not stop to speak to Louisa. She felt that a terrible injustice had been done and did not know which way to turn for friendship or comfort. Louisa had turned against her because of the chickens. She had believed Saint John who was a liar.

She slipped up the back stairs to her mother's room and opened the drawer in the walnut dresser which held her clothes. In the drawer there were dresses and underwear fresh from last Saturday's washing.

With the freshly washed clothes there were some

others that were not starched. Susan took out a dress to change into and then the soft clothes held her attention. They were the first petticoats she had ever possessed with lace on them. When Jennie's trousseau was being made she let Susan have her old petticoats and Mrs. Middleton had made Susan six new underskirts. These petticoats with lace around the edges and even on the waist around the neck were Susan's most prized possessions. Susan lifted all six of them from the drawer and laid them on the bed. Her face that had been gloomy and angry began to lighten. She smiled as she touched the lace-edged ruffles. As a dog goes away by itself to lick its wounds, Susan licked the hurts she had received by looking at her treasures. But looking at them did not satisfy her. She lifted one of the petticoats over her head and then another. The lace edged ruffles stood out about her knees. She could see them in the mirror above the dresser. It was so pleasant to see the lace Susan took all the petticoats from the bed and put them on. The last two she was unable to button even at the top. But that did not matter. The lacy edges whirled about her knees when she turned and there was a sound of rustling, like the sound the skirts of the cousins made when they moved about the house.

IX

ROBERT MIDDLETON went directly from his home to the bank where he met two friends, Richard Childs and James Bell, who signed his note for a hundred dollars. This was the fourth time he had borrowed money since early fall. The first was a five hundred dollar note he had taken out when he saw that the trousseau and wedding would cost more than had been expected. He thought this five hundred with the two hundred that Jennie had saved from her salary would cover everything. But additional and unexpected expenses came up. The sons must have new clothes and Mrs. Middleton and Susan new dresses for the wedding. And even from the early fall, because Jennie was at home for the first time in three years in the winter, and because the very atmosphere of the coming wedding had taken possession of everyone, Mrs. Middleton found it impossible to practice the little economies that she had learned during the years. The whole atmosphere of the house was against her. Also a sum of money did not rest for very long in Robert's pockets even when it was not actually in his pockets but in a checking account at the bank. With this money in the bank he felt a vast confidence and elation, a real joy, not in the money itself, but because for a little while he need not think about the next day's expenditures with the usual dread. Instead of holding himself to a rut, pressing his generous nature into a small compass, like a bale of cotton is compressed between great steel jaws for shipping, he was able to expand and when his wife asked for something that was needed he could say, "Certainly, Mother, I'll write a check."

But too many of these checks were written and the five hundred dollars soon vanished. Robert borrowed two hundred personally from his friend James Bell and a hundred more from the bank. On this morning he had asked James Bell to sign his note for another hundred. His salary was a hundred and fifty dollars a month.

After signing the note the three men left the bank and stopped on the sidewalk. Robert thanked short, rotund Mr. Childs. They shook hands and Richard Childs hurried away to his law office.

Robert patted his breast pocket where the bills he had just received lay safely in his wallet, "Well, that's done," he said. "I don't know how to thank you, Jim." He looked directly into James Bell's face. When he saw the warm sympathy there and realized that all his requests for help had not alienated this friend an unexpected emotion very difficult to control took possession of him, and his voice shook when he spoke again: "When Susan grows up and falls in love," he said, "I'll say to her 'Daughter, you have my blessing. Here's two dollars. The Bishop lives around the corner.'"

"I was just considering that myself," James Bell smiled. "My oldest is sixteen. I told my wife I'm glad we aren't like the French who must provide dowries for their girls. I drew up a marriage contract once for two French families. Holy Moses! it was a contract. My stenographer nearly swooned. There's a fixed amount a girl's father must pay for each profession. Doctors and lawyers come high. In France you'd have to shell out quite a sum for that Doctor of Jennie's."

"According to that I couldn't afford a hod-carrier." Robert's mouth twisted into a rueful grimace. He stood aside to let two men enter the bank and the friends began walking along the street. They were very different in appearance. James Bell was a huge man. He spoke with a slight drawl and his voice and his face expressed a kindly sympathy and a readiness to laugh at the least provocation. Robert Middleton was as tall as his friend, but was thin. He held himself with a simple and natural dignity, though at times the natural dignity became overemphasized as if he thought of himself as sitting on a horse at the head of a parade.

"When we planned the wedding," Robert said, "I thought it might cost five hundred dollars. Well, 'the best laid plans' you know. Since the first yard of valenciennes lace was bought for the first pantalets in the trousseau there has been one thing or another—especially another."

"Yes, in a large family it's always—another," James Bell said and laughed. "We were congratulating George English on the new addition to his family the other day. But George complained. He said, 'My wife presents me with another as soon as my back is turned.' And one of the men said, 'Soon as your back is turned? Oh, no, George, on the contrary.'"

Robert laughed with his friend but his laughter was not easy and natural. "That note this morning makes nine hundred dollars," he said gloomily. "I'll be forced to take Christopher out of college and even Bobby must work when he can. I'm glad Hugh has finished his law and is practicing."

"Hugh is a fine boy, a fine boy, steady and dependable," James Bell said, "and Christopher. I think Chris will make a brilliant lawyer."

As James Bell comforted his friend, he felt a deep sympathy for him and also a friendly contempt for this man who was so helpless about all the practical matters concerned with life. But his own life had been made more significant by helping his friend, just as in a larger way he had felt his own existence of more importance when he paid the doctor who saved the life of one of his children.

"Come to my office," he said impulsively to Robert.

"No, no, I can't this morning. Too much to be done," Robert protested, but he continued to walk down the street dreading to leave his stable and good-natured friend. As they walked he considered whether he should tell James about the quarrel. "Perhaps it would help to take him with me to see the Doctor," he thought and then rejected that idea. "Somehow the gossip would get out," he told himself, "and before an hour everyone would know about the quarrel and it would be exaggerated twenty times. No, we must keep that to ourselves. Jennie must be persuaded in some way to go on."

They turned off the main street and entered a short side street on which there was a long building with rows of offices on each side. This long two-story building was called Law Range.

In the hallway, just in front of the door of James Bell's office Robert stopped. James Bell walked lightly into the office, laid his hat on the desk, spoke to his stenographer, and came back to stand just inside the door. He looked over his shoulder and saw that the stenographer was busy. Nevertheless he lowered his voice.

"Speaking of your son-in-law, your future son-in-law," he said, "I see you didn't do anything about what I told you several months ago."

"What could I do?" Mr. Middleton asked irritably. He was especially irritated, not with his friend, but because he knew that he was at fault and that he should have done something about the matter. "What could I do?" he repeated, "when a girl is in love . . . I did speak to Jennie as you advised, at least I tried to, but she was so much in love she wouldn't listen, and then I neglected . . . I didn't try again . . ."

"Well, I suppose it isn't too important. But I feel a responsibility since I introduced them. We were in that hotel and he came in. I had gone to the cigar stand and Jennie was standing with my wife near the stairs. Jennie had just said one of those recitations for the guests, you know how informal a summer hotel is, and he had evidently heard her. He came over to me,—I had known him for several years,— and said, 'I must know her.' He is a man who never gets excited and yet he was . . . I could swear he was trembling. And he hadn't been drinking. I had never believed in love at first sight. But there it was . . . before me."

"Yes, yes, I know." Although he had heard this story before it was especially welcome to Robert at this time. "Yes, it must be the real thing," he said. "It must be a great love, and I believe everything should be sacrificed for such a love. Yes, and no one could know better than you, Jim. You saw them at the very first meeting, and you saw them last night. How did they strike you. Didn't it seem to you they were particularly fitted for each other?"

"Well, when you say particularly fitted. . . ."

"I mean Jennie is emotional, we know that so why not recognize it, and he is . . . I would say he has a great deal of plain common sense. Wouldn't you say this . . . so they will balance each other. . . ."

"Well . . . he is a splendid man, Robert. Only, up

in those mountains the boy babies drink whiskey instead of mother's milk. Everyone says he will be a brilliant surgeon. But I felt I must tell you because of the responsibility . . ."

"Yes, I understand. And yet, don't we all drink sometime or other in our lives. I did for a time until my wife . . . it all depends on the woman," he reassured himself, "a woman can influence a man . . ."

"Yes, that is true, absolutely true," Jim said hastily. He slipped his arm across Robert's shoulders. "I shouldn't have brought it up, Bob. But your daughter is so sweet. We all love her. She has had rare training and well . . . you might call it fastidious training. However, I'll see you at the wedding tonight. Will the minister intone the service," he asked, smiling.

"Dr. Grant will not officiate," Robert said in a stilted manner.

"Officiate is good, that is good," Jim laughed. "He is very officious. I must say I don't care for that man. And I don't care for that new-fangled intoning. You know of what it reminds me." He took his arm from Robert's shoulder, "You know what it sounds like exactly when he sings 'Oh Lord show thy mercy upon us'. Like this," Jim changed his deep voice into a singsong nasal tone and chanted, 'M-y-y dominecker rooster can beat your dominecker rooster, Amen."

A pleased smile came on Robert's face. And then the smile spread on his lips and he laughed out loud. "Yes, yes, like that, exactly like that," he pushed out his stomach in imitation of the stout minister, jerked back his head and intoned just as his friend had done, "No-o-o your dominecker rooster can't beat my-y-y dominecker rooster, Amen."

Jim swayed back on his heels and in the same pompous voice intoned again, "I-bet-you-ten-dollars my-y-y dominecker rooster can . . ."

At that moment some lawyers who had been detained at home by late breakfasts hurried into the building. The friends stood apart, trying to appear dignified and only looking as if they were little boys caught in some mischief.

"Getting rid of your daughter today?" one of the men who had just come in said to Robert.

"She's getting rid of me," Robert answered, "the old man's in the background now. The women have captured the citadel. It is theirs."

"You've got a clear day, after all," the lawyer opened his door. "I thought the ice was here to stay."

After these men had left the hall the two friends stood without speaking. Their little moment of pleasure was interrupted and the more serious matters were put into the background by the laughter they had enjoyed, so it was impossible to bring the serious thoughts into speech again.

Robert said, "I must be going."

James Bell, now thinking about the work waiting for him in the office, said good-bye.

"Thank you again," Robert said earnestly and hurried toward the street. His quick energetic steps sounded on the tiled floor of the hallway. As he passed an office with its doors open, a loud voice said, "Of course a promise made under stress is not binding unless . . ."

Robert thought of all these men in their offices going about the every day work and they seemed so free of care, in such a happy state of freedom from responsibility he envied them. What he wished most to do as he walked along the street saying good-morning automatically to friends and acquaintances, answering sly allusions to the wedding or good wishes, was to go to his own office, shut himself in and catch up with all the work that had been accumulating for days. This state of quiet industry seemed the only natural and decent way for a man to live and he longed for it. But this was impossible and he knew it was impossible. He took from his pocket the folded yellow sheet he and Christopher had worked on that morning and opened it. He scratched off the first item "go to the bank" with his pencil and this gave him a sense of having accomplished something. Below the first item was written, "Call on our guests" and under that a list of the guests. He raised his hand and gestured to the Negro driver of a hack. The hack drew up to the curb. Robert stepped in and gave the name of a hotel. As they drove along the street he thought of the hundred dollars which was in his wallet. "I will pay a part of each bill at the hotel," he told himself, for the Veterans who had come from a distance were staying at the hotel as his guests.

Robert was a lay-reader in the church and for this

reason knew more of the Bible than most men. As he realized that the next day he could not pay all of the hotel bill, but must ask them to wait he thought of himself as like the steward in the Bible who said to himself when he found that he was ruined, "What shall I do. I have not the strength to dig, to beg I am ashamed." But he remembered that this steward was receiving money, not paying it out and searched in his mind for the details of another parable. "I remember," he thought, "it was about the servant who went down on his knees and begged his Lord for time to pay up his debt. And yet I haven't reached the place where I must go on my knees. Everyone trusts me. My credit is good."

The Negro driver said "whoa" and pulled up his bony horse to the curb.

"All right, Uncle," Robert stepped out of the hack, "wait for me," he added and hurried into the hotel.

"General Stephens said to come right up, Mr. Midleton," the clerk said respectfully.

Robert smiled as he walked toward the elevator. He remembered again that his credit was good, that people trusted him. The hotel clerk spoke to him respectfully and these things helped him to recover his confidence. He stood outside himself and looked on Robert Middleton and spoke just as someone in the community, the clerk at the desk, for instance, might speak of him. "Robert Middleton is a good father," the clerk might say. "Though he has been poor he has given all his children an education and other advantages as well.

And though he is often behind, he has eventually paid
up every cent of his debts. He is not a great man and
never will be a great man. It is too late for that. But
he has given his children ideals and has made them
live up to these ideals."

In his room on the third floor of the hotel General
Stephens, the Veteran on whom Robert was calling,
stood before a long mirror. He was trying on the new
cadet-gray uniform which had been made by his tailor
for the wedding. All of his clothes were made to order,
but he was especially anxious for the uniform to be
exactly correct.

As he looked at himself in the mirror the fingers of
his right hand passed over the two divisions of his
gray whiskers that reached the top gold buttons of the
tunic. Everything seemed correct. The two rows of
gilt buttons, decorated with a raised eagle surrounded
by stars, the insignia for a General Officer of the Confederacy, were four inches apart at the top and three
inches at the bottom of the coat. The skirt of the tunic
swung gallantly halfway between hip and knees according to regulations. The tunic collar sloped at an
angle of thirty degrees and the General's parted
whiskers showed glimpses of a gold embroidered
wreath with three stars enclosed. On his sleeves four
rows of gold braid extended around the seam of the
cuff and up his sleeve to the bend of his elbow. It was
a magnificent uniform, and the General looked magnificent in it. He knew this was so, and turned before the
mirror admiring his appearance. The gray trousers

were pressed into a fine crease and had two stripes of gold lace on the outer seams. The gold flashed in the sunshine that came in the window.

But the most effective part of the uniform was not the gold lace nor the buttons. It was a sash of red silk with bullion fringes. The General felt uncertain about the sash, not because a sash did not belong with the uniform, but because instead of the duller buff sash which lay on the bed with the new white gloves, he had decided to use the red sash which was correct only for the General Staff and officers of the Engineers.

But he could not regret this breach of regulations. The red sash, wound twice around his waist, tied behind his left hip and hanging toward his knees with the fringes swaying as he moved, was exactly the right shade of red that set off the gray and gold of the uniform. It gave the whole uniform a dashing air that the buff sash could never have given it.

The General hoped secretly that none of the other officers would notice the breach of regulations, and comforted himself with the thought that few Veterans paid special attention to the regulations and many of them had forgotten them during all the years that had passed since they had fought together. Only the year before General Stephens' own camp had suddenly become agitated over the breaches of regulations in the uniforms and had resurrected the old order of June 6, 1861, Order Number 9.

The General turned before the mirror and the red sash swung from under the skirt of the tunic. He

thought with pleasure of how it might affect young
Lucy, the Middleton's niece. He had enjoyed the rehearsal at the church and the reception the evening before. The girls, rosy young and smiling paid little
attention to the younger men, but gathered about the
Veterans, so that the older men were taken back to
the days when they had gone out as young heroes to
fight for the South. As he watched the red sash swing
out from the tunic the General felt for the sword that
should have been there. A dreamy and vague impression of the first year of the Civil War came on him
as it had the evening before. He forgot the miserable
later years of the war when it had not been a romantic
experience but a bitter and grim reality and only remembered the beginning that was like the joyful first
flight of a young bird that has known nothing but the
comfort and security of a nest.

"Come in," he said as Mr. Middleton's knock
sounded on the door.

"This is a great pleasure, General," Robert said.
"As I told you last evening I would have called yesterday, only there was so much to be done, and I knew
you would understand . . ."

"Of course, of course . . ."

"Are you comfortable?"

"Absolutely, sir. Won't you sit down. I was trying
on my uniform for this evening."

"Yes, I see. It is splendid, splendid," Robert smiled,
"the girls will be dazzled . . ."

"It is exactly like the uniform General Lee wore at

Appomatox," General Stephens said solemnly. Though he had been thinking of the girls and of Lucy particularly, he did not wish Mr. Middleton to believe that he wore the uniform for them. "General Iredale was in the Engineers, was he not?" he asked.

"Yes, but later of the General Staff. You saw his uniform last evening. He wore it because . . ."

"Yes, I knew he was from the Engineers, the raised E in German script . . ."

"On his buttons, yes," Mr. Middleton interrupted, "General Iredale is a splendid type of man and soldier. He built the bridges your men crossed . . ."

"No doubt the Engineers were essential. But you must sit down," General Stepens insisted because Robert had continued to stand.

"I have only a few moments," Robert sank into one of the stuffed arm chairs. "We are sorry we could not have all our guests in our home," he said, "but it was impossible . . . you understand the house had to be given over to the women. It is like a young ladies seminary. I feel I don't belong there myself. You know, don't you, that the other groomsmen who do not live in the city are at this hotel . . . Colonel Sims of the Cavalry is just down the hall . . ." he went on to speak of the other Veterans who were to take part in the wedding.

"I came on the same pullman with General Doty," General Stephens said.

"You are both from the same part of your state. It must have been a tiring trip. . . ."

"We were talking about the history of your state, and about the Middletons, naturally," the General smiled, "no one who speaks of your state can fail to speak of the Middletons. They are part of its history."

"A cigar?" Mr. Middleton asked. He offered the expensive cigars he had bought that morning.

"You are not smoking?" the General asked.

"No, I prefer my old pipe," Robert said, "no, perhaps I will try one of these," he took one of the cigars from his pocket but did not light it. "We belong to the quieter branch of the family," he said, "my grandfather's place is still there—we were not in the line of Sherman's march. It is not one of the celebrated mansions, but it was a . . . home, quiet and unostentatious, just as my grandfather was . . ." he halted himself abruptly.

"That little niece of yours is a beauty," General Stephens said.

Robert listened while the General spoke about Lucy, but the words did not penetrate his thoughts. "The General thought we belonged to the wealthy and distinguished branch of the family," he told himself, "but there is nothing to apologize about. Why did I seem to apologize."

"Yes," he said aloud, answering a question from General Stephens, "Lucy is my only brother's child. She is beautiful, one of the beauties of the family. She has just had an unfortunate love affair."

They spoke of Lucy until Mr. Middleton rose to leave. As he was saying good-bye the General said,

"One moment, I almost forgot to tell you. Your wife called and left a message. I believe the Bishop wishes to see you on an important matter."

"Yes, the Bishop. Yes I will see him," Robert answered. "You must come to our home and feel that it is your own," he said as he shook hands with the General at the door of the room.

He repeated these words to the other guests whom he visited. When he had crossed the last of them off on his list he sighed. "Now for the Doctor," he said to himself, "I wish this did not have to be done. And perhaps it is already settled. Perhaps he has telephoned Jennie and everything is settled again."

But he did not feel very hopeful.

X

THAT morning old Mr. Bauer, who had given all the Middleton children music lessons and still taught Susan and Bobby, came from the German colony across the river to tune the piano for the reception. He had just recovered from an attack of rheumatism and walked with a limp, but he was very efficient and no one knew the old piano better than he did. It had belonged to Mrs. Middleton's family and was one of those instruments made with care and precision and the best quality of material. He loved it for its own sake as an instrument, and it always gave Mrs. Middleton great pleasure to hear him express his admiration. Mr. Bauer had become almost a member of the family and everyone knew his history.

The year before the Civil War when he was twenty-one years old Mr. Bauer lived in the household of an ex-ambassador to Russia and taught his daughters music. These daughters were born in Russia and the Czarina had been their god-mother at the christening. One of the daughters had a Russian name, Doushka. Those old days were very precious to Mr. Bauer and he often talked of them. When Susan did not know her lesson well he said, "Doushka, although of a more high altitude than you, a god-child of the Czarina, nevertheless knew her lesson." Although Susan knew that this Doushka was an old lady, a great-grand-mother Mr. Bauer made her appear in his talk as a little girl, a perfect legendary figure. And Susan felt an obstinate resentment against this perfect little girl, especially at the moment when her small fingers were trying awkwardly to find the note on the keyboard that corresponded to the written note on the sheet of music before her. Though Mr. Bauer was an old man he had great strength in his fingers and when a pupil struck the wrong note he rapped the knuckles of the fingers that had struck the note with his pencil. His high and cracked irascible voice could be heard all over the house when he became angry because Susan or Bobby had not practiced enough. At times he even made Susan cry, especially when the pencil came down on her bent knuckles just at the place where the bones were nearest the skin. And yet his old face with a halo of white hair was quite angelic and there were times when he was kind. Then his voice was quiet as he counted "one-two, one-two" and the pencil went up and down in his hand and his small wrinkled lips smacked together at each count.

Because his old pupil, Jennie, was getting married Mr. Bauer took a special interest in tuning the piano. He explained this to Bobby who was under the piano watching the process. Bobby watched every movement

that Mr. Bauer made but at the same time he kept
at a safe distance from the heavy tuning key, because
no one ever knew when Mr. Bauer might have one of
his spurts of temper and the key was much heavier
than a pencil.

From his place under the piano Bobby could see the
feet of people who passed through the room. There
was much activity on the lower floor of the house. The
bridesmaids and ushers were decorating the whole
lower floor. They draped the graceful smilax from the
corners of the rooms to the chandeliers and hung gray
moss from the corners and at the center. Over the doors
and above the mantels they tacked Confederate flags.

But the bridesmaids and ushers did not decorate in
a spirit of festivity. There was not much laughter in
the house. They had learned about the quarrel between
Jennie and the Doctor and were unsure of themselves
and of what they were trying to do. There was a feeling that everything that was done, like putting up the
decorations, might all be for nothing. The bridesmaids
who found it necessary to go upstairs passed the closed
door of Jennie's room with apprehensive glances as if
the room held an ogre who might spring out at them.

Mr. Bauer struck an out-of-tune key and it whined
across the strings that were exposed by the upraised
top of the old square instrument. The note whined
through the house. And when he struck a chord, dis-
cordant and rasping, it seemed to express the whole
feeling of discontent that was in the hearts of the
people who went about the house. Everyone was nerv-

ous and on edge. One of the ushers teased Lucy Middleton about General Stephens and instead of laughing at the implied flattery as she would have at another time, Lucy became angry and ran upstairs to hide in her room.

But in spite of the uncertainty all the small and large plans that had been set in motion days, even weeks before were carried along by their own momentum. The bride's flowers, which had been ordered at least a month before, were brought to the door by a messenger. Pamela and Janie, who answered the bell, called Mrs. Middleton and Nancy from the pantry where they were helping to get the dinner ready.

Mrs. Middleton untied the string of the box and let the three girls peep at the flowers. They were lilies of the valley and one white orchid. The girls exclaimed over the flowers.

"I do wish Jennie could see them," Janie said. Her voice was like herself, delicate and sweet.

Up in her mother's room Susan had heard the doorbell and her curiosity would not allow her to keep away. She slipped down the back stairs and very quietly joined the little group round the flowers. Standing on tip-toe she looked over Janie's shoulder.

To Mrs. Middleton Janie's wish was like an inspiration. She thought immediately that the sight of the flowers, her bridal flowers, might rouse Jennie. She covered the box and tied the string loosely about it and put the box into Susan's hand.

"Take these up to your sister," she told her small

daughter. And then she had another inspiration. "Pamela, why don't all of you go with Susan," she urged, "you and Janie," she added because Nancy was needed in the pantry.

The girls looked at her dubiously. "Do you think she'd want us?" Janie asked timidly.

"Let's go," Pamela said sturdily, "she can't eat us."

"Yes, go . . . go," Mrs. Middleton said with nervous emphasis. "It will do her good. Show her the flowers and make her . . . make her . . ."

"Yes, yes. I know," Janie said hurriedly because she saw that Mrs. Middleton was close to tears.

Mrs. Middleton did not wish to go up herself and she sent the bridesmaids because she thought they would help Jennie to recover, but she hurried them away because she did not want them to suggest that she go with them. Though she loved Jennie, she was a little afraid of this imperious daughter and felt obscurely, for she did not put the feeling into words even to herself, that there was an antagonism between them. She had felt this antagonism before at times and it disturbed her. She did not understand it, and was ashamed of it, but it was there.

The sheets that had been laid over the wedding presents early that morning to protect them from the dust and from scraps of moss and smilax made the large dining-room appear like a store that has been closed for the night when all the goods are covered away from the dust. Because of the sheets Mrs. Middleton did not notice that the largest wedding present, a silver bowl, was gone from the table. She and Nancy spoke to the ushers who were completing the decorations in the dining-room and entered the pantry. The door swung to behind them.

Mrs. Middleton felt closer to Nancy than to the other girls because Nancy was her own sister's daughter, and because she was willing to accept responsibilities. Nancy had the raw-boned look of the Scotch ancestor of Mrs. Middleton's family. This ancestor had gone to France from Scotland as a very unimportant member of the staff of the Scottish Queen Mary. He stayed in France because he was given some land and a title by the French king. But he became homesick for Scotland and returned there, taking with him his sons and a daughter and her French husband. The French husband stayed only a little while in Scotland. He and his wife came to America.

Nancy DuPre had sandy-red hair and deep blue eyes, with light sandy lashes. Her appearance, her tall raw-boned length had made her more mature and imaginative than other girls of her age. She was eighteen.

All morning she had respected her aunt's reserve and had not spoken of the quarrel. But her aunt had tacitly admitted the quarrel in the hall, and she went about the work in the pantry with a distressed look on her face and did not try to hide it. The night before Nancy had had a dream, and this dream disturbed and excited her. She had longed to tell someone about it, but did not feel close enough to the other girls to share it with them. She was more at home with older people.

Now as the pantry door swung to behind them she put her hand on her aunt's shoulder. "Aunt Carrie," she asked, "what has happened to Jennie, why is all this uncertainty?"

"What has happened?" Mrs. Middleton asked. Her voice sounded almost stupid, because all her attention was on her inward thoughts.

"Yes," Nancy said. She spoke emphatically as if she tried to rouse someone from sleep. "We know Jennie and Doctor have quarrelled, but why? What is it all about? Is it serious?"

Mrs. Middleton groaned. "I don't know what it is all about, Nancy. There has been a quarrel, a serious quarrel. Jennie says she will not be married tonight. That is the long and short of it."

"So that is why I had the dream," Nancy said in an awe-struck voice.

"What was it?" Mrs. Middleton stopped her work and looked straight at her niece, anxiously and curiously. "Not that I believe in dreams . . ."

"I dreamed," Nancy said mysteriously, "that we were standing outside the church, just as we stood last night after the rehearsal. Only Jennie had on her wedding dress. I could see the church clearly and even those tombstones at the left of the church. I am not sure whether the ceremony had already been performed or whether it was before. But suddenly a storm came up. There was thunder and lightning and a bolt of lightning came down and struck the bride and groom— they were standing together—and then a great cloud rolled down and I couldn't see them any longer. I couldn't see anything, the church or the tombstones or anyone. All had vanished."

"It was certainly a premonition . . . it could not be anything else." There was wonder in Mrs. Middleton's voice. "Perhaps at that very moment they were quarrelling . . ."

"My old nurse said I had second sight," Nancy said proudly, "and I was born with a veil over my face."

"The Scotch are supposed to have second sight," Mrs. Middleton agreed. "Do you remember when your uncle was in that train wreck? Just the night before it happened I dreamed . . ."

"And in the dream I saw everything clearly," Nancy continued. She had not even heard her aunt speak. "I even saw that old tombstone near the corner of the church and the letters on it. You remember the one that says 'scared to the memory' instead of sacred."

Although her voice was distressed, it had a sort of wonder in it and an excitement that was almost hysterical. Mrs. Middleton recognized the hysteria and put her hand on the girl's arm.

"You mustn't let yourself get excited about these things, Nancy. Remember you have French blood also. Your great-uncle Raoul was very practical . . ."

"Yes, I know, I know," Nancy said. But on her face there was still the look of a person who knows that she has been singled out by some unknown force to be the instrument of that unknown and mysterious force. But even while she was feeling this mysterious force in herself and acknowledging it, her capable fingers began to arrange the salad on the small plates which had been placed on the shelf of the china closet.

XI

SUSAN walked up the stairs very proudly carrying the box of flowers. She was an important person. Her mother had put a double responsibility on her, to carry the flowers and also to make Jennie feel more cheerful. It was flattering to be chosen for this mission. The petticoats Susan had put on in her mother's room just before she came down to answer the door-bell added to her feeling of importance. She moved her body so that the ruffles on the six petticoats touched her knees and swung about them.

Pamela and Janie followed Susan up the stairs but they went with less confidence, unsure of the way in which Jennie might receive them. They were under the influence of the feeling of insecurity and doubt that was in Mrs. Middleton's face and that they had felt in the house all morning. They mounted the stairs with their arms about each other as a sort of protection from this feeling, as people get closer to each other when there is any suggestion of danger.

Pamela glanced up at Susan and as she did so stifled a giggle. Her hand pressed against Janie's waist and she whispered, "Look at Susan." Janie looked and she also began to giggle. "What in the world!" she whispered.

The ruffles on the six petticoats above them swung outward over the steps as Susan's little body swayed importantly in a comic imitation of some grown-up person.

The girls let Susan go ahead to Jennie's door. But as they reached the hall Pamela ran into the room she was sharing with Lucy and dragged Lucy into the hall. "Look at Susan . . . Petticoats," she whispered. Lucy came reluctantly. She was still angry because they had teased her about General Stephens. But as she looked at Susan her sullen expression lightened. The three girls huddled together laughing. They tried to stifle the laughter, but their efforts only made them giggle more easily. And the sound of their own voices was pleasant and reassuring to them.

Susan heard the laughter, but was too much concerned with her responsibility to pay attention to it. Only it stirred in her a desire to smile. She flung open Jennie's door and said, "Here are the bride's flowers," in an officious and important voice.

Jennie was dressed. Her hair was combed and her face powdered and the room was in order. But she was staring into the fire with a look as if she did not live in the room, but was a long way from it living in some other place. Susan's abrupt entrance startled her. A shiver went over her whole body. When she understood that the person who had interrupted her thoughts was Susan she asked irritably, "Why didn't you knock?"

At once, when Jennie spoke, Susan's important and officious manner vanished. She tip-toed to the bed and laid the box there instead of taking it directly to Jennie. The tone of severe reproach Jennie had used was one she had no way of combating. If Jennie had smiled even a little everything would have been different. But the reproach took the spirit out of Susan and she became limp just as a starched dress loses all its stiffness when it is put into a tub of water.

But the girls in the hall were not affected by Jennie's attitude simply because they had forgotten to think about Jennie and were thinking of Susan's petticoats. They stood in the doorway and just as Susan had brought the flowers to cheer Jennie they brought their laughter with them. Janie and Pamela made ridiculous motions trying to attract Jennie's attention to Susan. Pamela lifted her own skirt to show her petticoat and pointed directly to the little girl. Susan's back was to them but she heard their giggles. And suddenly like a remembrance of something that had happened long before she heard the laughter of the girls on the stairs and in the hall, and at last she realized that this laughter was connected with herself. She became conscious of the six petticoats and as she became conscious of them and of their significance to the others they lost all the delight she had felt in them, and became instead of light and airy articles of beauty, something heavy that weighed on her. A red flush came into her face.

She wished more than anything else to get away from
the room. And as the girls came into the room she tried
to slip past them to the door. But Jennie at last understood what the girls were trying to tell her.

She called out, "Susan, come here to me. No, stand
out where I can see you."

Now it was impossible for Susan to go. She came
from behind the girls obediently. But the petticoats
weighed her down and her knees were weak.

"Turn around," Jennie ordered. Susan turned. Her
dress flared out. As it did so Jennie saw that in addition
to the new petticoats Susan had found an old dark
flannel that had belonged to Jennie long ago and tucked
it in with the rest. Jennie saw this. She tried to make
her face stern. But now the bridesmaids were laughing
out loud. They came further into the room shrieking
with laughter. And Jennie left the fireplace and joined
them. Pamela threw her arm about Jennie.

"Susan," Jennie demanded, "why are you wearing
all those petticoats?"

"Petticoats?" Susan asked with false innocence.

"Has she had them on all the morning?" Jennie
asked the others, "Surely Mother noticed . . ."

"I saw them for the first time as we came up the
stairs. You should have seen her . . . like a . . .
circus queen," Pamela said and went off again into
helpless laughter.

"Oh, Susan!" Jennie exclaimed and looked into
Susan's eyes reproachfully. And Susan knew that

Jennie was not only laughing at her but for some reason she was ashamed before the cousins.

"Don't scold her," Janie begged in her soft voice. She saw that Susan's face was crimson and that she was looking down at her feet and could not raise her eyes to them.

"Why did you do it?" Jennie asked. Jennie always went to the bottom of a matter. She did not leave any detail untouched.

Susan whispered, "I wanted to rustle." She shook herself to show them how the petticoats would rustle about her knees. She was very serious about it, but this only made them laugh again.

Jennie said, "Suppose I put on all my trousseau at once. You are greedy. That is Susan's worst fault," she said to the others, "she is greedy and wants everything and all at once."

Susan rushed to the door. She could not stand before them any longer.

"Yes," Jennie called after her, "go and take them all off except one. And put that ugly dark skirt in the rag bag where it belongs." She flung herself on the bed as Susan disappeared. "This is terrible," she laughed, but her laughter was almost like crying.

Janie untied the string on the box of flowers that was beside Jennie on the bed. She had been Jennie's roommate at college and was a closer friend than the cousins. "May I open it?" she asked Jennie. "Can't we see the bride's flowers?"

Jennie nodded indifferently. The other two girls came

to the bed and all bent over the box. Jennie did not
glance at the flowers as Janie held the end of the white
ribbon in the air. The lilies of the valley fell in a long
cascade attached to the white ribbon. The white orchid
was near the top. There were exclamations of pleasure.
Jennie heard them but did not turn her head.

Pamela said, "Let's try them in the prayer book.
Where is the prayer book, Jennie?"

"In the new trunk. But why . . . what's the use?"
Jennie asked. Her face was again sober and unresponsive.

Pamela unfolded the tissue paper wrappings from
around the prayer book. It was pure white leather. The
leaves were gold at the edges. Pamela kept one piece of
tissue paper at the back of the book to protect it from
her hands. Lucy laid the end of the white ribbon
inside the book.

"Look, Jennie, it's so beautiful." Janie smelled the
lilies that were closest to her. "Give it to Jennie. Let
her hold it," she told Pamela. Pamela laid the book
in Jennie's hands. But they did not respond. The white
leather book lay sideways and unwanted in Jennie's
limp hands. Pamela ran to the closet and took down
the white box in which lay the silk Confederate flags.
She lifted out three, gave one to each of the other
girls, and began humming the wedding march. The
girls held the flags as if they were bouquets of flowers,
just as they had held them at the rehearsal the evening
before, and walked before Jennie slowly to the time
of the march. But Jennie paid little attention. She held

the prayer book with its cascade of flowers in her hand, loosely, but her head was turned away. "The flowers will wilt," she said in a hard dry voice. She knew the girls were trying to coax her into a more gracious mood. She even guessed that her mother had sent them for this purpose. And a part of her longed to respond to them and become happy again or at least as gay as she had been before the quarrel. But the evil spirit that was in her put up a barrier between her and the whole world. It was just as if the quarrel had plunged her into a dark and evil dungeon. There was an escape from this dungeon. She knew she could get out of it if she would make the effort. But she could not make the effort. She saw the girls look at each other in despair as Pamela closed the box of flowers and put them outside the window on the roof of the porch, and the evil self that had possession of Jennie and would not let her make the effort to get out of the dungeon rejoiced that she had made them despair.

Pamela was a second cousin of the Middletons' and putting the prayer book in the trunk closed the top of the trunk with a bang. She went to the fireplace and stood before the fire with her skirts lifted to warm her sturdy legs. Her deep blue eyes looked at Jennie curiously and her broad little face with the small mouth and short curved upper lip looked determined and strong. She said, "Jennie, you ought to be ashamed."

Pamela was a second cousin of the Middleton's and was named for her own and Jennie's great-great-grandmother. She had a more determined character than the

other girls. In fact they secretly held a grudge against
her.

Lucy especially disapproved of Pamela. Though
Lucy was not yet twenty, she was plump and not in a
childish way but as if she were older. And she was
very beautiful with large black eyes and long black
lashes, and what people called a magnolia complexion.
Her eyes were coquettish and her mouth curved and
alluring. Yet hidden under this alluring exterior was
a nature similar to that of a prim mistress of a girl's
school. She had shuddered with disapproval when
Christopher said to Pamela the day before as they
went up to inspect the trousseau, "Take a look at the
pillow-cases for us," because Pamela laughed when he
said this, and because Lucy knew that this joke was
not a nice one. In the symbolic language Pamela had
already managed to share with the men "pillow-cases"
meant, not only the trousseau, but one special article of
the trousseau, the lace-trimmed pantlets.

And now she shuddered with aversion when Pamela
said to Jennie in such a harsh voice, "You ought to
be ashamed."

"What do you know about it?" she demanded of
Pamela. "You haven't quarrelled with your sweetheart.
In fact you seem to get on very well with the men."

"Oh, please, why should we talk about it," Jennie
begged. But she went on speaking as if she found it
necessary to justify herself to Pamela. "I think a girl
has a right to expect something from marriage, something beautiful. And he was so ugly last night. He

swore. I think a girl has a right to expect a little chivalry from the man she is to marry."

"Oh, chivalry!" Pamela said.

"Yes, chivalry," Jennie insisted.

Pamela let down her skirt, turned herself to the fire and spoke over her shoulder. "In school once in the fifth grade the teacher was explaining to us about chivalry. She said all male creatures have the instinct of chivalry toward the female. She said, 'Consider the rooster, how he scratches for worms and then calls the hens to share them'. And I broke right out and said, 'But he isn't chivalrous. I've seen the roosters in our yard . . .'"

"Look!" Lucy interrupted, "look what you're doing to Jennie."

Pamela looked and saw on Jennie's face an expression of misery. "You make me hate getting married," Jennie cried out, "you make me hate it." She flung herself on the pillow of the bed. "You make me despise everything," she said in a voice muffled by the pillow.

"Now are you satisfied?" Lucy said to Pamela. Pamela ran to the bed and put an arm about her cousin. "Jennie," she pleaded, "please, Jennie, I didn't mean to hurt you. What I said wasn't anything. You can love a person . . . and know . . . my brothers are kind, aren't they. Only I know they aren't naturally chivalrous, but have only what father and mother teach them. Sometimes they're mean. But they are kind, too, and I love them. I was just trying to say that people

are . . . well . . . they're people," she finished help-
lessly.

Janie and Lucy exchanged a glance which said much.
Lucy thought, "So this is the girl whose great-grand-
father was our ambassador to Russia, whose people live
in that big white-columned house in the low-country.
And her mother's people thought they were condescend-
ing a peg when they married into our family." The
glance and supercilious smile she exchanged with Janie
said all this and more.

Pamela pulled Jennie up from the pillow and wiped
her eyes with a small linen handkerchief she took from
Jennie's hand.

Lucy said out loud, "A girl has to get married, for
a home and children," she shuddered, "but that is what
I dread, the man and . . . and . . . everything. If
we could have it all without that."

"If we could be widows," Janie said. "I have always
thought widows were the happiest people. They have
the children and the income and a house . . ."

"Who is that coming along the hall?" Pamela asked.
She looked at Janie and saw that Janie was thinking,
just as she herself was, that it might be Mrs. Middleton
and that Jennie's mother would find her in tears. But
it was Nancy who knocked lightly on the door and
came in. She went directly to Jennie. "Miss Lizzie
Palmer is coming up the walk," she said hurriedly and
in a whisper. "Annie May has gone to meet her at the
door."

"Oh," Jennie put her hands to her face, "she'll come up here. I invited her to see the trousseau."

Nancy stooped over Jennie. "You must get your face washed," she said because she had seen at once that Jennie had been crying.

"I'll bring a wet cloth from the bathroom," Pamela said and hurried into the hall. When she returned Jennie was at the mirror brushing her hair vigorously. The thought of guests had put instant life into her. She snatched the wet cloth from Pamela and then the towel.

"Miss Bessie is with her," Nancy said. She stood behind the others so that she would not get in the way. She was very conscious of her height.

"We used to call Cousin Bessie the Kangaroo," Pamela said, but the others did not hear her. Jennie took the powder puff from Lucy and dusted her cheeks and nose. While she did this she spoke to the others, "I went to Miss Lizzie's private school one year when Father had a little money. It's nothing, really, except . . . my hand is shaking, isn't it? Miss Lizzie is very particular. Everyone was afraid of her. She thinks a gentlewoman shouldn't do this or that. I don't know why I should care."

"Neither do I," Pamela said.

"Suppose she had taught you," Lucy said.

"She didn't teach me, but she is my cousin on mother's side."

"I think we should go and leave Jennie alone," Janie suggested, but Jennie turned from the mirror and grasped her friend's hands, "No, please," Jennie whispered, "I don't want to see them alone. You see her brother Stuart was in love . . . I mean . . , it's embarrassing . . . well . . . you understand I couldn't . . ."

"Of course you couldn't," Pamela said, "Stuart is so dried up. And Cousin Lizzie supports him. He's too proud to work. . . . Here they come," she said, and everyone, listening, heard the voices of the cousins out in the hall. Miss Bessie was a cousin of Miss Lizzie's and lived in the country. Jennie wondered what they were saying out there in the hall. "What can I do?" she asked herself. "I am not to be married tonight. And yet how can I say this to them? I must go on for the present as if everything was just as it should be. I must smile and not let anyone know how I am suffering."

This thought, that she must smile in spite of her suffering, made her feel that there was a purpose in life, however temporary it might be, and she was actually smiling as she met the two women at the door and kissed Miss Lizzie's leathery cheek.

The bridesmaids had already lifted some articles of the trousseau from the trunk on to the bed. They stood near the bed smiling shyly as Jennie introduced them. Only Pamela did not need an introduction. She went to her cousins and kissed them dutifully, but as she turned her back to them she made a wry face as if the kisses had not been pleasant. The two women, one tall, the other much shorter and very large at one end like the kangaroo to which Pamela had compared her, sat on chairs while the bridesmaids fluttered around them bringing pantlets and petticoats, night-gowns and dresses for them to inspect. There were not many dresses, and these had been made by Mrs. Middleton and a seamstress who came to the house. The wedding dress also had been made at home. Jennie looked at the dresses more critically than she had before because she was seeing them again through the eyes of the two visitors.

The girls rushed to the trunk, to the closet and the drawers of the walnut dresser and came back holding in their arms all the dainty and new articles of the trousseau. They were like sales girls trying to please obstinate but influential customers. Miss Lizzie and Miss Bessie exclaimed pleasantly over the trousseau and looked down their long beaked noses dutifully at every piece that was brought to them. Jennie continued to watch them. She knew that the underwear was correct and that every stitch was small enough to please even Miss Lizzie. But she was not so sure of the dresses, because Mrs. Middleton had bought pieces of silk and velvet from the bargain counter and some of the pieces had flaws in them. But the wedding dress was of new and expensive material.

Pamela gave the wedding dress to Jennie and lifted off the white sheet that covered it with a flourish. Jennie held the dress against her. The train dragged limply on the floor. But the dress lay against Jennie in soft folds. The beautiful old lace at the throat made her olive skin look rich and deep and the cream cloth shimmering against her deepened the color of her brown hair and eyes. As Jennie saw that they were all admiring her, and as she caught a glimpse of herself in the mirror her imagination went forward and she saw herself walking down the aisle of the church dressed in this shimmering gown with the veil drifting behind. And the evil burden lifted and she felt joyous and helpful. But this feeling seemed improper to her, just as a person who is at a funeral feels that he has done something improper when his mind goes forward to the next day when he is to go on a pleasure trip.

But the excitement of the visitors and the sight of the whole trousseau which she had forgotten continued to have an effect on Jennie. Color came into her cheeks and her eyes shone with genuine pleasure. She laughed and talked with the visitors and even spoke of the wedding naturally and without hesitation.

Nancy slipped from the room and rushed down the stairs. In the living-room she tripped over Mr. Bauer who was adjusting the three brass pedals of the piano. She said, "Oh, excuse me, please," but did not stop to see the indignant expression on the old man's face. Bobby saw it and crawled to the other end of the piano.

Nancy flung herself into the pantry and caught Mrs. Middleton in an ecstatic embrace. "It's all right, Aunt Carrie," she panted, "Jennie is happy again. I am sure everything is all right now."

"Are you sure, child?" Mrs. Middleton asked. Her eyes begged Nancy to repeat that she was sure.

"Yes, sure," Nancy said positively. Then a curious mystical look came on her face. "Except my dream last night. I wonder what it could have meant. Because I saw it so clearly," she said.

"We won't let ourselves be disturbed by dreams," Mrs. Middleton said happily. "Are you sure about Jennie?" she asked again.

"Yes, of course," Nancy assured her solemnly, "she was laughing."

"Then if she was laughing," Mrs. Middleton said, "I am so glad."

"And she spoke of the wedding as if it was the most natural thing to be married tonight," Nancy insisted. "I couldn't be mistaken. And yet that dream. . . ."

Mrs. Middleton smiled. She saw that Nancy was glad of the change in Jennie. But she also understood that Nancy could not help but regret that she must relinquish the mystery of the dream, and that in the part of her that wished to believe in the dream she hated to give up the mystery, and accept what was usual and commonplace.

XII

THE groom and his best man, Dr. Greve, were staying at the most expensive hotel in the city. It had just been built in anticipation of the new business that would be brought to Lexington by the expansion of the city limits and was considered very luxurious by the citizens who had never travelled out of the state. Its elegance made little impression on the two doctors who had been spoiled somewhat by much finer hotels in large northern and western cities. But the service was good and Dr. Gregg's breakfast had been satisfactory.

Dr. Gregg was still using his toothpick—a habit which no contact with elegant tourists who scorned toothpicks could make him abandon—when he walked across the hall to the suite where Dr. Greve and his wife were staying. He had just heard Mrs. Greve call good-bye to her husband from the hall and knew that his friend would be alone.

As soon as Dr. Gregg entered the room the other doctor slipped a bottle of liquor and some glasses quietly on the table. Both doctors took their glasses and settled back into chairs to drink and smoke.

Dr. Greve was a slim and elegant little man. His clothes were always correct, and though he seemed not to give much attention to his personal appearance he was always so clean and neat that even after the hardest day's work it seemed he had just come from a bath. Above his upper lip which was full like a child's there was a small brown moustache. He was born in New York State in a small town near Saranac. His medical training was taken in New York City where he specialized in diseases of the lungs. In Mountain City he had his own large sanitarium for cases of tuberculosis and was often called in on difficult cases by other doctors. His own sanitarium could not hold all his patients, so his professional visits took him to most of the buildings for the sick that sat against the hills on the outskirts of Mountain City like huge rabbit hutches with screen-covered porches where the patients lay to get the mountain air. Though the little doctor sat quietly in the hotel room he gave the impression of continuous movement. His eyes were bright and quick and his whole face, with pointed handsome features, made him seem continually alert like a small wild animal that must be always watchful.

"So this is the wedding day," he said to his friend.

"Yes," the Doctor answered.

"You don't look like a happy bridegroom."

"Must a man look like a happy . . . I wish two people could get married without all of this damned fuss . . ."

"You never told me you didn't like it."

"Jennie wanted it," the Doctor said uncomfortably. Dr. Greve laughed.

"Why do you laugh?" his friend demanded.

"Nothing . . . only . . . 'she wanted it'," he quoted and laughed again.

"Compromise," the Doctor said, "but that's all over. I won't do it again."

"You mean get married?" the little doctor asked in an amused voice.

"Compromise . . . give in," his friend said. "You can spoil a woman until she thinks . . ."

"What happened last night?" the little Doctor asked.

"Nothing . . . that is . . ."

"Tell me . . ."

"Jennie broke our engagement. The wedding is off," the Doctor said abruptly.

"You had a quarrel?"

"I don't like quarrels."

"I know . . . but what happened?"

"She wanted teas. I think that was it . . ."

"Teas?" the little doctor smiled.

"Yes, but that wasn't exactly . . ."

"Go on . . ."

In a low voice the Doctor told about the whole quarrel with Jennie. It gave him a sense of shame to tell about it, but at the same time he felt a relief in going over the details of the quarrel.

"And you swore at her," Dr. Greve said at the end. There was a smile on his attractive mouth under the moustache. His eyes glittered with amusement. He

put his hands in his pockets and hunched his shoulders
as if he could only take this way of saying to himself,
"This is a fine and amusing situation indeed. And you
are very fine, Dr. Greve, yes, very fine. You and I
understand each other." As he put his hands in his
pockets and hunched his shoulders with his watchful
little smile showing under the moustache his whole person said that he was delighted with himself and with
the situation.

"What you don't understand, my friend," he said
and then did not continue.

"Go on. What is it I don't understand?"

"You won't be angry?"

"Go on."

"What you don't understand is the impulse that
made you choose Jennie instead of one of your hill
maidens for a wife."

"I didn't choose her. It was against my better judgment. But it was something I couldn't . . ."

"But what led you to her . . . what attracted you
to this poverty-stricken delicate well-bred child of the
upper crust . . ."

"I tell you I didn't choose her."

"Because you admired the . . . upper crust," Dr.
Greve said and added hastily, "Now don't get angry
. . . you told me to go on."

Dr. Gregg chewed on his cigar but did not speak.
Looking at him, his friend saw a red flush come up
on his broad cheeks. It showed even on the bald spot
at the top of his head. Dr. Greve could not tell whether

the flush was from anger or shame, but he was sorry
that he had spoken so frankly, and he was not sure he
was right.

"No," he said, "I was wrong to say that. I know
there is something else. Because in spite of your pride
in being a country boy who has made good, you are
greedy for delicacy and beauty. I have seen it in your
eyes at a concert, in your whole face as you listened.
You are sensitive under that rhinoceros hide. And that
is the trouble. You aren't articulate, except when you
swear," he laughed, "you can't express your sensitive
feelings . . ."

"I haven't read all the books in the world as you
have," Dr. Gregg answered dryly.

"And no one suspects how sensitive you are," Dr.
Greve continued. "Even I forget at times. Then I see
you blossom under praise and hurt by blame and I
know . . ."

"This is too damned personal."

"Then let it go."

There was a silence between them. It was plain that
the little doctor was unaccustomed to silence and that
it made him uncomfortable. He lit one cigarette after
another, and crossed his knees and uncrossed them.
He wished to speak but Dr. Gregg's heavy silence prevented him. So he waited. He never waited calmly.
And now he was especially ill at ease. There were no
patients calling him so that he felt himself needed
every moment of the day. This strange vacuum where
he had neither work nor the varied and temporary com-

panions who came into his life each day made him unhappy. He was lost. And his friend's silence, which
meant that he resented what had been said, made him
feel more alone.

The other Doctor was thinking of Jennie. And because he felt resentful toward her, that other resentment which had lain in him from the evening of the
storm when he and Jennie had stayed in the cabin all
night came up to him.

"Why must women dole out little bits of love?" he
asked, and his resentment showed in his voice.

The little doctor said, "I don't understand."

"Let it go," the Doctor sighed heavily.

The little doctor leaned forward. He had become
serious and attentive. But now again the live, glittering
look of amusement came into his eyes, the look that
said, "I know people and my only defense against them
is amusement. I can be amused at the world and at people, and if I am amused I can't be hurt."

He said, "You will admit I have said nothing before . . . against your marriage, I mean."

The Doctor nodded.

"Then I will tell you something. I have said nothing.
And yet all along I have had the most malignant hope
that it wouldn't come off."

"Why?"

"Because I don't think you are suited. It is nothing
personal against Jennie. But now that this has happened, my advice is . . ."

There was the sound of a key in the lock of the outer

door. The little doctor shifted his position and sank
back in his chair. His face became reserved and quiet.

The door opened. Into the room came a young
woman. She was blond and had large blue eyes, candid
and sweet. There was a worried frown between her
eyes. This frown did not go away but remained there
always. She was dressed in an expensive blue silk and
wore a fur coat over it. On her blond hair was a small
fur hat with the breast of a bird on it. The feathers
were the color of her eyes.

As she came into the room she stopped abruptly,
noticing the strained silence that had come on the men
as she entered. In the silence she went to kiss her husband's cheek. Her silk skirts rustled. She lifted her
head and looked at both men suspiciously. A discon-
tented look came on her face and then it changed to a
bright expression of affected interest.

"I heard you talking," she said brightly and laid
some bundles on the table and sat down. "I heard you
talking," she said again brightly and waited. She added,
"It's very cold outside." Her voice was a soft drawl
with a faint whine in it. This faint whine was disturbing and irritating like the sound of dripping water
from a faulty spout. "It isn't very warm here," she
added and shivered and drew her coat around her.
"What were you talking about?" she asked.

"We were talking about marriage, my dear," her husband said.

The cautiously sweet expression left her face and
in its place came one that was bitter. The frown deep-

ened on her forehead. "What do you know about marriage?" she asked. She spoke to Dr. Gregg appealingly. "He is an enemy of marriage," she told him.

"Not an enemy," her husband corrected her easily, "only an unbeliever. I was telling the same thing to Doc here. He and Jennie have had a quarrel."

"Oh, no. Have you really, Doctor?"

"I don't know. It's all foolishness," the Doctor mumbled. He was embarrassed and wished that his friend had not spoken of him or of the quarrel.

"But it will be such a beautiful wedding. What was the quarrel about? Perhaps I can make it all right with Jennie. I don't know her well, of course. But in these things, women understand each other. I am sure I can do something. Will you let me go to Jennie?" she asked eagerly.

The little doctor took a cigarette from his case. He did not look at his wife but at the match which he held to the cigarette. In a low voice he said, "Don't interfere, Sally."

"But why not?" she asked. "You may not like this wedding or any wedding," she said spitefully, "and I know you would like to interfere. Why did you come if you don't like all this. Because I know . . ."

"Ask Doc here why I came," her husband said casually. "He said he couldn't go through it without me. He's like a woman who can't go through childbirth without someone holding her hand."

"But I didn't . . . at least I only wanted you . . ."

Mrs. Greve saw the warning look on her husband's face and did not continue.

"He's lying to you, Mrs. Greve," Dr. Gregg told her. "I asked him to come simply to give you pleasure. I thought you would enjoy the wedding."

"Did you really?" she asked and a pleased smile came to her lips. "But then I don't know what to believe. You men sit here laughing . . . I can't understand you. When I had my first baby I heard Doctor Cobb tell my husband that I'd had an easy time. An easy time! It was twenty hours. And you laughed together, you know you did," she said to her husband, "out in the hall of the hospital just outside my door. You laughed together. You doctors. You two should have Dr. Cobb here, and then you would all be together like the . . . musketeers."

"One for all and all for one," her husband answered. His answer was almost like a sneer.

"Yes, that is what you are. And you are against women. Say what you please but you are, you all are. I feel sorry for Jennie Middleton. I do. I feel sorry for her." Her lips quivered. She flung herself out of the chair, gathered up her bundles from the table and went into the bed-room. The door closed sharply behind her.

Dr. Gregg looked at his friend and smiled, but with his smile there was a look on his face as if he did not completely approve of what the friend had done. "You aren't exactly kind to your wife," he said.

Dr. Greve lit another cigarette and said grimly. "All

the covert carnality and materialism that underlies a
loving smile. My wife was . . . is . . . beautiful.
She is a good mother. A woman's instinct says to her,
'get yourself a husband and children and a nest' and
that is good. But society reminds her, 'you can't go out
like the little birdies and build your nest with sticks.
Your husband must do it for you.' And so a woman
must be more practical than we are. She doesn't look
for a companion but for a nest. Even the little creature
that smiles the sweetest and looks most innocent has
a glint in her eye that says, 'can he make a nest for me?
and how good a nest? if I give what do I get?' And so
love and companionship are corrupted."

It seemed that he had finished, but the pause lasted
only a moment. He had known the other doctor for
many years, but this was the first time they had met
under such circumstances; in another city where the
usual methods of living and working had been disturbed and changed; where all the environment was different as it is on a voyage when people have been
temporarily separated from what is usual so that the
difficulties and problems of the every-day life stand
out vividly until the new experience absorbs them.

Dr. Greve smiled and it seemed that he was smiling not only to himself and the other but at himself.
He spoke in a low voice, half amused, yet it was evident that he was wholly absorbed in what he was saying
and that he had thought all this before, but had never
spoken it aloud, and was glad to say it at last.

"Love dies slowly. You keep on trying until you dis-

cover behind the little devices of love that hidden
mercenary gleam. Then you cynically furnish all that
she needs and wants, new clothes, a fine home, care for
the children. But there is no love. I don't want a
dowager, neither do I want a household pet. I want a
mate. Animals mate only to perpetuate their kind. But
human beings are more advanced than animals. They
mate at all seasons, and for that reason alone we are
different. We can enjoy and we should enjoy each
other. But why should I talk in this way . . . You are
in love. You think Jennie is different. Don't deny it
. . . I see it in your face. You are smiling and thinking, 'but Jennie is different.' "

"No," the Doctor interrupted, "I was only thinking
that you were right when you said you are cynical. But
I am not cynical . . ."

"No, but you are. Only in another way. Your work
is everything to you. And that is good. That is good.
And that work will save you. But you won't satisfy
Jennie. You haven't enough ambition."

"I thought I was ambitious," Doctor Gregg protested, "I thought I was nothing but ambition."

"No, you only love your work," the other said, smiling, "you go to the Mayo clinic every year to study.
You read and get the latest surgical instruments. You
are not lazy. But you are indifferent to fame, you don't
wish to outsmart everyone and stand on top with power
over others. And let me tell you I understand people,
and I have read your Jennie. She is ambitious. So you
will be unhappy or else it will be necessary for you to

change . . . that is if you intend to go on with this wedding?" His voice rose and he looked at the Doctor questioningly.

"I don't know," Dr. Gregg answered, "but if I do, why should I object to change. We are continually changing . . . you know that . . ."

"Yes, our bones and flesh change. But so do our moral natures. And nothing changes a person so much as living closely with another. At least it is usual. And let me tell you, your little Jennie has a will and if anyone changes, you yourself . . ."

"You speak as if I am helpless. I resent that."

"Don't be angry, my friend."

"No, only I am not helpless."

"You mustn't think this is personal. I was wrong to speak as I did. I have no wish to break up something that is good. And how can I tell. You say I am cynical. And yet I . . . I also look for the human being who can make the raw bloody edges of life fit together.

"No," he continued, "you are not helpless, because you go bluntly on your way. My wife says I am cruel, and I am cruel, but you . . ." he smiled, "do you remember our friend, your beautiful patient . . . *our* friend . . ." He emphasized the word 'our.'

"She was . . ." the Doctor lifted his heavy shoulders impatiently.

"I thought of her as a fungus, living materially on her husband and emotionally on others. But you were brutal to her. It hurt."

"That's over," the Doctor said impatiently. "Why

do you wish to plunge yourself into people's hearts and lives," he said angrily, "and analyze them and continue to analyze them. I can't understand it."

He turned away from his friend. There on the table near him was a picture of Jennie. And this picture brought her suddenly and vividly before him. And the contrast of Jennie's freshness with the remembrance of that other woman, made him feel a vivid sense of closeness to Jennie. He saw her as he had seen her in Mountain City at two o'clock one morning when they returned from a call in the country and he took her into the narrow little Greek restaurant where he often went for coffee. She sat on a stool at the counter beside him and was pleasant to his friends. That evening she was so small and eager and alive and friendly. He felt a great joy in her companionship and now he remembered this feeling of joy, and confidence in her returned to him.

"You have had a disappointing experience," he said to Dr. Greve, "and you believe I must have the same experience with marriage. But Jennie is different . . ."

"What did I tell you," the little doctor exclaimed, "I said you would think Jennie different, and you do. You have said it."

"And she is," the Doctor insisted stubbornly.

"But society is not different," Doctor Greve insisted maliciously. "Society will make her like the others. And we are particular, you and I. We want our women gentle, loving, thoughtful and loyal. But we want them intelligent, too, women who will be independent and allow us our independence. And that is impossible because . . ."

"And you want yours to be beautiful," Dr. Gregg laughed.

"I do. Yes . . . yes . . . it is a fact. I do," the little doctor acknowledged. "And so do you . . ."

"As for independence," Dr. Gregg insisted, "you forget what Jennie has done. She has studied and taught. She has been independent, and that is why . . ."

"But she is ambitious . . ."

"She has energy and enthusiasm and your jaundiced liver mistakes it for ambition . . ." For the first time since they had begun talking Dr. Gregg spoke cheerfully and confidently. The sense of Jennie's nearness, the nearness he had felt in the little restaurant, stayed in him so that his natural and usual confidence in himself, his work and in what he was doing returned.

Dr. Greve leaned forward and tapped his fingers on the arm of his chair. "You believe you will keep your independence. Perhaps you will, my friend. I hope you will. But my jaundiced liver," he smiled, "says no. Because if you do you will always give your wife the feeling that you are not tied down. And what woman can stand this. Not one. Not even the most intelligent. And that is why I am cynical," he added.

"You don't want me to go on with this marriage," Dr. Gregg stated resentfully.

"No, for God's sake, I think you should, if you are hell bent for it. I think you should. What will you do about the quarrel?" he asked skeptically, "will you beg her pardon?"

"No, I'll wait. We'll see what she does about it."

"Yes, we'll see, we'll see. And perhaps you are right. Perhaps Jennie will be the . . . what you wish. But I have a suspicion that you won't keep your independence. Or if you do you will be banished. But 'what is banishment but freedom,' " he quoted.

"And what is freedom?" Dr. Gregg asked.

"Just now your freedom consists in marrying your Jennie. Because that is necessary to you. What it consists of later, we'll see."

Dr. Gregg laughed. "I still don't know what freedom is."

"Well . . . then I don't know. Do you?"

"No, do you?"

"No."

They laughed together.

At that moment a knock came at the outer door. Dr. Greve answered it. A boy stood outside with a card on a plate. Dr. Greve said to the boy, "Wait a moment." He closed the door and came into the room. He was trying to suppress a smile but his eyes sparkled. He looked more than ever as if he could not keep still, as if his whole body danced because his eyes were so alive with pleasure and laughter.

"This is good. Oh, this is good," he said. "Your future father-in-law is downstairs, and wishes to see me . . . me. He has come from Jennie. I'll tell him to come up."

"Wait until I go back to my room," Dr. Gregg told his friend.

"No, you won't. No. Not at all. You will wait here." He hurried to the door and gave the boy a coin. "Tell Mr. Middleton to come up," he said.

"No," he insisted, as Dr. Gregg tried to reach the door, "you can't leave me. This is your responsibility. I didn't quarrel with Jennie. . . . You know, I like your father-in-law. He is one of those men who have principles. He is like Brutus, the noblest Roman of them all. That is the impression he makes, that he is actually noble clear through, that he would praise an enemy. We don't do that sort of thing. We condemn our enemies. We have lost that fine custom that says acknowledge the good in your enemy. I want to see more of him. I am glad he is coming. Here he is. I hear his step along the hall. What a light step and how eager it sounds. Like a very young man."

XIII

I WAS just going," Dr. Gregg said to Mr. Middleton when the three men had shaken hands, "I'll leave you two together."

Mr. Middleton bowed. He was glad to be left alone with Dr. Greve and was repeating to himself what he had come to say, that Jennie had refused to get married that evening and that perhaps Dr. Greve could think of some way in which the bride and groom could be reconciled. He was anxious to know the state of mind of his future son-in-law and looked at him curiously to see if he could determine from the expression on his broad good-natured face what he might expect. The face was pleasant and smiling. But instead of finding anything that might help him Robert Middleton suddenly noticed the Doctor's long lashes and deep blue eyes and a foolish thought came into his mind, "the children should have his eyes," he thought and then almost groaned.

Dr. Gregg tried to leave the room, but the little doctor took him by the arm and firmly urged him back again. "Oh no, on no account must you go," he said, "I am sure Mr. Middleton agrees with me. Don't you, Mr.

Middleton," he asked pleasantly. Anyone looking closely
at his face might have seen that he was quietly and inwardly enjoying himself. Dr. Gregg did see this and
cursed under his breath. But he remained in the room.

"Certainly, gentlemen," Mr. Middleton answered
formally, but he was puzzled and uneasy. As he sat
down his long fingers touched his chin. The middle
finger stroked his jaw. There was an uncomfortable
pause. Since the Doctor was there Mr. Middleton could
not begin the private conversation he had planned with
Dr. Greve. Dr. Gregg sat on the edge of his chair as if
he intended to go just as soon as the twinkling eyes of
the little Doctor had become interested in something
else. But the twinkling mischievous eyes did not change
and finally Doctor Gregg settled back in his chair and
lit a cigar.

"Will you have a drink?" Dr. Greve asked Mr. Middleton. He poured for each of them, and gave a glass
to Robert Middleton. Robert did not often drink. Now
he told himself that the whiskey would clear his head
and perhaps give him an inspiration about how to pro-
ceed with what he had to say. It was necessary to get
the matter settled at once for the wedding was only a
few hours away.

The little doctor sat back in his chair with his glass
in one hand and a cigarette in the other. And Mr. Middleton thought there was surely an amused gleam in his
eyes and a suggestion of a smile around his lips. His
moustache quivered. Robert had eaten little breakfast
because of his anxieties and now it was two o'clock,

close to the time when dinner would be ready at home.
Because he had not eaten, the whiskey did not clear his
head as he had hoped. It had an immediate effect but
this effect only complicated matters. His head felt light
and as if a thought might come into it at any moment,
but none came. He let Dr. Greve fill his glass a second
time. They spoke of the weather and the ice that had
formed and the sun that had come to melt the ice. And
as they spoke of the melting ice Mr. Middleton suddenly felt as if all his troubles were melting away. They
had held him straight and tense all morning like the
coating of ice on a bush and now the ice melted and he
felt the delicious warmth of the sun. It was amazing.
He was very sensible and told himself that it was the
whiskey that made him feel he had not a care in the
world. And yet it seemed like a miracle to have every
care taken from his shoulders and to feel the delightful
stimulating warmth. He associated the new sense of
well-being with the men in the room and was grateful
to them.

"Gentlemen," he said, "it is a pleasure . . . two
such illustrious colleagues, no, not colleagues . . . because I am a lawyer, or I was a lawyer, and you are
physicians. You know what the wicked men said to
Jesus, 'Physician, heal thyself.' "

"We were talking about women," Dr. Greve said
in a low voice, "that is, when you came in we were
talking about women, and brides and . . . and so
forth . . ."

"Yes, women, by all means. Gentlemen, women can

be the very devil. Excuse me, but this is so. They are incorrigible. You have a wife, Dr. Greve, and you must know. They go calmly and sweetly, and who can be sweeter than a woman,—for days, hours, months, and then, suddenly, there they are in your way. They block your path, obstinate as a mule. You can't make them budge, and you can't leave them. It is possible to leave a balky mule and walk down the road alone. But women . . . there they are, there she is. You must wait until she moves. You must wait. And that is the whole problem in a nutshell. . . . And what are we waiting for? Why do we wait?" he asked them. "Are we men to suffer such dishonor?"

"No, we are not men," he continued, "we are gentlemen, and that explains it all. Gentlemen wait.

"Why do you sit there like . . . like a clod," he said to Dr. Gregg, to his future son-in-law in an irritated voice, "I beg your pardon, but that is the way you impressed me at the moment. I know you are not a clod. But why don't you go to my home and tell Jennie . . . tell her to behave herself. It is as simple as that. You have the responsibility now. You are her husband, well . . . almost. My responsibility ends here and now. Why don't you go down there? I can tell you why. It is because you are afraid of her. And I am afraid of her. We are all afraid. Secretly, in our hearts we are afraid of women. Isn't that true, gentlemen?"

He understood dimly that he was talking more than he should and that he was not saying what he had planned to say to Dr. Greve alone. He knew that it was necessary to get to the heart of the matter soon. Otherwise there would be no wedding. But the presence of both doctors complicated everything and he could not remember the purpose of his visit. But he was enjoying himself. It seemed that these men sympathized with his burdens as a man and that they were not putting him in the wrong, but were agreeing with all he said, and not only agreeing but applauding him.

"How does Jennie feel about all this?" Dr. Greve asked him.

"Jennie? Yes, my dear sir. You speak of Jennie. She says that she will not get married this evening. And that is the whole trouble. You have diagnosed the real trouble at once, like a true physician. It was a stroke of genius. It was magnificent."

"You enjoy this," Dr. Gregg said to his friend in a low voice, like a growl, "but I am leaving."

The wicked amused gleam went from Doctor Greve's eyes. "No," he said quickly, "wait. I am serious. Wait."

"Mr. Middleton," he leaned forward in his chair and his face and voice were serious and intent. "Would you be willing for me to go and talk to Jennie? Or do you think it would be best for the Doctor here to go?"

"By all means go," Mr. Middleton said enthusiastically.

"Do you mean that I should go?" Dr. Greve asked in a respectful voice.

"Yes, by all means."

"Then with your permission, I will go," Dr. Greve

said. "Is it all right with you, Doc?" he asked his friend.

Doctor Gregg looked at him suspiciously.

"It's all right, it's all right," Doctor Greve assured him. "I am serious. I intend to do my best. I mean it. I mean it. And I think I will succeed. I know Jennie. I can see that you wish to continue with the plans, and I respect your wish. We talked it over and I respect and honor your decision. So I will do my best." He spoke directly to Mr. Middleton. "I will see Jennie immediately after dinner," he said, "and I think I can assure you the wedding will happen just as it was planned." He saw that the suspicious look continued on Dr. Gregg's face, "No, I promise you, Doc," he said in a sincere, almost a solemn voice, "this is a serious matter and I will treat it as a serious matter."

The door to the inner room opened. Mrs. Greve stood there. "Good morning, Mr. Middleton," she said to him shyly and respectfully, "how is Jennie?" She came into the room. Mr. Middleton rose and met her. He took her hand and bowed low over it with stately dignity. But as he bowed a strange feeling came over him. His head became confused. He could not see and sweat came out on his forehead. He clung to her hand to steady himself. She looked at him and at the hand in surprise and embarrassment. But in a moment he straightened himself, let go her hand and feeling about caught the back of a chair that was beside him.

"I interrupted you," she told him, "because Mrs.

Middleton telephoned. She asked me to tell you that the Bishop called again. He is anxious to see you."

"Thank you, Mrs. Greve," Mr. Middleton said to her. He held himself with exaggerated dignity, but his voice was too loud and he knew it was too loud but could not control it.

"She said it was something about Dr. Grant," Mrs. Greve said, "and it was important."

"Dr. Grant?" Robert repeated. His face became somber. Mrs. Greve went quietly back into the bedroom. "Dr. Grant," Robert said again. He sat down in the chair to which he had been clinging, "Dr. Grant is a fine man. I have no doubt he is a splendid man. He is an eloquent preacher . . . but the truth is I haven't a great respect for him . . ." and without any warning he went into a detailed story of Dr. Grant's stay in Lexington. He even told the doctors the gossip which had been circulated about Dr. Grant, the gossip about women.

Dr. Greve said, smiling, "But you must consider the temptations of a minister."

"Temptations?" Robert asked vaguely.

"Women," Dr. Greve explained, "and the temptations of women. They are literally on their knees to the minister once a week at least and it is hard, if the minister is attractive, for women to see beyond the man to heaven and God. A minister is like a matinee idol. And what a splendid position for such an actor. He is always the star of the show. He doesn't need to tramp the streets looking for a part in a play. He is not forced to take an insignificant role. Every Sunday from one year to another his position as star is assured.

"One of my patients had an affair with her minister. It speaks well for the ministry that most of them do not take advantage of the star part or the adulation of the women. Some of them hate it. But this man did not. He invited young women of his congregation upstairs into his bedroom whenever his wife was on a visit out of town. And he always, always mentioned some time during the evening how the prostitute had washed the feet of Jesus with her hair—or at least dried them— and how Christ had been so human that he turned water into wine at the wedding at Cana in Gallilee."

"Yes," Mr. Middleton laughed, but there was no enjoyment in his laughter, "the wedding at Cana. Dr. Grant now, I am sure he would use just such an excuse. And I can imagine a woman, some women, annointing the feet . . . a romantic position . . . with the hair . . . like Guinivere and King Arthur—'liest thou so low, my pride in happier hours' . . . But I must go," he said in a distracted voice, "I must see the Bishop. Did I leave my hat and coat with the bell-boy?"

"No, here," Dr. Greve said quickly, and with the quick movements that were natural to him he lifted the hat and coat from a chair and held the coat for Mr. Middleton.

"So we will expect you after dinner," Mr. Middleton said to Dr. Greve. "It is very kind of you, but I hope you won't talk of the wedding at Cana to Jennie.

I mean she is young and would not understand. It is
very kind of you to take all this trouble."

He shook hands with Dr. Gregg and as he did so
remembered that he had said something that was not
exactly complimentary, and tried to make amends for
what he had said. "Only this morning," he told Dr.
Gregg, "my friend James Bell was telling me what a
reputation you have as a surgeon. I knew it before. I
knew it long ago. But we are proud of you, proud of
you and your skill . . ."

As the effects of the whiskey wore off he remembered other things that he had said. There was something about Jennie he told himself, something that was
wrong. "And you must be patient with Jennie," he said
to them, "she is naturally wrought up to a fine pitch
. . . nervous because of the wedding. She is a splendid
woman. I can say this even if she is my daughter. I
love her very much."

"I know that you do," Dr. Gregg said to him. Dr.
Gregg's kindly deep and sincere voice was very comforting to Robert Middleton.

And yet as soon as he reached the sidewalk outside
the lobby of the hotel he remembered again that he had
said what should not have been said. And as his head
cleared the very words he had spoken came back to him.
He had a sense of guilt because of these words. There
was a sense that he had been disloyal to his wife and to
Jennie, the two women he loved best. He asked himself
why he had spoken in just that way about women. He
had never had those words even in his thoughts. And

yet he had said them. "It must have been the whiskey, and the . . . the sympathetic atmosphere," he told himself, "and that old fault," he added bitterly, "the everlasting instinct to be charming, to please everybody, to see everyone's side of a question so long as I am with them. If I hadn't possessed this fault I might have amounted to something."

"All right, Uncle," he said aloud to the driver of the hack, "now you can take me home."

As they turned the corner of Main Street into Lady Street another thought came into his mind. "I wonder what the Bishop wants?" he asked himself, "well, 'sufficient unto the day.'"

XIV

ROBERT MIDDLETON stayed in his home only long enough to eat the dinner his wife had kept ready for him. He found the house strangely quiet. The quietness disturbed him and he longed for the sound of the young people's voices. When he asked about them Carrie explained that the ushers had gone to meet Christopher and Hugh and that the bridesmaids were getting their beauty naps. She told him, smiling, that Susan also had gone to their bed-room for a beauty nap like the older girls. Bobby was out playing. Robert enjoyed hearing about the younger children. The thought of them made him feel that the ordinary life was still there to be taken up when the unusual and disturbing activities of the wedding were over.

The thought of the Bishop and his urgent message for Robert was stirring in Carrie's mind, but she did not speak of it. And Robert also said nothing about it. But he ate little and hurried to get away and she saw that he was anxious and that he wished to relieve the anxiety as soon as possible.

Bishop Allison lived in a simple frame house on a

cross street two blocks from the home of the Middletons. Robert had known the Bishop for a long time and like almost everyone else he loved this friend. No one ever left the Bishop without feeling that he had encountered a person who was entirely lacking in thought for himself.

As Robert stepped on to the verandah of the Bishop's house the front door opened. The old Negro man who served the Bishop was letting someone out of the house. This man was portly and tall and there was a benign expression on his rosy face. He was dressed in the clothes of a clergyman. This man was Dr. Grant, the rector of the Middletons' church.

Robert had come up the steps hastily, and the two men almost ran into each other. They drew apart. No one spoke. The old Negro man watched them as he held the door courteously for Robert to enter. Robert bowed slightly. Dr. Grant bowed. Robert bowed again and tried to pass Dr. Grant and go toward the door that the old Negro was holding open for him. But Dr. Grant did not move. He opened his mouth to speak and yet did not speak. Both men's faces became mottled and red. They were like two roosters that meet in a ring, their combs becoming redder and redder as they circle about each other, their spurs made harmless by covers of felt, but their anger and fighting spirit causing each to appear dangerous to the other.

The old Negro, bent with age, was shivering because of the open door. His master's home was receiving the cold air from the outside. He said, "Mr. Middleton,

will you come in, sir?" Because he said this and because Dr. Grant heard, the minister stood aside and
allowed Mr. Middleton to go past him.

The old Negro, walking softly, led Mr. Middleton
along the hall toward the Bishop's study. The house
had an atmosphere of suspended life. Though no one
had ever been asked to be quiet there, everyone knew
that the Bishop's tiny frail wife was slowly dying, and
they moved and spoke quietly as people do in a hospital
even on those days when visitors are allowed and the
halls and wards swarm with relatives and friends of
the sick.

As the old Negro man opened the door of the
Bishop's study and announced Robert the Bishop left
his chair at the fire and came forward to meet Robert
with his hand outstretched.

A young man, slim and fair-haired raised himself
from a chair behind a desk at one side of the room. He
was acting as the Bishop's secretary while he studied
for the ministry. This young man looked at Robert
Middleton critically. He knew that because of Mr.
Middleton the Bishop was being disturbed. Also he had
heard the Bishop and Robert discuss religious questions and he was sure that Robert was not an orthodox
churchman. He had heard Robert say out loud to the
Bishop that he did not believe in the apostolic succession. That is, that he did not believe that there had
been an uninterrupted succession of laying on of hands,
beginning with Jesus laying his hands on the heads of
his apostles and the apostles in turn laying their hands

on their successors, so that nearly two thousand years later the Bishop by the right of this succession, was as holy as if Jesus himself had laid his two hands on the Bishop's head. To himself the young man used a word to describe Robert Middleton, a word that had been used against those southerners who had not believed in slavery. The word was renegade.

In spite of the fact that Robert here in the Bishop's sanctuary was more controlled and quieter in his movements than usual he nevertheless gave a feeling of energy and life to the room. The young man felt this energy but did not like it. How much more splendid the Bishop seemed to him, calm, placid, gentle and kindly. To the young man the Bishop with his kindly face, his transparent skin, his bald head with a ring of white locks surrounding the bald spot, seemed the very spirit of God on earth and in contrast Robert seemed to him a wicked and rebellious spirit.

The young man took some letters from the desk, "Do you want these, sir?" he asked the Bishop, "you know the letters Dr. Grant brought."

The Bishop hesitated and then told the young man that he might leave the letters. Mr. Middleton had not seen the young man in the dim light of the study. Now he saw him and spoke to him pleasantly. The young man bowed and went silently through the door. After he had closed the door behind him he stood in the hall for a moment gazing back through the door anxiously as if he were a mother leaving a child alone with a playmate whose bad influence she suspects.

Bishop Allison motioned silently to Robert to take one of the chairs before the fire. Everything that people thought of him was true, that he possessed a genuine goodness and peace. But this had not always been true of him. Many things had happened to him before he attained the peace that he possessed. He became a captain in the Confederate army at the age of twenty. When the Civil War ended he was an idealistic young man, looking for justice and secretly glad that the slaves had been freed. He began his study for the ministry soon after Appomattox. During Reconstruction, still idealistic, he looked into the laws passed by the Reconstruction legislatures. He found that these laws were just and progressive, that they would benefit not only his own group but all groups and races in that part of the country. And because his imagination was stimulated by these laws he thought that other people would be stimulated by them. He thought other people would be glad to know the truth of what was going on about them and would welcome what he had to say to them about these laws. He spoke from his pulpit about them. He tried to persuade his congregation, his friends and even his Bishop that idealistic people should not condemn Reconstruction completely. He acknowledged all the evil that was a part of Reconstruction, but felt that if people of his group embraced the new laws and tried to enforce them with their own means of enforcing laws that they would emerge from their trials purified and strengthened with the knowledge that they had done what was right, and with a section of the country that could be a greater force for good in the nation.

He was ostracized and temporarily suspended from the ministry. When Reconstruction ended and both the vicious and idealistic politicians had been driven North young Allison was taken back into the church. But poverty and ostracism had made their impression on his life. He and his delicate little wife had endured many hardships, more than others, because they had not had the approval of their neighbors and friends. He entered the church again and ever after he concerned himself only with the spiritual aspects of his profession. He wanted peace more than anything else. And everyone wanted peace after the stress of war and reconstruction, so that once more he was at one with his people. He lived a deeply spiritual life. During his ministry his people went to him with their personal troubles and he helped them. They felt the peacefulness of his inward life which he had made for himself by shutting out all contact with politics or other stressful activities of the outside world. He was gentle and kind. When he became a Bishop he remained just what he had been as a minister. People came to him and were helped by his peaceful and detached attitude toward life. They recognized his spiritual detachment from the world and this very detachment made him different from all others, so that they could look up to him as a sort of idealized father who could comfort them and at the same time help them to resolve their difficulties.

When they were seated before the fire the Bishop said to Robert, "Do you know why I sent for you?"

"No, Bishop, but I suspect it has something to do with Dr. Grant. I met him at the door. Does he wish to take part in the ceremony tonight, because if he does . . ."

"No, that is not what he wishes, Robert. It has something to do with him, yes. But a different matter. You know the little silk flags the bridesmaids were to carry in the wedding this evening."

Robert interrupted, "Certainly . . . We told you about them and you approved . . ."

The Bishop continued, "Early this morning Dr. Grant telephoned me that we must not use the flags. I asked him why we should not and he said that he disapproved of having these flags in the church, that using them might promote sectional hatred. I told him I did not think this was so. But he called me again later and said that some of the members of the vestry agreed with him, and then, as you saw he came to see me about this matter. So it seems that we cannot use the flags. I know you and Jennie will be disappointed but I am afraid we must do as he says."

"But what reason, by what right . . ." Robert cried out, "this is my own daughter's wedding, Bishop."

"It is Dr. Grant's church."

"Why did he speak of it so late? I can't understand . . ."

"If you will let me speak . . ." the Bishop said quietly.

"Certainly. Excuse me, Bishop, but this . . ." Robert checked himself, but he could not control his anger. "I will not allow that man to dictate to me," he said angrily.

"But think, my friend. What can I do unless I am ready to make an issue of this. I can't go over Dr. Grant's decision in his own church. I can only advise him . . . as I did advise him. But he can appeal to the vestry. You know we are a democratic Church, and you yourself would be the last person to want it otherwise."

"It is an act of spite," Robert said, "because I asked him not to take part in the ceremony. I had your permission for that, Bishop. I apologized . . . I apologized profusely." Robert brought his fist down on the arm of his chair, "This disturbance, this unnecessary disturbance is the result of that innocent request. This spite is unbecoming a minister of God," he said in a loud voice.

The Bishop paid no attention to the raised voice nor the look of anger on Robert's face. He leaned forward in his chair and laid his white transparent hand on Robert's arm. "I was delighted when you and Jennie told me the plans for her wedding," he said. "Even the thought of the little silk flags was pleasant to me. I am disappointed that we are not able to use them. But after all they are a part of our sentimental feelings for the past. The past is dead and all our rebellion and bitterness cannot bring it back. We can only look over the little mementoes and sigh over them. Then why make all this disturbance . . ."

"Why do you speak as if I were making the disturbance," Robert asked reproachfully, "when it is he . . . he . . . and you support him," he said bitterly.

"No . . . I . . ." the Bishop flushed. "I will tell you a secret, Robert. But it must not go any further than yourself. I . . . I do not like this man. He has done progressive things for the church. He is building a parish house for the young people. He is planning to get a new electrically pumped organ. The old one is almost useless. I know that in some ways he is doing a fine thing and yet . . . I disliked intensely the way in which he made that collection in church to raise the money for the reredos."

"Yes," Robert said, "I hated it. How can he make any objection to the flags after that vulgar show, passing the plates during a service so that the women could throw their jewelry and silver spoons and what-not into the plates? It was showy, it was vile, and yet almost everyone in the congregation approved of it. Even my wife wanted to give some old silver, but I wouldn't allow it. 'The world is still deceived with ornament.' Shakespeare is not outmoded, Bishop. Do you remember:

> 'The world is still deceived with ornament,
> In law what plea so tainted and corrupt
> But being seasoned with a gracious voice
> Obscures the show of evil. In religion,

"In religion," Robert repeated maliciously.

'What damned error, but some sober brow
Will bless it and approve it with a text
Hiding the grossness with fair ornament?
There is no vice so simple but assures
Some mark of virtue on his outward parts.' "

"Yes," the Bishop agreed, "you are right. The reredos was not worth such a display." And now he also sounded angry and disturbed. Robert had never before seen the Bishop's calm and gentle manner shaken. He was startled as a person might be if the peaceful waters of a small lake should suddenly rise up in waves that threatened to overturn the boat in which he was sitting. But this show of emotion by the Bishop affected Robert in another way. It made him calmer. He was pleased that the Bishop also disapproved of Dr. Grant and at the same time he felt a responsibility for taking his part in working out a solution of the difficulty.

"Must we allow him to keep us from using the flags?" he asked, but he spoke in a different voice, calmer and more mature.

The Bishop rose slowly from his chair, went to the desk in the corner and came back with some letters. He gave the letters to Robert silently. One of them was from Dr. Grant and spoke of the flags and said that Dr. Grant was sure the Bishop would agree with him about not using the flags. The other two letters were from the most prominent vestrymen in the church. They were also the wealthiest. Both letters said that the writers agreed with Dr. Grant that the flags should not be used.

"You see, Robert," the Bishop said when Robert had finished reading the letters, "there are some members of the vestry who think highly of Dr. Grant. They agree with him . . ."

"Yes," Robert answered listlessly. He was silent for a little. In a low voice he said, "I am not wealthy."

They sat quietly. It was so quiet in the room the Bishop was startled when Robert suddenly rose from his chair and spoke in a loud voice, "Suppose we have a new parish house," he cried out, "Suppose we get a new organ and our reredos is the finest in the South. What of it," he demanded, "what of it? The rich men want all this. Dr. Grant and these men," he shook the letters in the Bishop's astonished face, "they wish to see our quiet city lose its dignity and traditions. Suppose our population becomes more than a quarter of a million and we bring new business to our city. What will it profit us if we lose our own souls?"

The Bishop smiled. "We won't lose our souls, Robert," he spoke quietly but there was a gentle touch of irony in his voice, "and as Dr. Grant pointed out to me, the city's prosperity will make it possible for our young men to make a better living than their father's have made. I said the same thing to him that you have said to me, and he pointed this out. The young men can grow up with the city and prosper with the city. It will benefit your own sons . . ."

"Yes," Robert stammered, "Yes, I see. I had not thought . . . my sons . . ." he paused, standing before the Bishop. "But I still maintain . . ." he said, though he did not finish the sentence and his voice was not confident as it had been.

The Bishop looked into the fire. Robert walked to the door, turned and paced back again and stood looking into the fire.

"Let the man have his way, Robert. And you and I will cling to our little mementoes and feel true to the sentiments that are dear to us . . ."

"If we are allowed to have them," Robert said bitterly.

"We have them."

"There is one thing," Robert said as he was saying goodbye to the Bishop at the door of the study, "I will not allow Dr. Grant to take part in the service tonight."

"No," the Bishop promised, "We will not allow that. But I think he is reconciled to that. He won't force himself on us."

As Robert walked from the house and the fresh air came into his face again he told himself, "That is settled then" and a little part of the weight that was on it lifted from his heart.

XV

AT the same time that Robert was arriving at the Bishop's home Mrs. Middleton was in the kitchen arranging a tray for Jennie. Two things had made her feel less anxious about her daughter. One was that Nancy had been so positive that Jennie was in better spirits and the other, that her husband had assured her that Doctor Greve would come and that they could depend on him to reconcile the bride and groom.

As she walked slowly up the stairs with the tray of food Mrs. Middleton groaned softly. During her girlhood it was the fashion for young women to squeeze their feet into the smallest shoes possible. As a result when she was on her feet constantly as she had been all this day she found it painful to walk or to stand.

She groaned again softly after she had set the tray of food on Jennie's table and sat down in a chair. At another time Jennie would have heard this groan and sympathized with her mother. Now she was not sensitive to any misery but her own.

"You must eat, Daughter," Mrs. Middleton insisted because Jennie paid not the least attention to the food but continued to stand near the window in the place where her mother had found her.

"I don't want anything, Mother. I sent word that *I* did not want any dinner."

"But you must," her mother said with patient insistence, "you must because you are going to have company. Dr. Greve is coming."

"Dr. Greve!"

"Yes."

"But why is he coming?" Jennie emphasized the pronoun.

"To see you."

"Why to see me?" Again Jennie emphasized the pronoun.

Her mother was silent.

"Why to see me?" Jennie demanded again. She left the window and went close to her mother. "Who asked him to come and interfere?" she demanded.

Mrs. Middleton laughed uncomfortably, "Why no one . . . why . . . who asked him . . . he wished to come . . ."

"Where is Father?" Jennie asked.

"Your father had to see the Bishop."

The odor of the food on the tray came up to Jennie. She seated herself at the table grudgingly. She did not eat as if she enjoyed the food and yet it disappeared quickly, suddenly almost as if by magic. Her mother watched her with satisfaction.

"Why do you watch me?" Jennie asked impatiently. Mrs. Middleton turned her head away. There was a look of sorrow and hurt on her face and this look of hurt resignation was even more irritating to Jennie. One part of her understood that she was in the wrong, and that her mother was right to make her eat and to try to make her come into the light of everyday things again, but because she understood that she was wrong any patience with this wrongness enraged her.

Annie May came up to say that Dr. Greve was waiting downstairs and Mrs. Middleton gave the girl the empty tray. She remembered that Annie May had not swept up the downstairs rooms since the decorations had been put up.

"Why haven't you swept the front rooms," she asked the girl. "Now we have company there and it is too late."

"I swept the rooms once this morning," Annie May muttered.

"I told you to sweep them again."

"No'm, I declare you didn't," Annie May said. She left the room hurriedly with the tray. The sharp tones in Mrs. Middleton's voice drove her out. It was necessary for her to feel the fifty cent piece knotted up in her handkerchief and resting in the bosom of her dress before she could get her feeling of pleasure in the wedding back again. But the fifty-cent piece was given her by one of the guests and there would be others. As she had told Louisa with a fifty-cent piece she could pay her own way to a dance and have a good time without any obligations to her escort for the rest of the night after the dance was over.

As soon as Annie May left the room Jennie said to her mother, "I didn't say I would see Dr. Greve."

"What will become of us," her mother said miserably, "what will become of us." But she knew that her daughter must see the doctor. She roused herself and looked at Jennie with authority, "You are going to see him," she said desperately. "You are still my daughter and you are going to obey me."

Jennie laughed. This laughter was reckless and irresponsible. It frightened her mother. "Then I will see him." She cried out and ran from the room. As she reached the bottom stair Dr. Greve appeared between the folding doors. He had his handkerchief out and was waving it like a flag.

"I am the ambassador of peace," he said, "here's my flag of truce."

He met Jennie, clasped her arm and led her into the living-room. "What's all this? What's all this?" he asked briskly, "you and Doc like two warriors sulking in their tents."

He released her arm and gave her a little push so that she stood immediately in front of him. She saw his eyes that were twinkling good-humoredly, and it was impossible not to return his smile.

"Now what are the terms of the treaty?" he asked, "being a woman I suppose you will say 'complete surrender'."

"It's nothing to laugh about," Jennie told him severely, but in spite of herself she could not look severe and a smile twitched at the corners of her mouth.

"Such a pretty girl, and so obstinate," Dr. Greve said. He shook his head dolefully. But she understood that the doleful expression was put on. Though Jennie was not conscious of it his attitude of amused admiration and affection stirred a feminine response in her, so that she had a desire to please him. Also she saw that she was attractive to him and this admiration for her as a woman in some indirect manner made up to her for the cold and critical attitude her own doctor had shown the evening before.

"Well," Dr. Greve repeated, "what are the terms of peace. What can I say to Doc?" He waited. Jennie strolled to the window and stared out at the automobile which waited at the curb for the doctor. This retreat from him was part of the coquetry which he had stimulated in her. But the little doctor did not see it in that way. He thought she was trying to ignore him, trying to make him feel that he and his friend were of no account. He decided it was time to speak plainly.

"Look here, Jennie," he said, "I came to see you because I am a friend of Doc's. Doc is in love with you. You are in love with him. He wants to marry you tonight . . ."

Jennie spoke from the window without turning her head. "Then why doesn't he tell me? Why does he stay there and brood over his wrong? I didn't do anything. Why did he swear at me?" Her voice was tearful.

"So that's it. I thought so. I thought so." He hurried to the window and took both of her hands in his. "Why I'm ashamed of you," he said speaking to her as he might speak to a child, "I thought you had more stamina than that." He had gone to the window and had taken Jennie's hands in order to persuade her as he might persuade a child, but when he took her hands and she looked into his face with her eyes soft and tearful, when he saw her mouth quiver a change came over his feeling toward her. There was a sudden and unexpected feeling of sympathy for her. But he continued to speak in the same cajoling voice. "Why don't you get your mother and drive to the hotel with me and have it out with Doc. You can have our whole sitting-room for the fight. Or don't have it out. Just go up to him and put your arms around him. He'll meet you half way. If a girl as pretty as you came to me and put her arms around me and said, 'I'm sorry' I'd surrender at once. Now get your mother and in that thing," he pointed to the automobile. "We'll be at the hotel in five minutes."

"He doesn't want me," Jennie insisted, "I know he doesn't want me. And you know it."

He had an impulse to put his arms around her and comfort her. The impulse said to him that it would be pleasant to press her round little shoulders with his hands. Jennie's quivering lips smiled. Suddenly a reckless look came on her face and a warm light into her eyes. Her eyes said that she was ready to dare anything. It was unconscious, and for that reason it was attractive. The reckless charm came like a wave of magnetic attraction from her whole body so that it communicated itself to him.

"What I would like to do," she said very low, "is go for a ride with you."

With the change in his physical attitude toward Jennie there came another change. The situation on which he had looked only a moment or two before with an amused tolerance suddenly took on a special significance. He was no longer out of the quarrel, but it became something that was threatening Jennie's happiness, and her happiness was important. Her whole body, her eyes, her mouth told him that it was important to her and that she, and she only must be considered. He said, "You want to go for a ride with me?"

"Yes, just a little ride," she begged.

"What would your mother say?"

"I don't know. I want to get out."

"Out? You mean the hotel?"

"No, out, out," she insisted and laughed into his face. He saw her mouth part over her teeth and the edges of her white even teeth.

"Well!" he exclaimed. His right eyebrow went up but his eyes laughed. "Out!" he repeated.

"Yes . . . out," Jennie laughed again. She did not know why she wished to go. She did not want any reasoning. Everyone was so reasonable. She did not long for attention or affection or patience such as her mother gave her. All day she had been so dull in her prison and now there was an opportunity to escape. She must become active. She must move, it did not matter where. Only she did not wish to go to the hotel with her mother. She saw that the little doctor would not object or put up foolish reasons for not going and said in an excited, shrill voice, "I'll get my coat," and ran out of the room.

The doctor watched her go. And when she had left a sudden realization of what he had felt as he held her small hands in his came to him. He shook his head and frowned, walked swiftly across the room and back to the window. "Poor Doc," he whispered. "Poor Doc."

On the stairs at the bend where there was a landing Jennie met her mother coming slowly down. Mrs. Middleton looked into Jennie's face and saw the excitement and recklessness there and that something out of the ordinary was happening and that Jennie wished to hide this something from her.

"What is it?" she asked anxiously. She stood in the middle of the stairs so that Jennie could not pass without pushing her aside.

"Let me by, Mother," Jennie panted.

"What is this?" Mrs. Middleton demanded.

"I'm going out," Jennie said recklessly in a loud voice almost like a shriek.

Mrs. Middleton looked over Jennie's head down into the face of Dr. Greve who had come into the hall. Her eyes said to him, "What is this? What have you done to my daughter?"

Dr. Greve shrugged his shoulders in answer to the questions her eyes asked. Then he smiled at her and looked at Jennie. The smile and the look said to Mrs. Middleton, "You and I know she is foolish. But let her be foolish. It is her own responsibility."

But Mrs. Middleton could not return his smile. She saw that this man would allow Jennie to do whatever she pleased, any reckless act, and would not stop her. She could not understand such detachment. To her it was necessary to brood and worry and pray in order to make things come right and even then they did not always do so. More often they did not. But it comforted her to feel that she had done her best by prayer and worry.

She was so concentrated on her family life it was always a shock when the outside world forced itself on her attention. At such times her imagination enlarged every small interference with the quiet family life into a huge menace. Any stranger appeared as an enemy or a potential enemy. She was sensitive and proud. She knew that people gossiped and that gossip could hurt and she wished to protect her family and herself from contact with anything that could hurt. It seemed to her so much surer to live a quiet unassuming life and go by the old rule, "out of sight, out of mind." If a family could live together with its books, its music, its little traditions and customs and keep its members from doing anything unusual then others would leave them alone to enjoy each other. She wished more than anything else to be left alone with her family, to enjoy it.

But Jennie's amazing behavior was threatening her peace and the peace of her family. And like a small animal that runs from its pursuers, but when it has reached its own burrow turns to protect it, she gathered together all her strength to protect the whole family as she stood before Jennie, just above her, on the stairs. Jennie and the little doctor stared at Mrs. Middleton. Because in one moment while she stood before them, above them where they could see her plainly, her whole character changed before them. She had come down the stairs tired and distressed and meek. Now she drew her body up stiffly and her face became haughty and commanding.

"Tell me where you are going," Mrs. Middleton said to Jennie in a haughty commanding voice that came naturally out of the face which had become so suddenly like the face of a person who has commanded all of her life.

On the step below her Jennie appeared like a small and ineffective child and even Dr. Greve appeared to shrink into a little boy who has got into some mischief or who has been caught just as he is about to do so.

"We are going for a ride," Jennie said quietly. But she looked up at her mother defiantly.

"You are going into that room and sit down," Mrs. Middleton told her.

"No," Jennie insisted, "I am going for a ride with Dr. Greve."

"Must I force you," her mother whispered. She was much larger than Jennie.

Jennie stared up into her mother's face, and it was the face of a cruel stranger. There was no familiar meekness in it and no sorrow, only a cold look that was frightening.

"Sit down in that chair," Mrs. Middleton ordered, pointing to a chair near the fireplace. She moved down the stairs with her arm outstretched and her finger pointing and as she did so Jennie moved backward before her until she reached the large chair and sank into it. She obeyed her mother. But for many years she did not forget this anger and humiliation. When she was seated in the chair by the fire none of the anger showed in her. She seemed to the others like a small child who has been terribly hurt. She crept further into the chair and as she did so Mrs. Middleton felt a deep sense of pity for her daughter. She was almost ready to let Jennie have her own way.

Jennie glanced at Dr. Greve and saw that his hands were in his pockets and that he was hugging himself and smiling as he watched her with amused eyes. He was smiling delightedly and this made her humiliation more painful. She thought, "if his hands were not in his pockets he would be clapping them as if he were at a play. He thinks we are amusing."

And Dr. Greve was pleased and amused. This encounter between the mother and daughter had entirely erased that other emotion of sympathy he had felt for Jennie. It was gone. Once again he looked on her, on

both of them with the amused tolerance which was
more natural to him. He was delighted with his recovery. But he had also come for a serious purpose and
must carry that out to the best of his ability. He saw
with the alert intelligence that had come back in him
with his recovery that Mrs. Middleton was softening
toward Jennie. He could see that her whole body softened. He went to her and said quietly, "I would like
to telephone."

She stood aside and held to the newel post of the
stairs because she had suddenly become very weak.
From her chair Jennie watched the doctor out of the
corners of her eyes. Both women watched him as he
walked to the stair landing where the telephone rested
on the little table. He had not said that he was calling
the Doctor at the hotel, but they knew this was what
he intended to do. He called the number. Presently
they heard him say, "Doc?" They watched and listened,
tense and silent.

He said, "Wait, Doc, wait a moment," and put his
hand over the mouth-piece. He beckoned to Jennie. She
went to him slowly.

"Jennie," he said in a low voice, "a woman can
make this world a paradise for a man if she will try,"
his voice was low but it had an immense urgency in it.

"But why shouldn't he make it for me?" Jennie
demanded in a whisper.

"I don't know," Doctor Greve whispered impatiently,
"only if you would just let that will of yours go, let
it go. Let it melt and don't care about it, don't care."

"But why?" she insisted obstinately. "Why must I do all the letting go?"

"Don't ask me why," he whispered. He spoke into the telephone, "Just a moment, Doc" and covered the mouth-piece again.

"I was willing to do anything for him," Jennie whispered dramatically. "I'd give my life for him."

"He doesn't want you to give your life. He wants you. He is warm and generous. I tell you so, Jennie. If you'll only get at him, only let him be so. As he is. Not as you want him to be. He takes you as you are. He is waiting in the hotel to take you as you are. Don't you understand, as you are. Take him as he is," he whispered fiercely.

But this was a stupid and foolish thing to Jennie. It was stupid for anyone to say this. Because she was giving up her individual life and so her energies must be used for her husband. And she must push him on to do more because he would be her ambition also. He must carry out her life in the world as well as his own. He must because she was giving up her individual life for him. So he must keep her individual ambitions alive in the world. She could not take him as he was any more than she could take herself as she was. She could not be satisfied with him any more than she could be satisfied with herself, but must urge him on to live her life in the world as well as his own. She could not say all this to Dr. Greve. She could not even put it into words. But it was so clear to her. It appeared suddenly after he had said, "Take him as he is." The reasons why she could not do so rang in her head as she told herself afterward "clear as a bell." Only it was impossible to say them. And even if she had been ready to do so she would have been prevented because with one of his quick and unexpected movements Dr. Greve put the receiver into her hand and closed her fingers over it and left her alone on the landing. He ran down the steps and stood beside Mrs. Middleton.

Jennie held the receiver but did not put her mouth to the other part which would establish communication with her Doctor. She could not make herself bend down to the mouth-piece.

"Go on," Dr. Greve whispered urgently.

Jennie hesitated. In herself she was thinking, "Why should I be the one to give in? Dr. Greve did not even say 'Jennie is here' so that Doctor could say he wished to speak to me. Dr. Greve wants it to seem that I wished to speak first. He wants to save Doctor's pride, not mine. He doesn't care about mine."

She heard a noise at the head of the steps, and saw that Susan was there looking down at her.

"Come here, Susan," she said almost without speaking at all, but Susan understood that Jennie wanted her and went down to the landing. "Talk to Doctor," Jennie whispered. She gave the receiver to the little girl and looked triumphantly down at her mother and Dr. Greve.

Susan took the receiver obediently. She was fond of the Doctor. She liked his almost indifferent way

of being affectionate, as if he loved her and yet did
not wish to impose his affection. She said, "Hello," in
her childish voice into the telephone, but no one answered at the other end of the wire. She said, "Hello"
again, and thought she heard the click of the receiver
going down over the hook in the far-off hotel room.

Jennie walked with a little swaggering step down
the steps to the room. "Now you see," she said to her
mother and Dr. Greve when Susan had said "Hello"
a third time and there was no answer. "He didn't want
to talk to me. You see I was right. And you wanted
me to humiliate myself. And I was right not to do it.
I'd give my life for him, but he doesn't care. Then I
don't. I don't care." She turned to her mother. "And I
am going out. What does it matter now? Dr. Greve,"
she begged, "will you take me? Of course you will,"
she laughed and ran up the stairs. "I'll be ready in a
moment," she called before she went into her room.
Her voice and shrill laughter echoed about the room
and Carrie Middleton winced as if the voice itself had
struck her across the face. Susan looked up the stairs
at the spot where Jennie had vanished. Once more she
said, "Hello," in a small questioning voice into the
telephone. No answer came. She put the receiver slowly
back on the hook.

With nervous excited movements Jennie went about
getting ready for the outdoors. She put on the new
coat, and adjusted her hat before the mirror. And
though she put the hat on the correct angle, tipped
toward the front, high in the back, she did not see

herself, did not meet her own eyes in the mirror.
And the same thing happened when she adjusted the
stole of brown fur which the Doctor had given her
the Christmas before about her neck and stood at the
mirror again with the large flat muff in her hands,
ready to go. Although she saw herself, the coat and
the green hat and the brown stole, she did not look
into her own face, and her eyes did not meet the eyes
in the mirror.

It seemed absolutely necessary to her that she get
away from the house. It was also necessary for her
to show Dr. Greve that she could get away. He had
looked at her with amusement and she must take that
smile of amusement from his face and put some other
expression in its place. She must do something that
would restore her lost dignity, her lost importance. She
could not go on until she had impressed her very self
on him.

Mrs. Middleton had not believed that Jennie was
actually going with Dr. Greve until she saw her coming down the stairs, holding her skirts up gracefully
with one hand and with the other swinging the wide
brown muff that went with the stole. The hat tilted
over Jennie's smiling and excited face seemed to say,
"I am going away, I am going away." And Mrs. Middleton knew that Jennie would go. And when she understood that she could do nothing further to prevent
her daughter from going her mind, which had waited
in a sort of dull dread of what might be coming, became active again, just as a person's stunned mind

which has refused to function after someone in the
house has called "Fire" becomes suddenly active in
order to save whatever can be saved from the fire.

Carrie said, "Susan, go up and put on your coat and
hat," and Susan ran up obediently. She passed her
sister on the stairs and looked up into her radiant face.
But Jennie did not see her.

Jennie stood before Dr. Greve and her mother. "I'm
ready," she said to Dr. Greve. And in the same way
that she had not looked at her own face in the mirror
she avoided her mother's eyes, looking at her, and yet
not seeing her.

"Dr. Greve is driving you out to see Old Rosin,"
her mother said.

"Old Rosin," Jennie asked, "but why . . . Old
Rosin . . ." she repeated in an astonished voice.

"Some things from the wedding," Mrs. Middleton
said vaguely, and then more firmly she added, "I have
been planning a basket." And it was true that she had
planned to send some of the leftovers from the reception the following day to Old Rosin. "And," Carrie
continued, "you and Susan can take the basket since
Dr. Greve is so kind and . . . and considerate. And
perhaps Dr. Greve will examine Rosin. She has tuberculosis," she explained to Dr. Greve.

Dr. Greve looked at Jennie and smiled. She understood the smile which said that he knew her pleasure
was ruined. But Jennie did not feel this. Her excitement and pleasure were localized, that is they were in
herself, and nothing that happened about her could

touch that excitement or the feeling of living vividly that was in her. She waited at the door while her mother went back to the kitchen for the basket. Dr. Greve saw that Jennie stood at the door on tiptoes as if watching and expecting someone and ready to put out her hand and rush away just as soon as that someone appeared.

Finally the curious little procession went down the walk to the waiting automobile. Carrie had brought Ed to carry the basket and had made him put on his white coat. She saw that Susan was placed in the center of the back seat and told Ed to give the basket up to Susan. Dr. Greve helped Jennie into the car and took the place that was left. The driver looked back questioningly. Dr. Greve said "Where?" to Jennie, and when she did not seem to understand, he repeated, "Where are we going?"

Mrs. Middleton heard his question and spoke to the driver. "The Penitentiary," she said.

XVI

D R. GREVE leaned slightly forward and looked at Jennie over the basket in Susan's lap. One of his eyelids came down over the eye, and his attractive mouth under the small moustache trembled with laughter that he was trying to control.

"Well chaperoned," she said and moved his head with a slight gesture toward Susan.

Jennie could not hear what he said but the slight gesture toward her small sister and the smile on his lips made her understand. She returned the smile and her smile said to him that Susan's presence did not interfere with her pleasure. The car went faster, faster than Jennie had travelled before. The cold wind blew on her cheeks and lifted her hat so that the straining pins made her scalp prick. But even this pricking sensation was pleasant to her. She felt that the wind could lift her just as it was trying to lift her hat, and that in a moment she could fly out of the car and away to another place. And yet she wished also to stay in the car and go on and on wherever they were going. She threw the fur stole over her shoulder and buried her

chin in the fur. Her eyes gleamed mischievously as she
looked again at Dr. Greve and he saw that her lips
were smiling against the fur. He lifted the basket from
Susan's lap and set it on the front seat beside the
driver. Then he lifted Susan to a place on the outside,
tucked the robe about her knees and over her hands
and took her place beside Jennie.

"Who is this Old . . . Old . . ." he could not remember the name.

"Old Rosin," Jennie said. They spoke in low voices
but with their heads close together so that they might
be able to understand each other under the louder
sound of the engine.

Jennie added, "Susan and Bobby were Old Rosin's
favorites," and hearing her say this made Susan feel
important. She listened while Jennie told Dr. Greve
about Rosin. She could not hear all the words that
Jennie said, because the wind blew the sound away
from her. But she knew the story, and it was true
that she and Bobby knew more than any of the others
about Rosin's life, because Rosin had talked to them
while she sewed on the mattresses. She was an expert
at repairing mattresses and upholstery and went out
by the day. For a long time Susan and Bobby did not
know that Old Rosin's name was Rosalind, and even
then they continued to associate her in their minds
with the rosin they pricked out from between the bark
of the pine trees in the country.

Rosin told them about her childhood in the mill
village near Lexington. Rosin was the ninth child and

at nine years of age she went into the mill to work. Her mother died when she was born. There was no one except Rosin to keep the house together because all the older children left home as soon as they were grown enough. Rosin kept the house together for her father until he, too, died when she was sixteen. Then she lived in the boarding house and continued to work in the mill. She did not know the members of her family. As she told Susan she might have met her own brother and sister on the street and would not have recognized them.

She tried to explain to Bobby and Susan why she liked to repair mattresses. It was because she liked cotton. She never enjoyed repairing an old-time feather mattress or a hair mattress as she liked to work with those made of cotton. And this was because she had learned to like cotton at the mill. There was one room in the mill which gave her special pleasure. It was the carding room. There she would go and watch the lap of cotton, "forty inches broad and as thick as a man's hand," she told them, pass over the cylinder. The lap was thick and soft. It was like a cloud. Rosin liked to touch it as it moved slowly to the place where the eye condensed it into a card sliver. She explained to the children what a card sliver was, a light rope of cotton only one inch broad. The soft card-sliver curled into the drums that waited at the foot of the carding machine. But it was not the slivers that Rosin loved. It was the lap that passed like a cloud slowly along the surface of the machine. The wide white cloudy lap moved noiselessly and the narrow soft slivers curled noiselessly into the drums. Watching this process made Rosin feel attentive and quiet.

And then one day she slipped on some oil and fractured her leg so that she could not stand up all day. That was when she began to repair mattresses, so that she could sit at her task. Susan always enjoyed the moment when Rosin finished a mattress and patted it down all over, and said, "Now it's done. Now you will sleep well and have good dreams." There was so much pleasure in Rosin's voice when she said this, and a sort of comforting feeling came into the air around them, as if everything was well and a person could go off to sleep without a worry or thought.

Rosin always said, "I didn't do so well this year, but next year will be my big year." But one of the years came and Rosin had tuberculosis. Because of this no one would hire her to repair their mattresses. There was prohibition in the state and Rosin made a living by selling liquor. One night, perhaps because she was drunk herself, she accidentally killed a man. Because she had worked for the Middletons and knew that Hugh was a lawyer Rosin sent for him. It was Hugh's first case that he pleaded in the courts alone. He proved that Rosin had killed accidentally, but she was put away in the Penitentiary for life.

As Jennie came to the part where Rosin had become ill with tuberculosis Susan leaned toward Dr. Greve so that she might hear better. She leaned toward him and as she did so she felt the rough coat which he wore and a smell of tobacco came up from the great pocket in his coat. She heard Jennie say, "and Rosin had a hemorrhage when Susan was there," and she remembered the day when she was watching Rosin. A fit of coughing came on her. It was frightening. Old Rosin's face was thin enough, but it became thinner. Her cheeks sunk inward. And Susan smelled the overpowering smell of blood as Rosin reached for some of the cotton batting and stuffed it to her mouth. When Rosin had gone, for she left at once, Susan's mother came in and asked for her and Susan told her mother, "Rosin was sick and had to go home. She was coughing and had a mouth bleed." Susan showed her mother the cotton with blood on it. She thought it was no more than a nose bleed which she had experienced herself and which was not too serious. It was surprising when her mother became excited and anxious. The word "consumption" was whispered over the house. The whole family moved to the country while the house was fumigated.

Interesting and mysterious words were added to Susan's knowledge. She did not understand fumigate because for a long time they were away in the country and she was not able to investigate that process. But she learned what a hemorrhage was. She knew the meaning of consume, but not of consumption. Bobby had read her a sentence from a book which said, "the house was consumed by fire." And because of this association Susan thought there was a fire in Old Rosin and that this fire was slowly burning her so that there

would be nothing left but the outward shell of flesh
and bones and finally even that would be consumed by
the fire of the dreaded consumption.

Now she knew better because she had been to the
Penitentiary before to see Rosin, and she was the
same, only thinner than she had been before. But it
was almost a year since she had gone on that visit, the
previous Christmas, and now as the automobile took
them from the streets of the town out into the country
and she could see the far-off walls of the prison, an
excitement came up in Susan, because she was to visit
that place again and see Rosin again.

As they came nearer to the prison she could see the
wide yellow Santee River that surrounded the walls
on two sides. The eighteen-foot walls went straight up
from the river as if they grew out of the mud. On the
other two sides the walls were built up from flat-baked
ground. There were no trees nearby and no cultivated
fields. It seemed that nothing could grow near that for-
bidding place.

The driver stopped the car just in front of the great
iron doors in the front wall. The sergeant who met
Jennie at this barrier knew her and let her in at once.
Visitors were not allowed in the women's division
without special permission so it was necessary to wait
in the office while the sergeant went to get formal permission from the Superintendent. Before he left the
sergeant looked in the files and gave Dr. Greve the
history of Old Rosin's case. Susan stood beside Dr.

Greve as he sat at the table and Jennie leaned over
from her chair. They read at the top of the history:

NAME—Rosalind Downs.

AGE—36 years.

It was true that this was Rosin's age. But because
she looked older, much older than that, everyone called
her Old Rosin.

COLOR—White.

CRIME—Murder.

TIME EXPIRES—Full Time. Death.

DISTINGUISHING MARKS—Red scar left fore-arm.
    Scar on right thigh just above knee joint . . .

MEDICAL HISTORY— . . . . .

The sergeant came, jingling his heavy keys, and led
Jennie, Dr. Greve and Susan through another iron
gate into the courtyard of the prison. Now the walls
appeared higher and thicker than they had appeared
from the outside. They seemed enormous. And far up
at intervals there were small green-painted wooden
sentry boxes with glass windows.

Along the back wall of the office there was a place
enclosed in thick wire netting. And sitting along the
wall behind the netting there were eight men in chairs.
The men leaned in their tilted chairs against the wall.
They appeared lazy and careless—and yet everyone
knew that at the slightest alarm they would be ready
to spring forward. They had long-barreled shot guns
slung under their arms. To the left there was a high
white-washed board wall. The sergeant unlocked a
small door in this wall and let them file through. In-

side this door Susan knew they would find Rosin because it was the woman's section of the prison. To the right after they got inside the wooden wall was a long low building divided in half by a thick wall. It was like a two-family dwelling. One half of it was for the white women prisoners and the other half for the colored.

The ground was flat and sun-baked. Even the rain of the night before had not taken off the baked appearance, nor had it filled in the cracks caused by the sun. There were three china-berry trees, with bare limbs. Now, because the ice on the limbs had melted in the sun there was a little dark pool of water under each tree. One of the trees stood just at the side of a curious little structure in the center of the yard. The structure was like a tent, only it was built of wood. On all four sides there was a wire screening from the roof halfway down the walls. This was the place where a consumptive patient was isolated.

Jennie ran forward and peered through the screen. "It's Jennie Middleton," she said cheerfully; "how are you, Rosin? I have brought a fine doctor to see you."

Rosin's voice came out weakly to them. They could not see inside. The sun came down on them as they stood there, but inside the little structure everything seemed to be in darkness. And Old Rosin's voice came weakly out of the darkness inside, as if it came not from a person, but was the darkness speaking. It was queer and unreal.

"Will you make an examination?" Jennie asked Dr. Greve.

He shrugged. "I will. But I told you I haven't any paraphernalia."

"Just to make her feel better," Jennie whispered eagerly. She put her hand on Dr. Greve's arm. "I want you to," she said, smiling at him.

"Of course, then," he said goodnaturedly. He imitated her voice, "If you want me to."

He walked to the front of the cabin, to the screen door.

"Do you want to see Rosin?" Jennie asked her sister.

Susan nodded, and Jennie lifted her until Susan could cling to the edge of the wood. She put her face close to the screening and said, "Hello, Rosin."

Rosin was propped up against two pillows. She turned her head. Her face was yellow and thin. It was cracked with wrinkles like the earth outside which was cracked from too much sun. Her eyes were deep and appeared very dark like the pools of water under the china-berry trees outside. A strand of oily brown hair lay across one cheek. She smiled at Susan and her mouth opened. Susan knew that she spoke but could not hear what Rosin's mouth said. She leaned closer and pressed her face against the screen. "What did you say?" she asked. "How's your mama?" Rosin said in a weak voice. Before Susan could answer Dr. Greve came to the bed and Rosin turned her face that way.

Jennie lifted Susan from the side of the little house.

As she was set on the ground Susan felt her sister's arms about her and Jennie's cheek close to hers.

As she stood with her arm about her little sister Jennie felt again an emotion that had stirred her before, the emotion that had come the Sunday morning when she had taken Susan to church and had received the bread and wine, the symbolic body and blood of Christ. She thought with a sort of wonder that this was a repetition of the Sunday morning experience. In her own mind she said "it is the same." Then she had Susan with her, and now Susan was there at her side. Today they were being kind to Old Rosin, and that morning the same thing had happened at the chapel steps. The strange old woman had come and she and Susan had helped the old woman up the steps of the chapel. It was very significant that this had happened twice. Jennie did not know exactly what the significance was, but it seemed to be a sign, if she could only find the meaning of the sign. And again the blood seemed very significant. The wine she had drunk symbolizing Christ's blood, and the blood she had just been telling Dr. Greve about, Old Rosin's blood on the cotton.

The sergeant came from the doorway of the white-washed brick building, the side that was for colored women. The great keys in his hand jangled together in the silence of the yard. A Negro woman followed him and took some dingy clothes from the line in the corner of the yard. She bent her head and looked back from the corners of her eyes at the visitors.

Dr. Greve joined Susan and Jennie and they walked to one of the china-berry trees.

"No," Dr. Greve said in answer to a question from Jennie, "both lungs. It will be soon." He put his hands in his pockets and shrugged as if he wished to say, "What con I do? They die. A Doctor is not God."

"She wants to see you," he said to Jennie.

Jennie took Susan's hand. In the structure it was not so dark as it had seemed from the yard. Old Rosin put out her hand from under the bed-clothes. She held it with the palm upward. Susan put her hand there because it seemed that Old Rosin was waiting for that. The long fingers closed around Susan's small hand. Susan felt the bones. It seemed almost as if there was no flesh, but only bones with a covering like a glove of rough leather that fitted the bones closely. The hand did not let go.

Old Rosin's skin with the inside light on it was transparent like rosin that comes out of the pine trees. Now her eyes did not look like the pools of water under the trees in the yard, dark and shadowy. They were deep blue and amazingly alive. And because they were so alive, and because of her bony hand that held to Susan's so almost desperately, and because Dr. Greve had said that Rosin could not live, Susan began to cry. She laid her head on the bed-clothes beside Rosin and sobbed. And this was the wrong thing to do. She felt Jennie take her hand and lead her out of the room.

Dr. Greve met them at the doorway in the high wooden wall. He saw that Susan was crying and that

Jennie had gone through some emotional experience. She looked at him with a pitiful expression of pleading and at the same time the expression said, "You and I have been through this together. And you are splendid. You can't save Rosin, but there are many others that you have saved." Her look was intimate and soft, and it gave him the feeling that the experience was important to them both, and that its importance was heightened because they were there together. Her whole body was soft and appealing so that he wished to touch her. He put his arm about her and held her close. "Well, are you satisfied?" he asked in a low voice, and in spite of himself there was emotion in his voice instead of the light tone which he had tried to use.

She nodded and looked up into his face and again he felt as he had in the living room of her home earlier in the day,—that what Jennie felt was important, and that she was more important than himself, than any of them, and that the pleasures as well as the sorrows of life were heightened when she was there, and that she must not be allowed to suffer. He tried to tell himself as they went on toward the entrance of the prison that the feeling he had of his own importance and of Jennie's importance was false. He tried to put himself back into the place where he looked on at the world and people from the outside and did not consider himself any more important than the others, but only one of them. But her tender smile and the expression of her eyes as she looked up into his, and the feeling of his fingers and the palm of his hand about her shoulder would not allow him to do so. He pressed her body closer to his own and the heightened significance of life and the rarity and unusualness of this experience came over him again.

And this feeling continued even after they had returned to the automobile with Susan. A generous and unusual impulse toward his friend came into him. He saw everything in a rosy glow of pleasure, and the qualities, his own and the qualities of others were heightened and increased in his eyes. He told Jennie about the operation which Doctor Gregg had performed just before he left Mountain City to come to the wedding.

"It has made him," he said. "I have always thought of him as a surgeon. And he has always wanted to be a surgeon. And this will make him. He is one naturally, instinctively. But now people will know."

When he saw the look of pleasure on Jennie's face he was glad that he had told her.

"I didn't know," she said. "I am glad. I didn't know you thought this . . . this . . . of him."

"Of course. I have always known it," he said to her. And he thought that this was true, and that he had always had a tremendous admiration for his friend.

He sat close to her in the car and her eyes looked at him above the brown fur that hugged her neck so closely, and her lips that were smiling above the fur, and her small round chin that was outlined by the fur drew his attention until she spoke and he looked into her eyes again and saw the soft admiration in them.

He felt generous and uplifted, and a tremendous confidence in himself and in Jennie's feeling for him radiated a warmth in him. He felt that he must insist that she see his friend. Without realizing it himself he knew that she preferred him, but that she must go on and be married to his friend. He did not wish to prevent it. His feeling for her was different. He did not understand in what way it was different. There was a reverence in it for Jennie and a sort of pity for his friend because he would not have Jennie's love and at the same time a great generosity toward his friend.

He said, "Will you stop by the hotel and see him?"

Jennie nodded and smiled and her nod and smile gave him pleasure.

At the door of the hotel Dr. Greve directed the driver to take Susan home and he and Jennie went to the back door of the hotel. They laughed together as they slipped up the back stairs so that Jennie would not be seen in the lobby on her wedding day.

Dr. Greve led Jennie into the sitting-room of his suite. "Excuse me a moment," he said to her and went softly into the next room. Jennie sat very still in one of the chairs. She heard Dr. Greve speaking in a low tone and knew that he was talking to his wife, but she could not understand what was said. She heard Mrs. Greve exclaim and then Dr. Greve's steps went from that room into the hall, and she heard him knock on the door opposite and call out. And then she heard nothing for a long while. Even Mrs. Greve did not come into the room to speak to her. She was quite alone. The loneliness became irksome. She felt that she was not herself, not Jennie Middleton who was to be married that evening, but a stranger who was sitting in a room which she had never seen before, and she was as strange to herself, as the room was strange to her. Then she heard footsteps in the corridor outside the door and started up from her chair.

XVII

AS Robert entered his own home after his visit to
the Bishop he felt again the almost uncanny stillness,
so different from the bustle and noise that had been
in the house for the past week. No one was in the
downstairs rooms. On the chandeliers, over the door
and from the corners of the rooms to the chandeliers
stretched garlands of smilax and gray moss. And hung
at intervals were the crossed red and white and blue
flags. The floor had been swept clean. The Confederate
flags above the mantel made him wince inwardly because they had some connection with the turmoil that
was going on within himself. "Did I mean it," he
asked himself, "when I told Christopher that he should
find a rich wife? Did I mean this? Does all my talk
amount to this . . . that I will give up anything so
that my sons will not experience my own poverty?"

He had always thought himself beyond the reach of
any material consideration. And yet he wished his
sons to live in a better way than he had lived. He
wished for them to have more luxuries and less anxiety
so that their sons and daughters might have every ad-

vantage without nagging worries, and the eternal notes
at the bank. And yet he understood that in spite of
these worries, all his life he had lived cleanly, at peace
with himself. There was a simplicity about this life
that pleased him. One of the wealthy vestrymen who
had written the Bishop owned the whole red light district. "Money comes from the rustling girls and goes
into the church," he thought bitterly, "from the whores
to God, whores and cotton mills." And yet these were
the men who would make the city grow so that his
sons might prosper. His own sons would become a
part of the whole structure, the evil part as well as the
good. He was bewildered by his own hesitation. It
was not that there was any immediate decision to be
made. This had been made for him. Dr. Grant and
his friends had won. But he was bewildered because
he had said to the Bishop, "What will it profit us if we
lose our own souls?" and when the Bishop spoke of
the way in which the city would grow and pointed out
that these very men would make it grow for the benefit
of his sons, he hesitated and stammered. He was
ashamed of this hesitation because it showed clearly
that he did value money and ease for his children. He
valued it more than he valued their integrity and his
own integrity. He was willing to compromise. What
did it matter if no one knew of this compromise? He
knew it within himself. And it was enough to make
him ashamed in secret. "Then I did mean it," he told
himself, "when I said to Christopher, 'find yourself a

rich wife.' I meant it coldly and cynically. It was not a joke."

In the living-room he sank down on the velvet cushioned piano stool. With one finger he picked out a tune slowly on the keys. He felt sad and disillusioned. He picked out on the yellow ivory keys the same tune which came to him whenever he felt that life was over and that there was not much more to live for, as he had felt when his wife went for a long visit to her relatives in another state. The tune he played with one finger went on. It sounded very loud in the quiet house:

> "There's a land that is fairer than day
> And by faith we may see it afar."

The clear sad notes were heard all over the house. The bridesmaids, who had waked from their beauty naps and were in Nancy's room talking softly together because they thought Jennie was asleep, heard them and hesitated in their talk as if someone had said an embarrassing thing that was hard to forget or overlook. The doleful hymn picked out on the newly-tuned keys was out of place and made them curiously uneasy.

Carrie Middleton heard the notes far back in the pantry where she was preparing dressing for the salad and knew that her husband had returned. She knew also, because of the song, that he was depressed, and hurried to the living-room. It was a family joke, or

rather a knowledge they shared together that when
the father sat at the piano and played that tune he
was melancholy.

Carrie laid her hand over his on the keys so that
the notes that were making her melancholy also would
stop.

"I can see you haven't good news," she said to him.

"No," Robert told her.

"Come and finish your dinner now," Carrie urged,
"you ate nothing before you left, not a thing."

"Is Jennie upstairs?" he asked her.

"Come and finish your dinner," she repeated.

"I wanted to tell Jennie . . ." he began, but she interrupted him again. Her voice was urgent, unusually
demanding. She got him into the pantry. "Tell me
what the Bishop said," she begged. She wished to
know what the Bishop had told Robert, and at another
time her curiosity and interest about the visit would
have been intense. But now she could only say to herself, "He mustn't know that Jennie went with Dr.
Greve. He will be angry and then . . . but he will be
angry with me, not with Jennie . . . because I let her
go. But I couldn't prevent it. And he won't understand."

She felt resentful at the injustice and a red flush
of resentment came up under the delicate white skin
of her cheeks. Her large gray eyes glowed with the
feeling of resentment and with other emotions.

Robert saw the flush and her large glowing eyes. He
put his arm around her and kissed her cheek. "Why

mother, you look like a bride yourself," he said. He felt grateful for her.

"Must you always call me mother?" Carrie asked resentfully. He looked at her in surprise.

"No, only . . ." he laughed good-naturedly and sat down to the rest of his dinner that Carrie had kept for him. As he ate he told Carrie about the flags and that the bridesmaids would not be allowed to carry them that evening. He told about the whole conversation with the Bishop, or about most of it. He was repeating the quotation he had used, "The world is still deceived with ornament," when Carrie heard a noise at the door that led into the dining-room. She looked up and saw that Susan was there.

"Just a moment, Robert," she said, "I'll come back. That is a good quotation and I know it was apt. I want to hear it," she said nervously, "I do want to hear it . . ." she hurried to the door and forced Susan through the dining-room and into the living-room. She looked everywhere for Jennie, but Jennie was not there. The room was quiet and empty and to Carrie the decorations seemed strange and unnatural in the stillness.

"Where is Jennie?" she asked breathlessly and in a whisper.

"With Dr. Greve," Susan told her. She spoke as her mother did, in a whisper.

"Where? Where is she?" Carrie gasped. "Tell me." She pressed Susan's hand.

"At the hotel," Susan whispered.

"At what hotel? Where? Why?"

"At his hotel. She's going to make up with Doctor."

"Are you sure?" Carrie let Susan's hand fall from her own.

"Yes'm, I'm sure."

"Don't tell your father about this," her mother said to Susan, "we must keep it a secret until Jennie comes. Do you understand?"

"Yes'm. I came in the automobile," Susan said proudly.

The door-bell rang loudly and emphatically. Susan ran into the reception hall.

"Is it Jennie?" Carrie asked. She was afraid to look for herself.

"No'm, it's Cousin Fannie and Saint John," Susan told her.

"Then let them in," Carrie said and then, "No, I'll let them in. Tell your father Cousin Fannie is here. And take the sheets off the tables. Cousin Fannie will want to see the wedding presents."

Susan walked reluctantly toward the dining-room. She put her head through the pantry door and gave the message to her father and then she turned to the tables that were shrouded in the white sheets. She stared at the sheets that covered the tables. Suddenly she had remembered what happened that morning. She had forgotten completely and now she remembered. Saint John had taken the silver bowl from under the sheet on the table. She lifted up the sheet from the large dining table and folded it across. There was the empty place right in the center of the table. Slowly she folded the sheets and took them back into the kitchen. In a moment they would find that the silver bowl was gone. And though there was no reason for her to feel so, a sense of guilt and dread came in her.

She laid the sheets which were rumpled by her awkward folding on a table in the kitchen, and sat down listlessly in the wide low hickory-bottomed chair that belonged to Louisa.

"Git up from my throne," Louisa said from the stove. Her voice was not unkindly, but it was firm, and Susan rose from the chair at once. To her own surprise she began to cry. It was the second time that day. She was a cry-baby. She began to cry silently and then with sobs so loud that Louisa heard.

Louisa laid a biscuit in the long black biscuit pan, dusted her hands and went to Susan.

"What's the matter?" she asked. "I didn't go to hurt you." She lifted Susan and sat down in the big wide low chair, and hugged her. "I didn't go to hurt your feelings," she said. "What you crying for? Now we both settin' on the throne."

XVIII

M RS. MIDDLETON kissed little Saint John and
Cousin Fannnie and welcomed them with as much
warmth as she could. But her affection was all on the
surface. There was no real feeling between them. The
members of the two branches of the family did not
often meet except on a special occasion, such as a
funeral or a wedding.

Cousin Fannie was the widow of Robert's cousin,
John Middleton. Long before she was a widow, in
fact during her whole married life she had managed
everything about her husband, who was not very com-
petent about business matters. It seemed to people who
knew Cousin Fannie that she had always possessed an
air of authority, that she had never been a child, or
even a young girl. Robert Middleton felt this just as
others did. He said that Cousin Fannie had sprung
full-grown from the head of Zeus.

She was a tall and solid woman with black hair and
a swarthy complexion and small black eyes. Everyone
thought her handsome, and though her features taken
separately were not good she did give an impression

of stateliness and dignity as she returned Carrie Middleton's kiss and walked into the house.

"Sit there," she said to Saint John when they reached the living-room, and pointed to a large cushioned chair. She looked at Carrie Middleton as if she wished to tell her also where to sit. It was necessary for her to get everything arranged to her satisfaction before she could function smoothly. She had a very orderly mind. Saint John obediently climbed into the large chair and squirmed until he had reached the back of it. He crossed his legs which did not touch the floor. His large protruding eyes stared at his mother and then at his Cousin Carrie. The sweet attentive expression did not leave his face. The two women sat together and there was a painful silence between them, at least it was a silence that was painful to Carrie who felt a responsibility for the conversation since she was the hostess. But she could not think of anything to say and anxiously waited for her husband to come back into the room.

Suddenly Cousin Fannie's voice boomed out so loudly it seemed to Carrie like the shot from a gun.

"Where is Jennie?" Cousin Fannie asked.

"Where should she be?" Carrie said brightly and knew that what she said was foolish, and yet there was no other answer she could give.

"I don't know," Cousin Fannie said, "but I stopped to see Ellen . . ." (Ellen was a cousin who lived a few blocks down the street) "and she said that she saw Jennie out riding with a strange man."

"Well, yes, in a way," Carrie stammered. She summoned all her energies and scattered thoughts to this problem. For she must present to Cousin Fannie the most orderly and conventional and reasonable excuse for Jennie's behavior. Finally she said in a solemn voice, "Jennie went on an errand of mercy."

"An errand of mercy?" Cousin Fannie repeated skeptically.

"Yes, an errand of mercy," Carrie also repeated and then the words of explanation came to her, they came almost faster than she could say them. "She went with Dr. Greve. He is the best man and happened to be here with his automobile when Jennie and Susan were just starting out to take some of the wedding refreshments to Rosalind—Rosalind worked for us at one time, and now she has tuberculosis. It is very sad. And Jennie is so tender-hearted. She insisted on taking the things herself. And Dr. Greve offered to take her. So I was glad. He is a specialist in the disease, a very fine man . . . his wife is a splendid woman," Carrie said although she did not know Mrs. Greve. "And I was so glad to trust Jennie to him. She insisted on seeing Rosalind herself. She made a point of doing this on her wedding day, and I couldn't refuse . . . an errand of mercy."

As she talked Carrie watched Cousin Fannie just as a small cornered animal might watch another and larger animal that is threatening it. At first she saw that the cousin was looking at her suspiciously, but as she continued the suspicious look went away, and at the end Cousin Fannie nodded her head, as if to say, "That's enough, I am satisfied. It is a proper explanation."

Carrie sighed with relief as she saw the expression of satisfaction on Cousin Fannie's face, and then suddenly she felt a strong resentment. "I am tired of explaining," she thought impatiently, "all anyone wants is the proper explanation. You can do anything, any wicked thing, if you keep it hidden and have the proper explanation."

"Why doesn't Robert come?" she asked herself. "Cousin Fannie is his relative." The thought came to her that perhaps Robert had left the house by the back door in order to escape Cousin Fannie. Robert and Cousin Fannie did not love each other. Once, long ago, Robert had played a practical joke on his cousin and she had never forgotten. At that time, on one of Cousin Fannie's rare visits, there was also an aunt of Carrie's staying in the house. Before the two women met Robert took each of them aside and in a serious and pained voice warned Cousin Fannie that Carrie's Aunt Kate was deaf, and warned Aunt Kate that Cousin Fannie was deaf. Then he brought them together and in a grave voice, putting his mouth close to the ear of Cousin Fannie and close to the ear of Aunt Kate, he introduced them, and then vanished into another room, where he looked around the side of the door and watched them shout at each other. Cousin Fannie was shrewd and discovered almost at once that

she had been fooled. She never completely forgave
Robert for the foolish and childish joke.

Carrie Middleton remembered that episode as she
sat in a chair opposite Cousin Fannie and the thought
helped her through the silence that was becoming more
embarrassing. Even after so many years she could
not remember the episode without a smile and the same
wicked little chuckle of amusement that had stirred in
her when she heard the two women shouting in the
next room and found Robert doubled over with laughter. The smile that had come to her face with this
memory was on it still when Robert came into the
living-rom. She was glad to see him at last and rose
to meet him, but as she looked at his face and saw
that he was disturbed about something she became
serious at once. But Robert said nothing to her. He
went to Cousin Fannie and kissed her cheek respectfully and spoke to little Saint John. He told Cousin
Fannie how sorry they were that her daughters could
not take part in the wedding. But Carrie saw plainly
that his mind was not concentrated on what he was
saying and she was not surprised when he said to
her, "May I see you a moment? You will excuse us?"
he said gravely to Cousin Fannie, and led his wife
into the dining-room.

"Look!" he said to her dramatically and pointed to
the table on which all the silver and cut glass wedding
presents glittered in the light from the chandelier.
Carrie Middleton looked at the table and at first could
only think how fine the mahogany surface, which had

been newly waxed, looked with the presents reflected in the polished surface. And then she saw that there was an empty place in the very middle of the table, and knew that the silver punch bowl was gone. She went closer as if by going closer she could find the bowl hidden somewhere on the table. But all that was left in that center space was a small white card which said the bowl had been presented by the United Confederate Veterans to their Daughter, Jennie Middleton, and by the side of the card a tiny silk Confederate flag which had come with the bowl. Robert came and stood beside her and he, too, stared at the white card and the tiny flag.

"Did you put the bowl away?" Robert asked. "Think, think!"

"No . . . no . . . it was there when Annie May and I covered the presents early this morning. Could Annie May possibly . . . Oh, Robert! Jennie will be so distressed . . . and the Veterans . . . to-night," she covered her face with her hands and groaned.

"Try to think back. You didn't put it away? Are you sure?"

"No . . . that is yes, I am sure. And someone was here all day . . . at least most of the day. I should have noticed, but those candelabra held the sheets higher than the bowl . . . I suppose that is why . . . I didn't look under the sheets or I would have seen," she talked nervously and as if she did not know when to stop and could not stop. "It couldn't have been Ed or Louisa. We know them too well, but we don't know

about Annie May. She may be light-fingered. You
must go in and talk to Annie May, Robert. I'll ask the
girls if they have noticed anything unusual about her.
I will go up now and see them. But you must speak
to the servants. But don't . . . don't tell Cousin Fannie . . . until we know."

She left her husband in the kitchen and hurried up
the back stairs so that she need not see Cousin Fannie.

But such a loss could not be kept from anyone who
was in the house. Presently the bridesmaids, holding
their dressing-gowns about them, were going about
the house asking, "When did you see it last?" They
looked under beds and behind cushions and in the
soiled clothes that waited for Monday to be sent to
Ed's mother for washing. Cousin Fannie joined in
the search and with her own hands opened the top of
the old piano and looked down into the strings that
were so much like a harp laid on its side. And because
she was very thorough she got down on her knees and
looked under the piano and under the tables.

Surprisingly enough, no one asked about Jennie,
though her room was searched for the bowl. But Mrs.
Middleton thought of her and had a peculiar feeling
of gladness that the bowl had disappeared, since the
disappearance had turned everyone's attention to the
bowl instead of to Jennie. But as she went about
the house and answered questions and searched with
the others, the thought of Jennie tugged at Carrie. She
asked herself, "What has happened. Why is she so
long about coming home?" She was so anxious about

Jennie she did not notice as she might have done or would have done under other circumstances that Susan was not joining in the search and that the little girl hung back in the corners keeping out of the way of everyone.

Every moment Susan was expecting Saint John to say, "I put the bowl out under the fig tree." But Saint John kept beside his mother and said nothing. And Susan did not go near him. She did not know why it was impossible for her to speak and say to them all, "The bowl is under the fig tree." This would have made everything very simple. Yet she could not say it. Was her silence instinctive, a natural part of her unformed character, or was the feeling that Saint John who had taken the bowl must be the one who told about it, the result of a code that she had absorbed from her very surroundings, at home or from her companions at school? Or was she, perhaps, protecting herself from some imagined unpleasantness? Whatever compelled her, she kept silent and no one thought to ask why she went about in an unnaturally quiet way with a disturbed and guilty look on her face. All the older people were far too busy and anxious to notice her.

Carrie Middleton did not have much confidence in the good in human beings. Her religion had taught her that the Old Adam is rampant in every person and this belief made her suspicious of her children as well as of others. So that she was always ready to believe sadly that people were capable of the worst deeds.

She was not fully convinced of Annie May's innocence even when Annie May, trembling and stammering with fear, swore to Robert and Carrie that she knew nothing about the bowl. Mrs. Middleton looked reproachfully at Annie May as if saying, "We trusted you and you have betrayed our trust."

Mr. Middleton shook his head and turned his back on Annie May who was crying into her checked gingham working apron. He thought he heard Bobby shouting in the next yard, and looked out of the small window high up in the wall of the pantry. He did not see Bobby, but nevertheless he said to his wife, "I think I'll find Bobby and ask him if he knows anything about it." He was glad to get away from Annie May's crying and from all the hubbub in the house.

Because the bowl had vanished from the dining-room everyone drifted back to that room when they had searched all the places where the bowl might have been concealed. Finally all were there. And except for little Saint John there were only women in the room. They did not look at each other but stared with blank faces at the place in the center of the table which was empty except for the small white card and the little Confederate flag.

From a corner between the end of the sideboard and the wall into which she had fitted herself Susan looked at Saint John, who, as usual, was beside his mother. His open little face looked with sympathetic alarm at the others.

"Have the servants been questioned?" Cousin Fannie asked.

"Mr. Middleton has spoken to them," Carrie answered in her most dignified voice, "and we know that Ed and Louisa are trustworthy." She spoke so to Cousin Fannie but secretly she thought that one of them might have taken the bowl.

"You have a right to your own opinion, of course," Cousin Fannie said haughtily. The tone of her voice said, "but as for me, I have my opinion also, and if you know what is good for you, you will accept it."

With a sudden energetic movement Cousin Fannie swung herself to the pantry door. She said, "I shall question them myself."

All of them looked at Cousin Fannie with horrified eyes. Because it was plain that she would make a commotion, and much unpleasantness. And then just as Cousin Fannie was about to open it, the pantry door was pushed from the other side, and there in the door was Louisa with Ed just in front of her.

"Excuse me, Miss Carrie," Louisa said to Mrs. Middleton. She gave Ed a little push and said, "Go on, Ed, tell Miss Carrie." Ed's eyes looked at them all with a frightened and appealing stare. He opened his mouth to speak. Before he could say anything Saint John went to his mother and took her hand. "Mama," he said in his slightly breathless voice, "I know where the bowl is."

When he said this all those who were in the room looked at Ed no longer. They gathered around Saint

John. Lucy knelt at his feet and put her arms around him. "Do tell us," she begged. Janie kissed him on the cheek.

"Tell us," Lucy and Janie begged. And Susan said to them under her breath, "Well, why don't you let him?" Her nose was out of joint.

"Where is the bowl, Saint John?" Cousin Fannie asked and in her voice there was the same tender solicitude that the bridesmaids showed toward him.

Saint John pointed to Ed. "He knows where it is," he almost shouted, "because he buried it."

"Did you take it, Ed?" Carrie Middleton asked and in her voice there was grief, but there was suspicion and almost certainty.

"No'm, Miss Carrie," Louisa burst out. "Only . . ."

"He buried it in the yard," Saint John shouted again.

"Where?" his mother demanded.

"No'm, I didn't take it," Ed told them in his soft melancholy voice. But no one heard him.

"In the yard," Saint John shouted again.

"Then show us," his mother said and looked at the others triumphantly. She marched out through the pantry, through the kitchen where Annie May sat in a corner, sniffling, out into the yard. Everyone followed, forgetting in the excitement that it was cold outside. Saint John led them to the fig tree. He pointed to the spot which anyone could see had been recently dug up. And because her son knew the place Cousin Fannie took full charge of everything. She was like a general, and now even Carrie did not question her authority.

"Dig it up," she said to Ed.

Ed got down on his knees obediently and began to dig with his hands. All the others gathered around the place. They were pressed close together around the place where Ed was digging like people at a funeral around a grave. Ed clawed at the dirt with his fingers and at last the newspaper covering appeared under the dirt. Finally Ed reached both hands under the bundle and lifted it out. Pieces of earth slid from the newspaper as Ed lifted the bundle up in his large hands. Before he could rise from his knees Cousin Fannie took the bundle from his hands. He stood up, wiping his muddy fingers on his overalls. There was a relieved expression on his face as if he felt glad it was all over, and he was finished with the trouble this had brought him.

Cousin Fannie pulled the newspaper away from the bowl and then slipped the torn coat away. And there was the bowl, shining in the late sun which just came over the housetops. Cousin Fannie asked, "Whose coat is this?" and she held up the coat.

"Mine," Ed told her. "It was hanging . . ."

"Never mind," Cousin Fannie said, and when he held out his hand for the coat she drew back from him. Carrie Middleton sighed, a loud sigh. She looked at Ed reproachfully and said, "Ed, how could you? Why did you do it?"

Ed cried out, "I didn't do it, Miss Carrie. This

little boy brought that bundle out here and tol' me to bury it." He pointed to Saint John.

"I intend to call the police," Cousin Fannie said.

Carrie Middleton said in an agitated voice to Susan, "Go and find your father. Go and find your father. He is next door, looking for Bobby . . . Wait for Mr. Middleton," she said to Cousin Fannie.

Cousin Fannie said, "You have a right to your own opinion, but I am calling the police. I would not have thought of it if this boy," she nodded toward Ed, "had not tried to blame my child."

Saint John buried his face in his mother's dress. He howled, "I didn't do it, Mama. I didn't."

Susan heard his crying as she ran to the front of the house next door. "But you did," she muttered, "but you did."

XIX

SUSAN did not find her father next door. He had followed Bobby to the home of another neighbor. She was not sorry to stay away from her own home, because in that house there was a problem that disturbed her. She was regretful that she had not told them all, while they stood under the fig tree, that Saint John had taken the bowl from the dining-room. This regretful feeling was unwelcome. She wished to forget Ed and to remember only the wedding and the pleasures of the wedding, but she could not forget his unhappy face. It was painful to her to remember it, but it was also impossible not to remember.

Two different experiences had recently made her conscious of certain things that were happening outside of her own little world. Unconsciously she was trying to bring these two separate experiences together in herself and make them fit into each other. It was very difficult.

She did not like Saint John, but he was a cousin. Also Saint John was white and Ed was colored. She had been taught through some process of living, although the words had never been said to her, that white people were more important than colored people, who could only wait on others in a house or work in the fields, and that colored people were unable to do anything else because their dark skins prevented.

This difference had been impressed upon Susan the very first year that she began school. That year a Negro was entertained at lunch in the White House. As a result of this many things happened in Susan's world. Her father and his friends who came to a supper which was called Tea on Sunday evening, talked about the luncheon and went back to their memories of Reconstruction and spoke of what had happened at that time. Some of them became very angry and indignant. And at school even the smallest children talked about the luncheon. The Negro children had been given a school that was abandoned when a new school was built for the white children, so they had to walk through the white part of town to reach it. The colored children and white children went along the same streets to school, and there were fights between them in the morning and on the way home in the afternoon. Susan had seen the boys throw rocks at each other. The white children marched together clear across the sidewalks and made the colored children walk in the road where vehicles were passing. It became necessary for the Superintendent of Schools to visit every class room from the first grade up in both the Negro schools and white schools. He told them that two colored boys had been taken to the hospital and said there must be no more fighting. A rule was made and enforced by the police that the Negro children must go to their school only along certain back streets. White children were not allowed on these streets unless they lived there. Very soon the white people who could moved away from these streets where the colored children passed.

This experience became a part of Susan. She understood that there was a difference between herself and Ed and Louisa and that she was superior to them, and that in order to be loyal to her own people she must preserve this difference.

But there was another recent experience, slighter and more intangible than the first, which had nevertheless become a part of her. There was a book which Bobby had read aloud to Susan that excited them both strangely. Susan did not know where Bobby had found this book. Perhaps their father had brought it home. Perhaps Bobby had discovered it at old Mr. Byer's second-hand book store when he went to buy his second-hand school books, and where there were many interesting and curious volumes for sale that did not have anything to do with school.

This book Bobby had read to her was a prophesy. The idea of a prophesy was itself interesting and made Susan and Bobby think of the Bible where events were foretold and dreams interpreted. The story said that many years in the future all people in the country except a few would be made into miserable slaves. They were the victims of machines and of the few rich men

who owned the machines. All the rest, except these
few rich men, were slaves who worked underground,
beaten and starved and chained. The rich men had
abandoned the ideals of the republic and called themselves princes. They lived in luxury and sin with many
beautiful women to wait on them.

And then a powerful workman, the son of a blacksmith, came up from the South and roused all the
poor ones who were in slavery. And when he and his
followers had killed all the rich people, the blacksmith
leader had his followers build a great pyramid on a
public square. The pyramid caused shivers of excitement and dread to go over Bobby and Susan. Because
that terrible pyramid was built of the dead bodies of
the rich. A layer of cement was laid down in the
square and before it was dry the bodies of the rich
were thrown on it. Then another layer of cement was
cast and on that another layer of the bodies of the
rich.

It was especially interesting to Susan and Bobby
that the man who did this, who freed the enslaved
people and revenged them in this terrible way, came
from the South. They wondered if this mysterious man
were already hiding there, or if he were a boy growing
up, or if he had not yet been born. If he lived already,
they might see him. They might meet him somewhere
along a country road or he might be dodging in and
out in the shadowy alleys between the stores on Main
Street, or hiding in the cellars. When they lived in the
country it was sometimes necessary to take the horses

to the blacksmith shop. Susan and Bobby always made arrangements to go when this was necessary and at the blacksmith shop they looked at the blacksmith with wonder and awe, thinking, "this might be the man" or "this might be the father of the man."

At the end of the book the man who wrote it said that people must prevent all these things from happening. This made the book more than ever like the Bible in which the prophets warned the people of the cities of their wickedness and then told them what they must do to avoid God's wrath. One day Susan and Bobby took a Bible out to a rock. They pricked their fingers with the end of Bobby's knife. They crouched over the rock and let the blood from each of their fingers drop on the stone so that it became one large drop of blood on the stone. And when this was done each raised a hand as Bobby had seen witnesses raise their hands in court, and with their other hands on the Bible they said together, "We do solemnly swear we will not let the poor people suffer and we will not let the rich people make them suffer, so help us God."

Susan did not find her Father and Bobby. At the neighbor's house on the corner she was told that Bobby had been there playing, that her father had found him and that they had returned to the Middleton's home. She walked slowly along the street, hoping vaguely that everything would be settled when she reached the house again. The air chilled her, but she continued to loiter. The sun was almost down. It had come that day and had taken the ice from the bushes and trees, and now it was going away, leaving the trees stripped of the covering which had changed every bush and tree, even the small blades of grass, into something mysterious and unknown. As Susan walked slowly along the street, the trees were again familiar and everyday as they had been all her life. The excitement of the morning was gone. She saw herself and Bobby as they let the blood drip on to the stone from their fingers and heard again the words they had repeated as they crouched over the stone. She saw the colored children running with frightened faces into the road as the white girls and boys spread across the sidewalk laughing to each other and calling out, "Run, nigger, run, the patterol'll get you." She did not question the white children's right to do this. But because she loved Ed and Louisa, and because of what had just happened to Ed, all this came back and became a weight on her heart. She felt weighed down in the same way that the branches of the bushes and trees had been weighed down by the ice.

At the house she slipped in the back way in order to go up the back stairs and avoid everyone in the front of the house. Louisa was in the kitchen at the table cutting up chicken for the salad they were to have at the wedding reception. Annie May was shaking out lettuce leaves. Susan tried to slip past them without being seen.

But Louisa turned away from the table and faced

Susan. "Ed tol' me you saw little Saint John make him bury that there bowl," she said to Susan.

Susan lifted a piece of chicken and put it in her mouth. She usually sampled what Louisa cooked or what was in the process of being cooked. But because Susan chewed the piece of chicken as if she enjoyed it, it seemed to Louisa that this child had no feeling. She asked harshly, "Did you?"

"Do what?" Susan asked.

"You know what."

"You mean did I hear Saint John tell Ed to bury that bowl?"

"Yes ma'm, that's exactly what I do mean."

"Well . . . yes, I did. Where is Ed?" Susan asked.

"Ed is gone," Louisa said.

The thought came into Susan that they had taken him to the police station. She was afraid to ask, but she wanted to know. "Did they . . . did they take him?" she stammered.

"He run away," Annie May said.

"You hush your mouth," Louisa said to Annie May.

Susan's throat filled. A feeling of immense sorrow came up in her into her throat. "He run away?" she whispered.

"Yes ma'm, he run away," Louisa said. Since Annie May had spoken of it she was willing to do so. "Nobody knows where he's gone. He was scared of the police. And he run away. I don't know what his Mama will do. And Lord knows how he'll ever live."

Susan ran through the pantry, through the dining-room and into the living room. Her father and mother were there alone with Cousin Fannie and Saint John, who had their hats and coats beside them waiting for their carriage. Susan walked straight to Saint John. As she came near to him she saw with pleasure that a look of fear came on his face. He tried to slip behind his mother's chair but it was against the wall.

"You know Ed didn't take that bowl," Susan told him, "you know it, you know it."

Almost before the words were out of Susan's mouth Saint John screamed, "I didn't, Mamma. I didn't. She hates me. She called me a bad name."

"I did not," Susan cried out. She did not know what she was doing and did not care. She did not stop to think whether she should do one thing or another, but did what was necessary to her. "You took the bowl," she said, "and made Ed bury it. I saw you and I heard you. We were playing Yankees and Confederates . . . General Sherman," she said, trying to explain to her mother and father. And suddenly she began to sob.

"She called me a bad name," Saint John insisted to his mother.

"What is this, Susan? What do you mean?" her father asked.

"I mean Ed didn't take the bowl. I mean we . . . were playing and Saint John took it . . ." Susan tried to tell him, but her crying interfered with the telling.

Her father saw the misery in Susan's face. "I believe Susan is telling the truth," he said.

"You have a right to your own opinion," Cousin Fannie said, "but I believe my child. I think Susan has some obscure resentment against Saint John."

"I didn't do anything, Mamma," Saint John said in his quiet, sweet breathless voice.

"Of course you didn't," his mother assured him.

"Ed run away," Susan told her father. She still used the words that Annie May had used, "Ed run away. And you did it," she said to Saint John.

"But I sent for the police," Cousin Fannie told Mr. Middleton. "He can't run away."

"But he did," Susan insisted.

Mr. Middleton went out to the kitchen. When he returned he said, "It is true. Ed has run away."

"I won't have it," Cousin Fannie said, "he accused my son of stealing. He tried to . . ."

"That's enough, Fannie," Mr. Middleton said sternly. Cousin Fannie's mouth that was open to continue her speech closed shut. There was a look of surprise on her face. She opened her mouth again but Mr. Middleton said again, "That's enough, Fannie."

Saint John peered out from behind his mother's shoulder. He looked more than ever like a frog peering from behind a log of wood at the side of a pond.

"Tell us what happened," her father said to Susan. "Don't cry any more. Tell us."

"Saint John knows," Susan told him. "Tell them," she said to Saint John. But Saint John would not speak to her nor look at her. He spoke only to his mother. He said, "I didn't do it, Mamma."

Susan had seen that Cousin Fannie obeyed her
father. She was very proud and felt victorious and
able to accomplish anything. She went close to Saint
John. "Tell them," she commanded, "you tell them.
Ed has run away and Lord knows how he'll live. And
you did it."

It gave her pleasure to put the whole blame on Saint
John. Her misery at Ed's going away, running somewhere out in the night, and her sorrow because she
had not spoken sooner, the courage that had been
given her because her father had spoken so firmly to
Cousin Fannie; all these things came together in her.
They made her face Saint John without any fear but
with pleasure and exultation. She said to him, "Tell
them. Are you going to tell them," and reached out
her hand and slapped his face. "Now tell them!" she
said.

Cousin Fannie gave a little shriek and pulled Saint
John to her. She hid his small head against her bosom.

"How dare you!" she cried out to Susan.

Susan felt her mother take her hand. She knew by
the firm clasp that her mother was angry and ashamed.
Her mother held the hand so tightly the bones of
Susan's hand ground together. Susan did not know
what was happening. It was as if suddenly she had
gone blind and deaf. She knew dimly because her feet
stumbled against them that she was going up the stairs.
She felt herself pushed into her mother's bedroom,
and heard the door close sharply behind her.

But she had slapped Saint John and the thought

that she had done this, even though she was punished for it, gave her satisfaction. Even her small hand felt satisfied though it was still red from its contact with Saint John's cheek. A smug and proud expression came on Susan's face.

Mrs. Middleton stared at the open door of Jennie's room. The room was empty. How much she would have given to know that Jennie was there and that she did not have to go down and face the questions about Jennie that she knew must come. But it was necessary to face them and with a resolute expression she went down. She saw the bridesmaids in the lower hall as she reached the landing. She wondered if they were talking about the silver bowl or speculating about Jennie. If it was about Jennie she thought they would be speaking of her in a friendly way, and she looked affectionately at the heads below her. Pamela's feet were stretched out and crossed straight in front of her as she lounged on the stairs. Her elbows were on the steps above but she was craning her head forward to hear better. Her brown hair was parted in the middle and rolled back into a simple knot. Lucy's black head of hair shone glossily where the knot rested on her neck and then at the front projected into the vine-like kid curlers that surrounded her face. She sat primly on a chair with her skirts arranged sedately about her. She, too, was leaning forward. Nancy stood with one knee resting on a chair. Her sandy hair, tied with a ribbon, hung back over her shoulders. Janie sat on the floor. The pale yellow dressing gown billowed around her and parted at the front where part of the lace-edged petticoat showed. Her ash-blond curls were piled high on her small head. She was like one of Susan's small china dolls. While Carrie looked at them Janie put her hand on Pamela's knee and spoke earnestly, and then all of them began to talk at the same time. But when the front door opened and Robert came in from the outside their talking hushed.

Robert said to them, "Well, I think I appeased Cousin Fannie. I apologized for everybody, for Ed and Susan and all of us," he said ironically, "even for you, Mother," he added as he saw his wife on the stairs. "Don't be too hard on Susan," he said to her and then he asked the very question that Carrie had been dreading. "Where is Jennie?" he said. When no one answered he asked the question again. He saw the expression of guilt or anxiety on his wife's face and ran up the stairs quickly, and looked into the open door of Jennie's room. Carrie followed him. She laid her hand on his arm. The bridesmaids were coming up the stairs and in a low hurried voice Carrie told him that Jennie was at the hotel. "But Mrs. Greve is there," she said and repeated the words, "Mrs. Greve is there," because she knew that her husband would at once get a picture of Jennie alone at the hotel with the two men, and that this picture would enrage him so that he would do something or say something that he would regret later. She had no time to go through the whole explanation beginning with the visit of Dr. Greve and she herself did not understand why Jennie had stopped at the hotel instead of coming home. "Mrs. Greve is there," she said again. But she saw Robert's face become flushed with anger and that he was about to speak and that he would speak in anger. She heard the steps of the bridesmaids on the stairs and pulled at Robert's arm until he faced the stairs and could see them also. He did see them and did not speak, but his mouth remained fixed in a straight line of anger and when he looked at her his eyes were filled with anger and reproach. He turned away from her and went down the stairs. The bridesmaids parted to let him by. He bowed to them courteously. They stared at him and drew away a little as if they understood that he was angry and did not wish to be too close to his anger.

Carrie heard the front door slam and knew that her husband had gone to find Jennie.

XX

MRS. GREVE did not go into the living-room of the hotel suite to speak to Jennie because her husband had told her that he was taking the Doctor in there at once for a reconciliation. But when Dr. Greve entered his friend's room he did not find him ready. Just as soon as he entered he saw that a bottle of whiskey stood on the writing table. There was no glass beside the bottle and yet half the whiskey was gone. Some of it had spilled and seeped into the blotter on the table and made a dark spot there. He was still completely absorbed in the feeling of generous exaltation toward his friend and Jennie and the sight of the bottle irritated him.

"Mama Whiskey is no solution," he said briskly and slipped the bottle into his coat pocket before he sat down.

Dr. Gregg lit a cigar and as he did so the little doctor watched him intently. Dr. Gregg's face was flushed and his beautiful deep eyes glistened under the long lashes, but his hand was very steady as he struck the match and his broad short fingers did not tremble as they held the match to his cigar.

"Son," he puffed out a whole mouthful of smoke. The smoke surrounded his head and hid his face, "that little bit hasn't touched me. I go for months without it . . . and . . ."

"Yes, and then . . ." Dr. Greve interrupted, "but Mama Whiskey is a bitch and you know it. Only don't call me Son." He took a watch from a side pocket. "It's about four hours before the wedding, did you know that? I have the license, your train tickets, your drawing-room for New York. All material evidence of the wedding is here. Only the spirit lacketh. You must supply the spirit. I don't mean Mama Whiskey," he tapped his pocket where the bottle rested and rose from his chair abruptly. "Jennie is across the hall," he said.

"Jennie?" the Doctor asked.

"Yes," Dr. Greve's voice became serious. A different and wholly earnest appeal came into it. "There's something about Jennie," he said, "I don't know what she does to you. Do you know we were talking about changing water into wine. It is like that. She takes your humdrum everyday life, as usual as the water that you drink, and makes it significant, sig-nificant, so that you feel that you really live. She turns your blood into wine. And it is worth everything to have that . . . though you must first make her feel that she is everything, I know that," he said impatiently, "I know it is hard to give in and it is a sort of tyranny of the spirit, but it is worth everything, because she will make your life significant and make it . . . but it will be hard for you, because you need to be understood. And when you are not undertsood you become a lout—forgive me, but something like that, and again when you are given warmth and affection and appreciation, you become lovable . . . more than lovable . . . but you must do this for her." He took his friend by the arm urgently, "Go across there," he said in an excited voice, "and tell her that she is beautiful . . . that you are the finest surgeon in the country and that you need her, need her . . . because you do. Go . . . go and tell her. I can't do your courting for you," he said impatiently. "By God, I wish I could, I wish I could."

The Doctor shook his friend's hand from his arm, walked firmly to the dresser and took up the brush there. He arranged his hair and changed his tie with steady fingers. It was true that the whiskey had made no impression on him. His mind was clear. He felt the stimulation of the whiskey for the first time when he learned that Jennie was across the hall. Then for the first time since he had taken it, the liquor began to go through his body and into his head so that he felt a dizziness and excitement that he had not felt before.

While he was sitting in his room waiting for Dr. Greve to come back from the long absence with Jennie he had thought of Jennie and the same remembrance of the experience with her in the little restaurant at two o'clock in the morning came back to him. There, in the ugly little place he had lost a sense of loneliness that had been with him all his life except when he was at work. He had felt that here was a companion whose love and loyalty could take the place of his loneliness. This was what he felt then and what he felt again in the hotel room while he waited for his friend to come back. He waited because he could do nothing else. He could never force an issue, no more than the mountains where he was born could force the seasons to come on them. He waited, and perhaps this was one of his greatest faults, that he was negative, and yet waiting, feeling that things would turn out one way or another, and that they must turn out that way whether he did anything about them or not, sometimes made them develop in just the way he wished. He did not know this about himself, but his friends, those who were closest to him, knew this about him. He was a fatalist, not by conviction but by his nature.

As he went across the corridor the alcohol flooded him as if it had burst from a dam. It quickened his senses and he entered the room with the longing to take Jennie in his arms at once. He saw that Jennie half-rose from her chair as if she was impulsively coming to meet him and he was glad. But she sank back into the chair, and this gesture, this half-greeting, made him feel cold and turned back on himself.

Jennie said, "Good evening," in a small voice which even to her own ears sounded supercilious and cold.

He did not answer, but took a place in a chair a long way from her. They looked at each other shyly and then away. The Doctor settled further down into the cushions of his chair. He looked at Jennie and thought that she stared at him resentfully, and his own look became resentful. Each of them looked away again. The Doctor lighted a cigar. There was a long silence. The Doctor cried out, "For God's sake say something."

There was something painful and pitiful about his cry. But Jennie did not understand this.

"I would," she said angrily, "if I had anything to say." She added, "I thought I had something to say. But I haven't. Not a thing. I don't know why I came." She lifted her muff angrily from the table.

Dr. Greve knocked lightly on the door and came in from the bed-room of the suite. He said, "Well, has anything happened?" He was restless and walked from one place in the room to another. He lifted Jennie's muff from the table and examined it closely. The others did not answer. Dr. Greve sat down abruptly on the couch next to the chair in which Jennie sat.

"Nothing happened?" he asked her. His voice was intimate.

Jennie shook her head. As she did so she smiled at him. He leaned across the arm of the couch and took her left hand in his. With his own left hand he fumbled in the pocket of his vest and brought out the wedding ring which the Doctor had given him that morning because he was to have it ready for the ceremony.

"With this ring I thee wed," Dr. Greve quoted mischievously, and at the same time there was a seriousness in his voice which Jennie understood, and she saw that there was a queer tenderness about his mouth, a tenderness that was not often there. He slipped the ring on Jennie's finger. "It's a lovely hand," he said. Jennie smiled at him and he felt again the pleasure in making her happy, because when he first came into the room he had seen the expression of blank despair on her face. Her small hand was warm and responsive in his. And he wished to do more than take her hand. He wished to put his arm about her and draw her to him, but he could not with the other Doctor there. And yet, though they knew that the Doctor was in the room it seemed that they did not know and that they were concentrated on each other only as two people can be when they are alone.

The Doctor stared at them and saw this concentration. He felt himself forgotten, and he sat very still with a peculiar smile on his face.

A voice from the next room called the little Doctor's name. He said, "Yes, Sally." Jennie drew her hand from his. The little Doctor's wife called again. He sighed, waited a moment, and left to go to his wife.

The door had just closed behind him when the Doctor rose from his chair and went directly to Jennie. He took her hands and drew her roughly into his arms.

"Who are you marrying tonight," he demanded, "that little shaver or me?"

A pleased look came on Jennie's face. "You, of course," she said self-consciously.

"Then behave so," he told her. He leaned down and

kissed her on the mouth. And suddenly for both of them as their lips came together there was a recurrence of the joy that had come over them and in them when they had kissed for the first time by the night-blooming cereus. He said, "I love you."

"Why didn't you tell me that before," Jennie cried out impatiently. She was almost sobbing. "I was so proud," she whispered, "when I heard about that operation you performed. I am so proud of you."

He laughed and his arms tightened around her. He was so grateful for her pride, and now he wished more than anything else to tell her about the operation, to explain all the details. He said, "It was this way. They woke me at three in the morning and said there was a man with a bullet in his brain. . . ."

She drew away from him and he saw the look of disappointment on her face, and this look of disappointment made him feel cold again. But he still held her in his arms and did not let her go.

Dr. Greve came into the room again. They had not heard him knock. When he came in they drew away from each other self-consciously. Dr. Greve's smile was mischievous. "Do you know what Sally wanted?" he said and continued without waiting for an answer. "She wanted me to stay in there. She said, 'They want to be alone.' Do you want to be alone?" he asked mischievously. He took Jennie's arm and pulled her down to the couch beside him. It seemed impossible for him to stay away from her. And it seemed to the Doctor that Jennie was pleased with this attention.

"Sally was right," he told his friend, "we do want to be alone."

"So you've made it up?" the little Doctor asked. He spoke to Jennie.

"Yes," Jennie laughed. "Yes, aren't you glad?"

Dr. Greve looked at his friend. He rose to his feet and looked again. The two men stared at each other. Their eyes were hard and cold. The little Doctor said, "Well . . ." Then a warmer light came into his eyes. The corners of his eyes wrinkled in the familiar lines of amusement. He lifted Jennie's hands from her lap and drew her from the couch. He put Jennie's right hand into the Doctor's hand. "Bless you, my children," he said solemnly.

The Doctor put his large arm about Jennie. She felt that he was laughing. She could hear the laughter rumbling in him. It was comfortable and comforting. The Doctor held out his other hand to his friend. They shook hands solemnly. Jennie glanced at Dr. Greve. There was a crestfallen look about him. As she thought this, Jennie said to herself that this word expressed just what had happened to the little Doctor. His crest had fallen, she thought. He seemed to have lost much of his jauntiness and confidence. And a feeling of contempt for him came into her. He stood there helpless, and it seemed that he did not know what to do next or what to say next. She knew without saying it to herself, that she was in control of the situation, that they would do what she said, and be what she said, and this feeling gave her a peculiar joy.

"I forgot," she said happily and joyfully, "you'd better take the ring . . . to use tonight for us." She slipped off the wedding ring and gave it to him.

"Shall I take you home?" Dr. Greve asked and his voice was diffident, without its usual confidence.

"I'll take her," the Doctor said positively.

"Of course," Dr. Greve told him courteously. "Only the groom is not supposed . . ."

"Supposed . . . hell," the Doctor said and put his strong fingers about Jennie's arm.

There was a harsh peremptory knock at the door into the hall. The door was flung open and Jennie's father stood in the doorway.

All the distance from his home to the hotel Robert had been angry, angry with his wife and with Jennie. How could his wife, he asked himself, allow Jennie to go away with a strange man on the very day of her wedding? But this most unreasoning and bitter anger was toward Jennie herself. He asked himself if she was to be trusted. Was she as innocent as he had thought? After all, she had been away from him for months at a time. What had she done, what had happened to her during those months? "She has behaved like an abandoned woman," he told himself. He said the words out loud as he rode along in the carriage which was taking him to the hotel, "Like an abandoned woman," he said and groaned. His imagination formed a terrible picture of Jennie from which he shrank and yet which he kept seeing. He had liked to think of her as an innocent child, and now he could not think of her in that way any longer. She was a woman, not innocent, abandoned and shameless. She had deceived him. He wished to strike her down, to feel his fist against her face. His fist clenched and unclenched at his side, and he longed to reach Jennie so that he could express all the anger that was in him against her.

But when he flung open the door the angry words did not come from him. Because he saw before him a natural and peaceful picture. He saw Jennie with the Doctor's arm about her, and this was natural. The Doctor was the man she was to marry that evening. And there was the other doctor near them. He looked at Jennie's face and saw that there was pleasure and satisfaction and a curious triumphant joy there. She was safe and happy. She was his young daughter, not the abandoned woman his imagination had been picturing to him. When he understood that this young innocent girl, standing with her lover's arm about her was his daughter, and that she was not that other vicious woman he had expected to find, a sort of agony of joy came in him as if someone had said, "Your child is dead in the other room," and he had gone into that room expecting to find death and had found the child living.

Jennie saw this look of joy on her father's face. She had seen his first look of anger which had frightened her, and now she saw that he was relieved and that he loved her. She ran to her father and put her head against him and slipped her arms about his neck. He said, "Daughter . . . Daughter," in a wondering voice.

And there were other things in his voice, all those feelings and emotions that Jennie had longed to hear that morning, appreciation of her and loyalty to her and emotion. It was the emotion which gave her greatest pleasure. She wanted emotion, and if she could not have it in love she wanted it in anger. Emotion made her feel that she was living, and she could not live without it.

Robert looked over Jennie's head to the two men who were standing silently across the room. All his anger was suddenly directed toward these two men. He looked at his future son-in-law and wondered how he could ever have thought of trusting his daughter to him. And the thought came to him—it had never come before—that this strange man was to take his daughter that night to a far away city and that his daughter would be alone with that strange man in a hotel room, and that strange man, massive and sturdy and with the peculiar smile on his lips, was to take possession of his daughter, this young innocent girl whose head was pressed against him. And that other stranger, the little Doctor, had imposed on his daughter. He had taken Jennie away from her home, from his protection on the day of her wedding and exposed her to scandal and gossip. He was older than Jennie and he was a man and should have protected her.

"Why did you bring my daughter here?" he asked Dr. Greve angrily.

"We thought . . ." Dr. Greve began.

"Did you think? Did you stop to think?" Robert

demanded. "God Almighty, did you stop to think of her, a young, innocent girl that you exposed to gossip? Did you stop to think of her?"

The little Doctor put his hands in his pockets, shrugged and turned away.

"And you . . ." Robert said and turned to the Doctor.

Dr. Greve faced Robert again, "After all," he interrupted, "Jennie is old enough to be married. She should be old enough to think for herself. She wanted to go . . ."

The peculiar ironic and yet understanding smile remained on the other doctor's face. His generous ugly mouth smiled at Jennie and at Jennie's father. But gradually a red flush spread all over his face. He felt a sense of shame at what Robert was saying. It seemed a shameful thing to him that they should be standing there angry at each other. And he saw the look of happiness and pleasure on Jennie's face as she lifted her head from her father's breast. He saw the look of triumph on Jennie's face and to him it seemed shameful that all of them should be unhappy and angry and that Jennie should be taking their misery and making it into her joy. At the same time he had an impulse to go to Jennie and take her from her father, to put his arm about her and keep her, just as he had felt the same impulse to do so earlier when he saw Jennie and Dr. Greve together.

"Come, Daughter," Jennie's father said to her. What Dr. Greve had said to him had cooled his anger. "After all Jennie is old enough to decide for herself," Dr. Greve had said, and this had been like a cold bath to the fever of Robert's anger.

Jennie said brightly, "One moment, Father." She ran to the Doctor and lifted her face to him. The wide square muff of brown fur hung from her arm and as she raised it the muff swung like a banner. The Doctor took her in his arms and kissed her on the mouth.

"Goodbye, Doctor Greve," Jennie said demurely and held out her hand to the other doctor. His hand met hers and as it did so his eyes smiled into hers. He whispered, "Got your way, didn't you?"

Jennie heard the words that he said. But she did not understand them, and smiled at him radiantly.

"I must tell Mrs. Greve goodbye," she said over her shoulder to her father, and went into the other room.

"My car can take you home, Mr. Middleton," Dr. Greve said courteously.

"Yes," Robert answered. "Yes, thank you, yes."

The little Doctor remained courteous and solemn until Jennie and her father had gone, then he sat down on the couch and began to laugh. He shouted with laughter. His feet came up on the couch and his heels beat on the couch as he continued to laugh. It was a crazy performance. The other looked at him with a puzzled frown and then looked away as if he was ashamed of what was happening. But Dr. Greve continued to laugh. His feet continued to beat on the cushions of the couch. He was still laughing when his wife came into the room.

"What is wrong?" she asked in her slightly whining voice, "What is it. What is so funny?"

"Sally," Dr. Greve laughed from the couch, "sometimes you have called me a fool. But I never agreed with you before. Now . . ." he held his hands across his stomach and laughed again.

"What is wrong?" Sally asked Dr. Gregg, "is something wrong?"

"No, only a little trouble with his stomach," the Doctor said dryly.

"Not the stomach, Doc, not the stomach," Doctor Greve shouted. He sat up on the couch. "But I have fully recovered, Sally, I have fully recovered. I give you my word, Doc," he said.

"Did you and Jennie . . . make it up?" Mrs. Greve asked the Doctor.

Her husband answered for his friend, "Yes, Sally, it's all arranged, everything, everything her own way," he went off into laughter again. "Water and wine," he said mischievously and winked at his friend, "water and wine," he repeated and shook his head.

His wife looked at him just as the Doctor had looked a few moments before. The habitual worried frown between her eyebrows deepened. "It's very late," she told him.

She saw that in some way he had become less confident. She understood this just as Jennie had understood it. And as he rose to go with her her voice became imperative. It held the sort of resentment that people have at any sign of weakness in those of whom they have been afraid, and of whom they are still afraid, but whose weak moment gives them an opportunity for saying those things they have not had the courage to say before.

She said, "Hurry. Do you think you are so important they are going to keep the whole ceremony waiting for you?"

XXI

As he and his daughter drove home through the quiet streets Robert told Jennie about the loss of the silver bowl, about Cousin Fannie and little Saint John and how Susan had slapped Saint John. The great relief Robert had experienced when he found Jennie safe, the relief that the quarrel was over, gave Robert a sense of sudden release from a great dread, and this relief gave his wit a special joyful tang. Jennie laughed at his picture of Cousin Fannie at the moment when Susan slapped Saint John. They laughed together and were happy together. But Robert became more serious when he spoke of Ed. He was genuinely concerned about Ed's disappearance, not only because they knew and liked Ed, but also because they needed him for the reception that evening. He said, "I telephoned Hugh at Natalie's and he promised to go to Ed's mother and find the boy if he is there. Susan insists that Ed has run away."

Robert did not tell Jennie what the Bishop had told him, that they could not use the silk flags. They were happy together and he hated to say anything that would

disturb their pleasure, for he knew that Jennie would
be disturbed. The flags had been so much a part of their
plans for the wedding.

It was dusk, because dark came early in winter and
the houses along Lady Street showed lights in some of
the windows. But on the block where the Middletons
lived their house shone out beyond all the others. Every
room was lit up, and the lights, especially those from
the downstairs windows through which it was possible
to see glimpses of the decorations, made the whole place
stand out in a sort of romantic atmosphere as if behind
all those lighted windows almost any exciting thing
might happen.

And when the car drove up to the front of the house,
so that everyone heard it, those inside became excited
and active at once. The whole house stirred. Carrie
Middleton hurried to the front door and opening it
peered down the walk anxiously as if she would like to
project her very self to her husband and daughter so
that she could find out immediately what had happened
in the hotel.

The bridesmaids were eating their suppers which had
been sent upstairs on trays so that the downstairs would
not be disturbed. But when Susan called out, "Jennie is
coming," they picked up the long skirts of their dressing
gowns and rushed down the stairs, getting in each
other's way, tripping over each other's long skirts until
they had crowded into a little group on the stairs just
above the landing.

As Jennie came through the front door they saw that

her face was relieved of all the dissatisfaction they had seen on it last. Her cheeks were rosy with the air that had blown on them during the drive. And the rosy cheeks made her look especially radiant. They saw that she hugged her mother and flung off her hat and fur stole and muff with a gesture that said she was confident and ready for the wedding or for anything that might come. They saw Mrs. Middleton go to her husband and ask him a question anxiously and that when he answered her he was smiling, and the expression of her face changed from anxiety to pleasure. And they knew from these things that everything was right and that the wedding would go on.

Nancy called from the stairs, "Oh, Jennie, did you know Dr. Grant won't let us carry the flags tonight?"

Jennie said, "What?" in an astonished voice. She looked at Nancy and then at her mother and father.

"Yes," Mrs. Middleton said, "the Bishop told your father!"

"Dr. Grant won't allow it?" Jennie repeated, "but why not? What has he to do with it?"

Her mother explained, "He said it was a great concession for him to allow a Confederate wedding at all. Because we should not do anything to arouse the old controversy. Your father says there is nothing we can do."

"Dr. Grant doesn't care about the controversy," Jennie said indignantly, "he is angry because you asked him not to take part in the ceremony at the church. But that was so natural. Why couldn't he understand that

it is a Confederate wedding," she lifted her chin
proudly, "and that he is a Northerner? Even the Bishop
was a captain in the army. Isn't there something we can
do, Father? Must we stand here like this? . . ."

"I am afraid so, Jennie," her father said, and Jennie looked at him in astonishment. His voice was so
mild.

"But don't you see," Jennie stood before her father,
"he wants to feel his power. He wants to make us feel
he owns the church. But he doesn't own it," she argued.
"It isn't his church. Are you going to allow this . . .
this Yankee to dictate to us?"

Mrs. Middleton put her hand on Jennie's arm,
"There's nothing we can do, child," she told her sadly,
"it is his church so long as he is here. The Bishop said
so."

But Jennie continued to stand before her father
urging him to become indignant as she was indignant.
Her whole attitude was saying, "Why don't you do
something about this?" He knew that she demanded
some active resentment from him. He remembered with
a sort of nostalgia as if this had happened long ago, the
moment when he had said to the Bishop, "What will
it profit us . . ." and had felt the same indignation
that Jennie was feeling. He looked back on that moment which had happened only a few hours before as
people sometimes look back with pleasure to their childhood when it seems to them in restrospect that living
was at that time a simple matter of deciding between
right and wrong, black and white. "But how can I ex-

plain it all to them?" Mr. Middleton asked himself and remained silent.

But Jennie was not silent. She saw at last that her father would not respond to her indignation. Her mind became active at once and asked itself what could be done.

"Can we get any flowers for the bridesmaids?" she asked.

Mrs. Middleton shook her head. "I telephoned both the florists," she explained.

"Then we will do without," Jennie said cheerfully. "We won't let Dr. Grant know that what he has done hurts us. And it doesn't hurt us. It doesn't at all. We will go on as if we had never thought of the flags."

"If we haven't any flowers, what can we do with our hands?" Nancy asked dismally.

Jennie laughed. This crisis was stimulating. She felt herself strong and purposeful. Everything depended on her. Now she had something to do. Now she was needed and could love people and give herself to them and do for them and tell them what to do. When Carrie Middleton saw this look of strong purposefulness on Jennie's face and heard her laugh she knew that her anxieties about the wedding were over and that now she could rest for a little. As she let herself into a chair she groaned softly, because when the pressure of standing was lifted and the pressure of anxiety from her heart she became conscious of the pain in her feet.

"What is it, Mother?" Jennie asked.

"Only . . . my feet," her mother said.

"Susan," Jennie commanded, "go upstairs and bring Mother's bed-room slippers. Now," she said to the bridesmaids, "all of you come down here."

"Just as we are?" Lucy screamed. Her hair was done up in curlers and she covered the kid-curlers with her hands.

"Just as you are," Jennie commanded.

"Someone might come," Janie objected.

"Let them come," Jennie told her recklessly and laughed. "Come down here," she commanded, "come!"

Susan hurried down the stairs with her mother's slippers. She knelt in front of her mother and with the skill that came from having done this many times before she slipped off her mother's shoes easily and softly so that she would not hurt the corns and just as carefully put on the slippers.

Mrs. Middleton sighed gratefully, "That is such a relief," she said happily. Jennie smiled at her.

"Take mother's shoes upstairs, Susan," Jennie ordered. The bridesmaids came trailing down from the stairs and stood obediently before Jennie. Susan watched them, not wishing to miss any moment of what was happening or what might be going to happen. "Go on, Susan," Jennie said impatiently and Susan obeyed at once. On the second floor she rushed to her mother's room, flung the shoes inside, and hurried down again.

Mrs. Middleton said to her husband, "Robert, there is some supper for you in the pantry."

When her husband was going, she asked, "Shall I come?"

"No," he answered.

"Tell Louisa to give you some coffee," Mrs. Middleton said.

Jennie looked critically at the bridesmaids who stood obediently before her. "Let me see," she said, "we must find some way, some natural way for you to hold your arms. Nancy, hold your hands like this as if you carried the flags or flowers. No, not that way. You are carrying something, realize that, you have something in your arms."

She lifted her eyes and saw the flags on the wall above the mantel. Quickly and with a flash of energy she stood on a chair and wrenched one of the flags from the nail that held it, and returned to the girls. "Hold this, Nancy," she said and when Nancy held the flag in the way they had practiced holding them she took the flag away. "Now, when I take it let your arms stay just as they were." She gave the flag to each of the girls. When the flag left their arms they held them in the same position. "Now march," Jennie said. She hummed the wedding march.

But the bridesmaids walked stiffly. Their elbows protruded from their bodies in an absurd and affected manner. Their wrists were curved unnaturally.

"No," Jennie said impatiently, "that won't do. That is terrible." She flung her hands to her hair and with the tips of her fingers shook her hair until it stood on end. The pins fell from it and it stood out about her face. "No, that won't do at all. Try your hands at your sides, just let them hang loosely." She ran to Janie, took her shoulders in a firm grasp and shook her. "Loose, let your arms loose," she commanded. She went to each of the others and shook them just as she had shaken Janie. When Jennie came to Pamela and shook her, Pamela relaxed not only her shoulders and arms but her whole body so that she shook like a rag doll. Everyone, even Mrs. Middleton laughed. "How confident she is," Mrs. Middleton thought proudly as she watched her daughter. "I am not surprised, not surprised at all that she made such a good reputation in her teaching."

Robert Middleton heard the laughter and came to the door of the dining-room with a cup in his hand. As he saw what was happening he went closer to his wife. He watched his daughter and a smile of pleasure and appreciation came on his lips.

Jennie saw her father come in. She saw his smile of appreciation, and the pride in her mother's face. She understood that all of them looked on her with admiration and confidence. Everything and everyone depended on her. She had regained their confidence and they would do whatever she wished and what she wished was for the good of them all. She was good once more and happy and joyful once more.

"Now," she said, to the bridesmaids, "let your arms hang loosely as I showed you, at your sides. Now march," she hummed the wedding march again. The bridesmaids began to hum the tune with Jennie. They giggled. There was a sound of joy and laughter in the house again. Carrie Middleton smiled. Her feet were comfortable, relieved from the pressure of the shoes. And the laughter and talk and the sight of Jennie so happy and full of energy made it seem that a pressure of sorrow and anxiety had been lifted from her heart along with the pain that had been taken from her feet when Susan had taken off her shoes.

Jennie watched the bridesmaids critically as they marched around the room in single file with their arms at their sides. "No," she said, "that won't do either. Let me see," she flung her hands into her hair again. Again her fingers shook it until it stood out about her face. The girls looked solemn and thoughtful, each trying to devise a way to help.

"This way?" Janie asked. She folded her arms loosely together as if she held a baby.

"No, no," Jennie said.

"The only thing for me to do," Nancy moaned, "is cut off my arms. There isn't any other way. They are so lo-o-ng."

"I know," Jennie shrieked suddenly. "Now," she began to explain, but interrupted herself, "wait." She hurried to one of the book cases and took a small book from an upper shelf. "See, this is the way I must carry the prayer book . . . like this," she walked sedately before them with the book held loosely in her hands, "Now," she ran to the bookcase again and took other books from the shelves and gave them to the girls.

"Now hold them like this, just as I will hold the prayer book. Now march again."

Again the girls' high sweet voices hummed out the wedding march. Lucy held her book carefully and tightly, and then at a look from Jennie relaxed her fingers about it. She lifted her head and peered in a dignified manner through the ends of the kid curlers which came down over her forehead. She marched solemnly just as the others marched, and hummed the tune with them.

"Now give the books to Susan," Jennie called. "Susan, stand there and take the books. And leave your hands just as they are," she screamed when she saw that Nancy was about to move her hands from that position. "Don't move your hands at all. Let Susan take the books from your hands."

Susan lifted the books carefully out of the unresisting hands of the bridesmaids as each passed her.

"Keep your hands as they were," Jennie said, "No, not that way, Janie, not like you were praying, but lower, clasped loosely." She went to Janie and shook her. "You must do what I say. You must. There, that's right. Now, isn't that better? That's right, isn't it, Mother? That will be splendid. They will have their hands in the same position as mine. It will carry out the same idea. When you go upstairs, practice it so you can show the other girls at the church," she said to the girls, "take the books with you. Susan, take the books upstairs for them."

The girls left their poses and gathered around Jennie. "You are wonderful," Janie said to her and put her arms impulsively and lovingly about Jennie. "No," Jennie told her modestly, but her face was gleaming with pleasure in what she had done and in the praise, "only I like things to be right. And we mustn't let him get the best of it," she said, thinking of Dr. Grant.

Susan was at the front door with her nose pressed against the glass of the door.

"Didn't you hear me, Susan?" Jennie asked her. "I said take the books upstairs."

"Yes," Susan told her, "Only, Hugh and Chris and the others are coming up the walk."

"Oh, my curlers," Lucy screamed. She clutched her hair with both hands and ran up the stairs, tripping over the hem of her dressing gown at every step.

"Run," Jennie laughed. She flung out her arms toward the other bridesmaids and shooed them away. But they did not need any urging. They flung themselves hastily up the stairs after Lucy.

"Take the books upstairs," Jennie said to her little sister, "didn't you hear me?" she asked impatiently. Susan went up the stairs balancing the pile of books in her arms and steadying it with her chin.

From the stairs she heard the brothers come in, heard her father ask Hugh about Ed, and heard Hugh say, "His mother hasn't seen him. He must have run away, afraid of the police."

Suddenly a terrible sadness came in Susan, as if some heavy weight like the books she carried had got into the pit of her stomach. She thought of Ed running.

She could see him running in some place that was like
a desert. And he was alone. He was running like the
song that Louisa sang, "Keep arunnin', Keep arunnin',
the fire gwine overtake you. Keep arunnin'. Keep arunnin'. The fire gwine overtake you." She saw Ed running with fire trying to overtake him, a fire in a cloud,
like the fire that came down over the ark of the Israel-
ites in the Bible. The fire moved forward swiftly over
the desert-like place so that Ed must keep running to
escape it. She saw the great ball of fire enclosed in a
cloud and a dark form, frightened and alone, hurrying
before it.

Susan felt a terror, as if she had been caught in the
dark and a hand had touched her on the shoulder. She
stumbled up the stairs, and paying no attention to the
books that dropped from her arms ran down the hall
and into Nancy's room where the bridesmaids were
waiting for her.

XXII

As eight o'clock, the hour for the wedding, approached people gathered at the church in crowds and were shown by the ushers to those pews which were not roped off from the others by white ribbons. The crowds came not only to see the bride but to catch a glimpse of the Confederate officers in their uniforms. They were interested in the whole pageant. So many people came the two ushers assigned to the side aisles found it difficult to keep these aisles open. It was necessary to do this because the bridesmaids were to walk down the side aisles to the chancel.

Some of the guests were shocked at the crowd and the display of open curiosity. And they criticized the Middletons for it. Miss Lizzie Palmer, as she walked down the aisle with her hand on Christopher's arm while Christopher whispered joking asides to her, lifted her large nose as if she sniffed the air about her and did not find it wholesome. Behind her marched her brother Stuart with Miss Bessie. Stuart was very like Miss Lizzie in appearance. And as he went down the aisle behind her he also lifted his nose. Miss Bessie turned her head aside not because she was distressed about the large crowd, but because Stuart's breath smelled of whiskey. She was rather ashamed because that evening at home as Stuart went up to dress he leaned over the banisters and was very sick. It had been necessary to clean up after him as if he had been a child who could not control himself.

Christopher unhooked the white ribbon bow and holding it in his hand led the Palmers to a pew near the front. He bowed Miss Lizzie into the pew and waited as the others followed her. Then he closed the door of the pew and walking back to the place from which he had taken the ribbon bow replaced it. He felt as he walked along the aisle that people looked at him with smiling admiration and this gave him pleasure. His mirror had told him that he was handsome in his new evening clothes. He knew some of the girls in the pews and smiled at them without looking directly at them. His smile was generous and included them all. He loved all young and pretty women. Augusta, who at that time was his favorite, was sitting at the end of a pew. She had confided to him as he showed her to the pew that she had broken her engagement the day before and this knowledge stimulated him. Brown-haired, rosy-cheeked Augusta was one of the most popular girls in the city, and her eyes, when she told him that she had broken her engagement to another man, said that she had done so because of Christopher. Christopher was not yet ready to concentrate his affections on one girl. But the knowledge that Augusta was complimented by his admiration and that other girls were complimented if he paid them attention made him happy. The organist was playing an urgent and passionate love song. The music came softly and spread over the church. It reached Christopher and spread through him urging him on to some romantic action. He leaned over the side of the high pew and whispered a few words to Augusta. She lifted her face to listen and he let his cheek brush hers. He felt the softness of her cheek and the contact gave him an indescribable feeling of joy.

The loud murmurs went on throughout the whole church. People talked above a whisper. Miss Lizzie Palmer had never heard this sound in the church before. She wished to say to them all, "Hush, be quiet. Silence," as she said it when she went into the schoolroom and found the girls talking above a whisper. But she had to content herself with pressing her own lips together. Stuart began to talk to Miss Bessie and he also spoke above a whisper. Miss Lizzie motioned to Miss Bessie to change places with her and she moved next to Stuart. Even this did not prevent him from making remarks as people were brought down the aisle by the ushers.

"The decorations are so pretty," Miss Bessie whispered, "at least I think so," she added as if she did not wish to compromise any other person's opinion and especially that of Miss Lizzie.

The church, like the Middletons' home, was garlanded in smilax and gray moss. The gray moss and green smilax suited the old gray fluted pillars that supported the center roof of the great church. Smilax was wound along the altar railing, and behind it many candles gleamed on the altar against the new reredos.

Hugh escorted Cousin Fannie and Saint John down the aisle and put them in the pew directly in front of the Palmers. This was the pew where his mother and the two youngest children would sit. Miss Lizzie leaned across the back of her pew and nodded smilingly to Cousin Fannie. Hugh returned to the vestibule of the church. He looked for Christopher, but did not find him. "He is off talking to some pretty girl," Hugh told himself resentfully, "and I haven't time to even speak to Natalie." Then he remembered that Christopher had said he must go back to the vestry room to make sure the two doctors had arrived safely. Hugh glanced outside the wide front doors of the church and saw that there was a crowd of people on the sidewalk. No more places were left inside the church except those reserved for the family. The bridesmaids and most of the groomsmen had arrived. Natalie, lovely and dignified in her lacy dress, smiled at Hugh and at the same time continued to listen to one of the Veterans who was telling her that she looked exactly like an old portrait. It was difficult for Hugh to keep from going to her and remaining with her. He wished to have her close to him, to put his head near hers so that he could see the tender, expressive mouth and her warm eyes that had become so dear to him.

The whole vestibule was like a picture of the days before the Civil War. Each Veteran in his gray officer's coat with gold braid and swinging sash, looked at once strange and yet as if they fitted into a frame that had been built for them. They were strange in contrast with the evening clothes of the ushers, but the old church with its peeling walls and gray and red stone and the flounced dresses of the bridesmaids made their gray uniforms appear in place, as if they belong there. The Veterans held themselves with dignity and alertness as if they were listening for the call of a bugle. Coming back from one of his trips down the aisle Hugh saw the picture that was made by the Veterans and the girls for the first time and for the first time saw what had been in his father's and in Jennie's mind when they had planned this elaborate wedding. He saw that General Stephens had Lucy over by the north door and was talking to her earnestly. "That will be a good match for Lucy," he thought. It pleased him that this special good should come from the wedding.

"If my mother comes while I am in the church," he said to one of the ushers, "ask her to wait for me."

When he returned the next time his mother had just arrived. The precious bouquet of violets that Hugh had selected for her was at her waist against her gray silk dress. An amethyst bracelet shaped like a diadem was in her soft white hair. Susan and Bobby were on either side of her. As they walked slowly down the aisle while people whispered or said in louder tones, "That is the bride's mother," Christopher pressed his mother's hand against his side. He felt her trembling. Ever since he could remember she had always trembled in moments of crisis. At times this had irritated him, because he thought a grown person should have more self-control. But now, with an insight that the excitement and pleasure of the wedding gave him, he saw that she was unable to help this trembling. She could no more control it than a tree can control its shaking limbs when a high wind comes.

Susan had asked her cousin, who was an usher, if she might walk down the aisle with him like a grown young woman. She was delighted that this cousin had remembered and had stepped forward and put out his arm to her. She walked proudly behind her mother with the tall young man, though it strained her to reach far enough so that her hand would fit into the crook of his arm. On her other side, lagging somewhat behind, came Bobby in his new suit with long trousers. He looked as if he wished people to think that he had no concern with this wedding, but was merely strolling down the aisle of the church by accident.

Hugh bowed his mother into the pew beside Cousin Fannie, and to Susan's delight her cousin also bowed her in. Mrs. Middleton placed herself between Bobby and Susan and they sat down without kneeling to say the small prayer which was usual when they came for the regular church service. The music of the organ swept through the church solemnly. The arches of the roof above them seemed to stretch clear up into the heavens. They were dim and remote. Up at one side of the church at the left Susan saw that Louisa and Annie

May had come into the gallery which was reserved for colored people. It was the old slave gallery.

In the vestibule Hugh moved about restlessly, his watch in his hand. It was five minutes of eight and Christopher had not come. The bridesmaids, in flounced, billowing dress of lacy point d'esprit with wreaths of small red roses on their hair, were moving about, rehearsing the position of their hands. The position, heads bent over the loosely clasped hands, gave them an especially demure even religious appearance, as if they had just come from praying in the church.

Hugh spoke to the bridesmaids and groomsmen, "I think you should get in line," he told them in a cold, formal voice. But no one did as he said. They moved a little toward their places, but did not hurry to them as they would have done if Christopher had spoken.

Hugh was at the north side trying to get the bridesmaids there in line when he heard a disturbance at the south entrance of the vestibule. He saw Christopher and Christopher beckoned to him. They met and Christopher drew his brother into a little alcove where the sexton kept his coat. Hugh saw by the look of anxiety on Christopher's face that something out of the ordinary had happened.

"Isn't the groom here?" he asked.

"Yes, the doctors have come. They are in the choir room. Something else has happened," Christopher said anxiously.

"Why were you gone so long?"

"I couldn't help it. I was talking to the Bishop. He

wanted to explain to me so I could explain to Father."

"It is eight o'clock."

"I couldn't help it, Hugh. Weddings are never on time. You should have seen the Bishop. I have never seen him angry before. But he was angry."

"You'd better get everyone in line."

"I will. But this is important. The question is, shall I tell Father now? The Bishop said after he had put on his vestments he opened the door into the minister's room and there was Dr. Grant, all ready in his own vestments. And the Bishop promised Father that Dr. Grant should not take part in the ceremony. He wants me to explain to Father that he could not help it . . ."

"Father will be angry . . ."

"That's just what I'm saying. Shall we tell him? The Bishop wants me to tell him. He said he reminded Dr. Grant that he was not to take part in the ceremony . . . sentimental feeling about the Confederacy . . . but Dr. Grant said this was his church and he intended to do his duty. He said, the Bishop told me he said, 'I will go into the chancel and unless you throw me out'—he said 'throw me out, Hugh'—I shall read the preliminary service.' The Bishop can do nothing. And you know they have the preliminary service at the foot of the chancel steps. Dr. Grant will meet Father there. I think we should warn Father . . . you know his temper."

"Father wouldn't make a scene."

"Of course not . . . I know . . . but I think it's only fair to warn him so he won't . . ."

Someone at the door said, "The bride is here," and

the words were repeated by others. Christopher heard
them and swung away from Hugh toward the front
door. Hugh followed him. They ran down the steps to
the carriage and stood on the sidewalk. They saw the
mysterious white figure in the dark interior of the carriage, and each of the brothers took a place at the side
of the carriage door, waiting for the mysterious figure
to come out into the light and become their sister Jennie. Robert Middleton stepped out of the carriage first
and stood aside. Jennie smiled at her brothars as they
helped her to step down to the sidewalk. She held her
long train and the veil carefully from the ground as
they passed up the walk between the crowds of people
and mounted the steps of the church. In the vestibule
the dressmaker who had been waiting for this moment
came forward and knelt down to arrange Jennie's train
and the veil. All the Veterans left their place and bent
over Jennie's hand. With a significant look at Hugh
which said, "I will see to this," Christopher drew his
father to one side and began speaking to him.

Jennie did not know that her father had left her.
She did not notice when he and Christopher slipped
out of the side door of the church. The gray-uniformed
Veterans crowded close to Jennie, each one trying to be
the first to pay her courtly and exaggerated compliments. Everyone in the vestibule was looking at her.
She was the center of attention. A warm and loving
emotion of gratitude came up in Jennie. Her smile was
bright and there were unshed tears of emotion in her
eyes. She received all the attention with gravity and

dignity. And though she was grave and sedate, on her mouth at the corners of her lips a loving smile trembled. She was the daughter of the Veterans and they were proud of her and she knew they were proud. She was not only herself but a symbol of their past.

But presently an atmosphere of strain settled on the people in the vestibule. Hugh walked restlessly up and down in the space under the stairs that led to the back gallery until Natalie came and touched his arm, when he stood and quietly talked with her. But he continually glanced at the side door of the church through which his brother and father had vanished. The Veterans had exhausted their compliments and did not know whether to take their places again or to remain near Jennie. She felt the constraint and for the first time saw that her father was not there. The organ droned on, but it seemed that even the organ had a complaining note as if it were asking, "How long, how long?" The bridesmaids looked anxiously at each other. They left their places and gathered together at the side door and whispered. Their white ruffled skirts stood out about them. Their heads were close together as they whispered. The ushers, except Hugh, lounged near the doorway wishing they could go outside to smoke.

Christopher had told his father that Dr. Grant insisted on taking part in the ceremony and he was not surprised when Mr. Middleton wished to see Dr. Grant. Christopher followed his father around the church to the outer door that led to the robing rooms. They soon reached the door of the choir room. Beyond this was

the minister's room and then came the smaller place reserved for the Bishop. Mr. Middleton flung open the
door of the choir room and strode through it without
looking to the right or to the left. He paid no attention
to the groom and his best man who were waiting in
that room for the signal to go into the church. He did
not see them. The doctors had heard the Bishop tell
Christopher about Dr. Grant, and they saw by Christopher's anxious face as he followed his father's swift
strides that some comic or tragic happening was about
to take place. Dr. Greve took his friend's arm and they
followed Mr. Middleton and Christopher through the
open door of the minister's vesting room. No one was
there, but the other door, the one leading into the
Bishop's room, was open.

Both men of God were standing near the steps that
led up into the chancel. The small door at the top of
these steps was closed but the music of the organ could
be heard. But louder than the sound of the organ was
another sound. In this room behind the organ pipes
was the place where the bellows pumped air into the
pipes. At one side, just behind the pipes a Negro boy
leaned over and worked the long curved arm of the
pump. There was a wheezing, creaking sound from the
bellows as if someone were breathing painfully. The
colored boy bent over and worked the handle up and
down ceaselessly. Sweat dropped from his forehead to
his hands.

As Mr. Middleton and Christopher entered this small
room both the Bishop and Dr. Grant turned toward

them. Both were in their vestments and in their hands were the prayer books with ribbons marking the place where the wedding ceremony was written.

"Dr. Grant . . ." Robert Middleton halted inside the door. He tried to speak, to go on speaking, but his breath came in gasps. It was like the painful gasps that came from the old bellows of the organ. Finally Robert continued . . . "My son tells me that you have forced yourself . . . that you have decided to take part in the wedding ceremony." Robert suddenly faced the Bishop and asked, "Did you agree to this?"

"No," the Bishop answered sadly. Above the white linen ruff, at his neck his face was pale and sad, "But I must remind you again that this is Dr. Grant's church."

Dr. Grant took the hem of his black robe in his fingers and pulled the robe to his waist. His trousers looked incongruous and out of place as they were exposed beneath the lifted robe. He reached in his pocket under the robe and took out his watch and looked at it significantly.

"It is past time for the wedding," he said coldly. He appeared cold and contemptuous, but his red face had turned a deeper red.

Mr. Middleton's fist shot up into the air in an uncontrolled gesture of anger. Christopher reached forward and touched his father's arm and pressed it, until the arm dropped to Robert's side.

"If you go in that door," Robert said to Dr. Grant, "I warn you, I warn you. I humbled myself to this man," he said to the Bishop, "I explained all the good reasons why we asked him . . . no, why we begged him not to take part in this holy sacrament and yet . . . I won't allow it. I tell you, Bishop, I will not . . ."

Dr. Grant said in the same cold voice, in which he had spoken before, "I intend to take my part in the ceremony, Mr. Middleton."

His voice was so cold, so measured, so contemptuous, even Christopher, though he wished to keep his emotions entirely detached and himself free from anger, felt his fists clenching themselves at his side.

The Bishop spoke to Dr. Grant. "Let me beg you again," he said in his sweet quivering voice, "not to do this. What satisfaction can you get out of it, my friend?"

"That is my affair," Dr. Grant said. He did not explain and never did explain why he wished so much to take part in the wedding. He looked at his watch again significantly, slipped it into his pocket and let the cassock fall over his trousers to his shoes.

"Then," the Bishop said steadily, "I must order you as your Bishop not to do this, not to make this confusion and bitterness. There is no reason in it . . . it is unseemly for a minister of the church."

"As I told you yesterday," Dr. Grant said to the Bishop, "I will report to the House of Bishops that you are fomenting strife and that you are provoking sectional hatred if," he said in a low voice that the others could scarcely hear, "if you don't keep out of this. I am only doing the will of my Father in heaven," he said out loud piously, "who sent his only Son to the wedding at Cana . . ."

"This is hypocrisy," Robert cried out.

The young Negro boy at the long handle of the bellows stared at them. He continued to pump rhythmically but at the same time he stared and listened and was astonished.

The two doctors looking in at the door smiled at each other. Dr. Greve put his hands into the pockets of his carefully pressed evening trousers and hunched his shoulders so that the stiff bosom of his shirt protruded like the breast of a bird. He smiled with a wicked sort of pleasure as if he were saying to himself, "What a show, what a show. What could beat this?"

Robert Middleton strode to a place just in front of Dr. Grant. Christopher followed him anxiously. "Now I believe," Robert said, "now I do believe the stories told about you, that you lust after women. Now I know you belong with those men who take their money from whores and give it to the church. And I will have nothing to do with you. If you go into that chancel I will never enter this church again. I will not countenance such hypocrisy."

The Bishop said, "I would like to have peace in this church." He spoke to Dr. Grant. "I feel that I must use my authority as Bishop to tell you that you must not go into the chancel tonight," he said.

Dr. Grant did not listen. He went directly to the steps leading to the little door and walked up the steps to the door and took the knob in his hand. He lifted his cassock as he had done before and again looked at his watch significantly.

Christopher tugged at his father's arm. "We must get back, Father," he said, "we must get back. They are all waiting."

The Bishop lifted his hands. Christopher saw the full white linen sleeves of the Bishop's robe. Before this he had always looked on the robe from the choir or the congregation and had not noticed the details. But now the details were clear to him. He saw the black band that held the fullness of the white sleeves at the Bishop's wrist and the ruffles of linen that almost covered the Bishop's hands and made them appear small and white and delicate like the hands of a woman. The Bishop laid these hands on Mr. Middleton's shoulders and turned him in the direction of the door into the other robing room.

"We will stand together in this, Robert," he said, "but that will come later. Now we must think of Jennie. Now you must go . . . go."

"Yes," Robert promised. But he walked past the Bishop to the foot of the small flight of steps. Christopher and the Bishop looked at each other anxiously. But Robert did not go further than the steps and he spoke quietly.

"Dr. Grant," he said, "I asked you to come to our home this evening to the reception. You had an engraved and formal invitation and I gave you a personal one, a special and hospitable invitation to come to my home. But now . . . now . . . I wish to engrave this on your heart, if you have a heart. I wish to say that this invitation has been cancelled, not by me, but by yourself, by your behavior, which is not the behavior of a gentleman and is not the behavior of a man of God. I do not like to be inhospitable, but I must ask you not to . . ." his controlled voice broke, his face suddenly flushed red as blood and he spoke quickly and angrily, "I do not want you in my home and if you dare to come, if you dare . . ."

He turned away and stumbled toward the outer door. The two doctors, handsome in their evening clothes, stood aside as Christopher led his father through the room to the door leading to the gravel walk.

In the Bishop's room the two men were silent. The bellows wheezed painfully. Dr. Grant still held to the knob of the small door and stared at his fingers on the knob. His portly form took up all the space at the top of the steps. His face had recovered its usual appearance with the red of good health shining through the skin. The Bishop remained at a little distance from him. When the first notes of the wedding march sounded, Dr. Grant did not wait for the Bishop to go first as was customary, but slipped into the chancel behind the choir stalls. After him the Bishop walked slowly into the space between the stalls, opened the gate of the altar railing and took his place in the large chair reserved for him at the side of the altar.

XXIII

BEFORE he and his father entered the vestibule Christopher pressed his father's arm. "You must brace up, Dad," he said, using the same words his father had often used in the family when any trouble came.

"Yes," Robert said, "I probably made a fool of myself, Christopher. But it couldn't be helped. It couldn't be helped. Even now when I think of that man!"

"What does it matter? Let the old villain do what he wants. It can't hurt us. And now we must go on with the wedding. You know you must take Jennie down the aisle and give her away. You must brace up," he repeated good-naturedly. He continued to press his father's arm affectionately until they were well inside the vestibule, until he had led him to Jennie.

Then Christopher's face took on a bright commanding look. He glanced quickly over all the people in the vestibule, the Veterans and the bridesmaids and ushers. And when they saw Christopher and that he was not disturbed but that his expression was cheerful and confident they felt that nothing was wrong and that the delay which had made them so uneasy was not im-

portant. They took their places immediately in response
to his look.

Jennie put her hand into the crook of her father's
arm. Christopher went to the side aisle, walked a little
way down, stripped off a white glove and lifted it high
in the air to give the prearranged signal to the organist.
At once the music changed from a quiet monotone into
the wedding march. Christopher returned to the center
door and glanced at everyone again. He saw that the
bridesmaids, dainty and fragile looking in their flounced
point d'esprit dresses and wreaths of small red roses on
their parted hair, were in single file at the side doors.
The Veterans, with their gray heads held stiffly above
the gold-braided gray uniforms, had taken their places
competently in a soldierly manner with heels together
in a double line at the center door. He heard Nancy,
who was in front of Jennie, say, "You're beautiful, Jennie." Then he took his place beside Hugh and waited
until the ushers just in front of them had reached a
certain place. He smiled at Hugh and gave him a slight
nod to show that he was ready and they started forward. As they moved forward slowly and reached the
tenth pew he heard a great concerted sound all over the
church. The people were rising to their feet and he
knew that the first Veterans had appeared in the aisle
behind him.

Miss Lizzie Palmer heard and saw the people come
to their feet, and she also rose to her feet. She had
watched a coronation procession in England from the
streets with other people in a great crowd, but she felt

that this mighty surge of curiosity exhibited in her own church was somehow indecent.

In front of Miss Lizzie Susan strained her neck trying to get a glimpse of the bridesmaids in the side aisles. She could not see them. But she could see the Veterans clearly. General Iredale passed close to her and she saw the long saber cut on his cheek and was intensely proud that she knew him. She had a special feeling for him because the evening before at the reception General Iredale lifted her to a chair and kissed her. He said, "If I were only as young as you." She answered, "If I were only a Confederate Hero like you." Everyone near them laughed and applauded what she had said. General Iredale kissed her again. She understood that they approved of what she had said, but she could not understand why anyone could wish themselves a child when they might be such a hero, with a saber cut that was a living and everlasting proof of heroism.

There was a loud murmur among the spectators. Susan leaned far over the top of the pew door to look back and saw that her father and Jennie were coming. Her mother's hand came down on her shoulder and pulled her gently back into the pew. Nancy passed just beside her. She looked really handsome, and held her hands very nicely, loosely clasped in front just as Jennie had told her. The three point d'esprit flounces of her skirt fluttered gracefully as if they were moved by a wind. As she passed Susan heard the rustle of her taffeta petticoat.

Robert Middleton and Jennie walked slowly. Their

chins were raised high in the air. There was a look of noble solemnity on both their faces. People said afterward that Jennie and her father were curiously alike that evening. No one had noticed the resemblance before.

Mrs. Middleton put her arm about Susan and Susan felt her mother tremble as the two passed. Behind her she heard Stuart Palmer say in a loud whisper, "They are like a couple of aristocrats marching to the guillotine."

Susan felt ashamed, not at the words, which she did not understand well, but at the tone of Stuart's voice which suggested that he was laughing at her father and Jennie. She looked quickly at her mother's face to see by the expression there whether her mother had heard. It seemed she had not. Mrs. Middleton was leaning tensely forward and Susan heard her mother give a painful gasp or sigh. She looked in the same direction and saw Dr. Grant come out from behind the choir stalls and walk down to the very center of the steps below the stalls. He waited there benign and holy.

As Robert passed the pew in which his wife and children stood he felt his wife's presence. But he could not turn and look at her. He thought he heard her sigh as Dr. Grant came from behind the choir stalls and appeared at the steps and wished that he could say to her, "I know. I knew that this would happen." The Bishop stood up before his chair near the altar. He came forward slowly to the gate of the altar railing and stood there in his black and white vestments. The full white sleeves of his vestments looked enormous against the candles.

The two doctors came forward and stood just below the steps of the choir stalls waiting for Jennie and her father. Robert saw that the groom's large, generous mouth was smiling under his moustache. His deep blue eyes gleamed in the light that came from the great chandelier above them. The eyes were deep-set and there was a kindly and uncritical expression in them. They were smiling or seemed to smile and his whole face, the eyes and mouth seemed to say to Robert, "What of it, what of it? Here we are. That is the fact. That is what we must acknowledge."

Robert thought, as he had thought that day at the hotel, "Their children will have eyes like his. And perhaps they will smile in the same way," he went on thinking, "but they will also have something of myself, of Robert Middleton. And they will belong to that future which I have dreaded. They will belong to the new things, not to the old as I do." He saw that the Doctor belonged to the new world in which Dr. Grant lived and like Dr. Grant he was indifferent to the old memories. But Robert did not resent this indifference in the Doctor. He could not resent the broad good-natured face that smiled and said, "What can we do? Here we are. And because we are here we can not be in another place."

Perhaps Robert imagined that he saw these things in the Doctor's face, but they were very real to him and, suddenly he thought, "That is it, that is it. We must discover our own nature and be loyal, that is the word, we must be loyal to our own nature, whatever it is . . . whatever is natural in us and not put on us by others." But it was hard for him not to question and he asked himself, "How can we tell what has been put on us by others?"

Dr. Grant lifted his large red face above the book in his hand. He looked out over the congregation. His sonorous cajoling voice began . . .

"Dearly beloved," it said, "we are gathered together here in the sight of God and in the face of this company to join together this Man and this Woman in holy Matrimony; which is an honorable estate, instituted of God in the time of man's innocency, signifying unto us the mystical union that is betwixt Christ and his church: which holy state Christ adorned and beautified with his presence and first miracle that He wrought in Cana of Galilee . . ."

The words "Cana of Galilee" brought to Robert's mind the conversation in the hotel that morning when Dr. Greve had spoken about the minister who used the wedding at Cana and the story of the woman anointing the feet of Jesus as an excuse for lax behavior with women. He glanced involuntarily at Dr. Greve. The little doctor, handsome in his evening clothes, was standing solemnly beside the groom. As Robert looked at him Dr. Greve's face did not change from its solemn expression. His mouth did not smile. But at the words, "Cana of Galilee," his shoulders gave an almost imperceptible hunch as if he wished to hug himself with

delight. His eyes gleamed with pleasure and mischief.
His right eyelid came down over his eye. He winked
solemnly.

Silent laughter came up in Robert. A picture of Dr.
Grant came to him. He saw Dr. Grant lying back in a
chair, a comfortable and satisfied and portly figure.
His great belly protruded above his bare feet. A woman
knelt at his feet and wiped them with her long hair. It
was a ridiculous picture. A smile came on Robert's lips.

Dr. Grant said, "Who giveth this Woman to be
married to this Man?"

The Doctor stepped forward. Robert laid Jennie's
hand on the arm of the Doctor. He stepped behind
them. Now his part was finished. He stood behind them
alone. Just beyond him up the steps in a straight line
were the Veterans. On their faces was a dignified
aloofness. Opposite them the bridesmaids smiled down
at Jennie.

The sound of the organ became louder. Dr. Grant
led the wedding party to the chancel where the Bishop
was waiting. Robert went back to join his wife. As
he opened the door of the pew and looked down at her,
Carrie Middleton saw with surprise and relief that
her husband was smiling.

The same smile was on Dr. Greve's face as he saw
Jennie give her prayer book with its cascade of flowers
to her maid-of-honor. He smelled the lilies of the valley. The smile remained on his face as he took the
ring from his vest pocket and gave it to the groom. He
was delighted with himself because he was able to look

on it all with his usual detachment. He saw the Doctor's broad hand take Jennie's small one and thought of
his friend.

"He is the real one," he said, thinking of the Doctor,
"he is the positive one here. He wants his joy to come
from reality. It is an instinct with him. He doesn't
know joy or pleasure that do not come from reality.
He does not fool himself. And that brings sorrow, too,
and yet it brings a hard joy, and sometimes a soaring
joy. She," he said, speaking to himself of Jennie,
"wants the joy that comes from above." He held his
hands closely to his sides for he felt a desire to gesture
with them to emphasize this aloof place from which
Jennie would get her ecstasy. "But Doc is the right one.
Only I wonder if they can bring about a fusion of joy
from reality and joy from imagination—too much imagination," he added. "Well, it's none of my business,"
he thought and his shoulders moved. The organ was
playing the other wedding march and he held out his
arm to the maid-of-honor for the return down the aisle.

But in spite of himself the little doctor wondered
again as he stood with the others at the train looking
up into the faces of the bride and groom. He saw that
Jennie was exhilarated. "She is feeling holy," he said
to himself impatiently. He saw that his friend, on
the steps of the train just above Jennie, was looking
down with a kindly, steady good-natured smile. "Perhaps it will be right," he told himself.

The car wheels began to move. They creaked and
groaned against the iron rails. The train moved on.

Jennie and the Doctor vanished from the steps of the pullman. The little group left on the station platform stared after the last car with a sort of lost intensity.

Someone said, "Well, they've gone." One of the girls wiped her eyes with her handkerchief. Christopher said cheerfully, "Let's go to the Opera House and see the last act of that play."

The little Doctor sighed and turned away from the empty tracks.

Afterword

By Lillian Barnard Gilkes

One day many years ago, I sat before an open fire in the apartment of Georgia-born Grace Lumpkin in what is now New York City's East Village, reading bits of her last novel in manuscript. We sat long over a delicious lunch Miss Lumpkin had prepared—she is an accomplished cook, as most Southern women of her generation are—talking of art and life and who, besides Hemingway and Wolfe and Faulkner and Fitzgerald, would write the great American novel. My contribution to the literature of the American novel is still mouldering in a desk drawer, Grace Lumpkin's quiet masterpiece is here in these pages of *The Wedding* (New York: Lee Furman, 1939).

I took the manuscript away with me. She had asked me to read it because we were friends; I had taught courses in creative writing and written on the subject, and she lacked confidence in her own genius. If I had any editorial suggestions then, I have completely forgotten what they were. They must have been about as important as the placement of a comma or a word change here and there.

Then one day in 1974—thirty-six years later—I came upon an article somewhere which said that the work of a sizable group of writers who came out of the 1930s and 1940s was being given that rehabilitative "new look," and reassessed. The list was long, but Grace Lumpkin's name—surprisingly—was not included. I went to my library shelves and took down my first-edition copy of

The Wedding—the only printing the book ever had—
and started reading and couldn't stop until the last line
was reached. Then I gave it and Miss Lumpkin's first
novel, *To Make My Bread,* to a friend who said, "I haven't
read anything so fine and so wonderfully written as these
two books in many, many years!" So next, in some
excitement, I telephoned my good friend Dr. Bruccoli in
Columbia, South Carolina: "Matt, here's a book that
belongs in your 'Lost American Fiction' series!"

He said, "Send it to me."

Here it may well be asked, how many novels of today's
crop are likely to survive the freshets of time? How many
are remembered at all from one year to the next? But the
astonishing thing was that the dramatic outlines of this
beautifully structured novel, its charm and freshness of
characterization, its *quality*, were not only as I remembered them but actually outshone—outdiamonded, you
might say—the impression I had carried in memory all
those years.

So then began what looked like a hopeless wild goose
chase: the hunt for the author of *The Wedding.* Our
paths had diverged. With no clue to her whereabouts, not
even knowing if she were still alive, I wrote to the
Georgia Historical Society. They could tell me nothing,
but relayed my letter to the State Archivist, Miss Carroll
Hart, who in turn had no information but referrred me to
the Librarian of the the University of Georgia at Athens.
Mr. John Bonner's name is emblazoned in stars on my
grateful memory. Miss Lumpkin, he said, was alive and
well in a little township of Virginia with the delightful
name of King and Queen Court House.

"When I left the New York area," Miss Lumpkin
wrote, replying to my letter, "I was technically on my
way to Columbia, South Carolina where I grew up from

my tenth year. . . . I stopped, as I had thought, only for a year or two here in King & Queen Court House, because our Grandpa Jacob Lumpkin (1644–1708) is buried at the old colonial church . . . nearby, and had built his home ['Newington'] on the Mattaponi River here."

Her arrival in the quiet little village, on this pilgrimage to the tomb of the ancestor of all the Lumpkins in America, is pictured in detail in her fourth novel *Full Circle* (Boston: Western Islands, 1962), which is fictionized autobiography. Intending only a short stopover, she fell in love with the tree-shaded beauty of the place, its remoteness from the noisy distractions and confusions of a troubled world. Here among her flowers, her vegetable garden, the grape arbor she rescued from an old root that "looked as if it was trying to crawl back into the ground," she was at peace. The "year or two" stretched to twelve. But it was more than an escape, it was a return to the place of her ancestral roots. A rebirth and a rejoining with family.

Born in Milledgeville, an historic old town in central Georgia which at one time was the state capital (1804–67), Grace Lumpkin comes of a distinguished line of governors, jurists, and members of Congress. The family is of English stock, though Miss Lumpkin herself speculates from the fact that Grandpa Jacob was a Cavalier and loyal to Charles II he might have been Scotch. But Goldsmith's use of a family name for the character of Squire Tony Lumpkin, in *She Stoops To Conquer*, seems to leave no doubt of English origin. "Anthony" was a Lumpkin family name in successive generations.

A hardy individualist, Grandpa Jacob's Cavalier loyalties got him into trouble when he refused to drink to the health of William and Mary who succeeded to the English throne after the fall of James II, the last of the

Stuarts, in 1688. In the local tavern, the old man would
neither take off his hat nor raise his glass when neighbors
tried to force the issue, but angrily fought them off. "I'll
be God-damned if I will drink to those usurpers!" They
made out a case against him, but he ignored the court
summons and "just naturally went along with his life at
Newington. . . . He never did appear to answer the
charges." Something of this cranky spirit of independence is reflected in the character of Grandpap in *To
Make My Bread* (New York: Macaulay, 1932), the old
mountaineer and ex-moonshiner who forfeited his land
to his creditors rather than become a sharecropper, and
walked fifty miles to attend a Confederate reunion in
Columbia.

About 1768 three brothers, George, Joseph, and
Anthony Lumpkin, moved farther south and settled in
Oglethorpe County, Georgia, where they built a church
and a brick courthouse for record keeping. "That
Joseph," writes Miss Lumpkin, "was my own direct
ancestor,"[1] first chief justice of the Georgia Supreme
Court and the first professor of law at the University of
Georgia, for whom the law school is named.

Grace was ten years old when her parents moved from
Milledgeville to a country home near the capital city of
South Carolina. Place is important in all of her work, as a
voice, a motivating influence on character. In *To Make
My Bread* it is the mountain country of western North
Carolina whence the McClure family eventually migrates
to a textile mill town (Gastonia, N. C.), in the failed hope
of finding a better living. In her second novel *A Sign for
Cain* (New York: Lee Furman, 1935), and the remarkable
short story "The Bridesmaids Carried Lilies," it is the
landscape and plantation area of central Georgia.
Readers of *The Wedding*, if at all familiar with the

Columbia locale, will easily recognize the wide street abutting on the Capitol; the main hotel where Dr. Gregg has immured himself like an Achilles in his tent; and Trinity Episcopal Church, where the ceremony is performed amid pageantry of Confederate flags and uniforms. Again, in the first novel we are inside the old auditorium with Grandpap and the boy John McClure, where the South Carolina Division of the United Confederate Veterans met in 1901, 1903, and 1906.

After high school graduation, Grace Lumpkin taught school and organized a night school for farmers and their wives. Her first stories were published in school magazines. Later she had a government job as home demonstration agent for the county, and learned more about the economic problems of the people on the land. "I lived out in the mountains of North Carolina most summers, and stayed with people who worked in the cotton mills. . . . I liked to write, and wanted to write, but at that time I seemed to be concerned with only two things, the hard details of making a living and enjoying myself with dancing and other pleasures." Then for two years she was industrial secretary of the South Carolina Y.W.C.A. and at twenty-five had saved enough money to get to the capital of Dreamland, New York City, which drew the youth from the hinterlands and small cities all over the country seeking the rainbow's end. The third day in New York her money was stolen, but she got a job in an office almost immediately, which paid for evening classes at Columbia University. She remained three years in her first job, "and then thinking it would give me more time for writing, I became a chamber maid. But with fifty beds to make and rooms and bathrooms to clean I found not much time or energy left for writing." So then it was back to office work. On borrowed money between jobs she wrote her first novel, and somewhere in this roller-coaster existence she got married.[2] The marriage seems to have ended unhappily.

To Make My Bread was widely reviewed, with high praise, and won the Maxim Gorky award for "the best labor novel of the year" (1932). The *New York Times* reviewer called it "one more milestone on the road to the return of 'social consciousness' in American fiction." "Solidly and honestly and graphically composed," said *The Nation*'s critic Robert Cantwell, of Miss Lumpkin's book, while calling it "propaganda . . . very good, very effective propaganda." Amid this little fanfare it was adapted for the stage by Albert Bein, and under the title *Let Freedom Ring* opened at the Broadhurst Theatre in New York on November 6, 1935. Afterwards transferred to the old Civic Repertory Theatre in Fourteenth Street, it had a successful run of almost six months.

Grace Lumpkin has been superficially tagged with the propagandist, "leftist" label. But the comment of the *London Times* critic—*To Make My Bread* was published also in England—is both a more perceptive and more accurate appraisal: "Miss Lumpkin conquers by the depth of her human sympathy, by the fidelity of her characterization." These elements, embodied in superb artistry, far outweigh in importance any period "message" from the Depression years that the "social consciousness" critics have recognized in her first novel. Was Thomas Hardy a propagandist for the English tenant farmers? Or George Eliot? *The Wedding*, in particular, is a work which resists easy classification under any of the conventional labels. There is social consciousness, a great deal of it in its portrayal of the lost fortunes and psychological peculiarities of a Southern middle-class family, its emphasis on outmoded values in the changing world of the early twentieth century; but no one would dream of calling this "propagandist" or revolutionary. In fact, Miss Lumpkin was criticized by some ultra-leftists for having in this book abandoned the class struggle!

Her second novel *A Sign for Cain* (1935), it is true, is marred by patches here and there of leftist didacticism, which accounts in part for its inferiority as a whole to the other two—a judgment with which the author herself agrees. Another flaw is the fact that the main characters, familiar Southern types who come close to being stereotypes, just aren't very interesting by comparison with the McClures and the Middletons; and the race relations theme is handled so much better, indeed with the highest art, in the wonderful "Bridesmaids," the long short story which appeared two years later in the *North American Review*. But with respect to character drawing, one must exempt from this criticism of *Cain* the portrayal of the Negro youth Ficents, and the wretched little kitchen slavey Selah. These and the minor figures of the lazy, ignorant, sentimental windbag Mr. Bridie who lets his women drudge to support him, and poor little filthy, overworked Gramma, are as fine and true to life in a provincial, economically depressed pre–1914 South, as anything in Thomas Wolfe's boardinghouse kitchen in *Look Homeward, Angel*.

It seems never to have occurred to anyone to call attention to *The Wedding* in conjunction with Eudora Welty's fine novel, *Delta Wedding* (1946). Analogues do not necessarily presuppose an influence, always something extremely hard to pin down. A wedding in a Southern family with all of its ceremonial ritual and tribal implications, its social importance, its emotional ramifications in a closely interwoven clan and community life, is a natural subject for any Southern novelist of the period these authors are writing about. Similarities of theme and title are therefore, in this instance, insufficient evidence on which to base a claim of influence. Furthermore, her emphasis on locale in the title of Miss Welty's book suggests other differences as well. For in treatment and style, no two authors could be more dissimilar: Miss Lumpkin direct and swift, sparser in her use of simile and symbol; Miss Welty slow-paced and deliberate, relying heavily on allusion, myth, and distortions of focus to convey meanings which, when she is not at her best, seem commonplace and contrived, rather than subtle. Yet in view of the fact that both bridegrooms are outsiders, representing a grafting of new blood onto a weakened and overly inbred family tree, I would risk a guess that Miss Welty had read Grace Lumpkin's novel before writing *Delta Wedding*. Both Dr. Gregg and Troy Flavin are tough, earthy mountain men: the doctor a more complex and engaging figure than Miss Welty's overseer, who in a demonstration of managerial "firmness" shoots the finger off a black fieldhand when threatened during an altercation, exactly fifteen minutes before going to the altar with a daughter of the big house.

But if one must give a label to *The Wedding*, I would say it belongs in the tradition of romantic comedy: the tradition of Shakespeare's comedies, of certain novels of Ellen Glasgow and Edith Wharton. In its richness of character delineation and of texture, the ease and swiftness of movement, one is reminded also of *The Great Gatsby*, though its informing irony rises to no great climax of overwhelming tragedy as does the mood of *Gatsby*. The mood here remains subtly low-keyed to comedy, with the central entanglement in all of its spiralling relationships finally resolved in a happy outcome. This tonal unity contributes to an expectation, an emotional conviction within the reader that the lovers' quarrel will somehow be healed, the wedding *will* take place, even while the situation appears hopelessly deadlocked and tension mounts to the breaking point of everybody's nerves. One of the most interesting and engaging features of the story is the way in which the sub-plot, involving the children, contributes to the overall suspense. Meanwhile, at no moment in time or point of sequential development does the author's technique ever show through the delicately meshed weave and inter-weave of surface and subsurface action.

The Wedding, in sum, is a beautiful affirmation of the continuing vitality of the story teller's art. It is a ringing rebuttal of those who sing the decline of the novel and the "literature of exhaustion." If the modern novel since the fifties has, with few exceptions, languished in a condition of stagnation verging on *rigor mortis*—and few, I think, would deny that this is so—what the critics presiding over the wake fail to recognize is that "exhaustion" lies not so much in the form, as in the writers themselves. *For there must, first of all, be a story to tell.* People to whom things happen, a seeing eye, and a skilled hand to put it all together.

There is a Grace Lumpkin Collection now at the University of South Carolina, consisting of manuscripts, published and unpublished, scrapbooks, book reviews, and correspondence. The Collection was originally destined for Boston University, having been asked for there, but a nephew who is a faculty member at South Carolina felt that the novelist's papers should remain in the city most closely identified with much of her work, and where, besides numerous relatives, she herself is now living. Regarding this gift, Miss Lumpkin wrote the

Director of University Libraries: "I would like to make it clear that there are two distinct 'phases' to consider. First the Communist, and second, the return to God."[3]

The distinction is useful only in point of time. Like many other writers here and abroad during the Depression years, Miss Lumpkin came momentarily under Communist influence. But it is questionable whether she ever really accepted Communist ideology, the whole kit and kaboodle, at the hands of the truly dreadful bunch of bigots and rigid dogmatists she fell in with; her outward submission to party discipline seems to have resulted in an emotional block which backfired, all the more intensely by reason of her earlier docility. According to Whittaker Chambers, whose friend she was, she testified at a hearing that she had never joined the party, though had written for it under pressure, and broke with Communism in 1941. Chambers further states in his book, *Witness* (1952), that at the time he was preparing his own dramatic break from the party Miss Lumpkin, long a friend of his wife's, loaned him all her savings.

It was, at any rate, an experience both searing and damaging to her art. Exposure of an international Communist "conspiracy," real or fancied, is a soil so far overcultivated that it has little left to yield but briars and burdocks. Small wonder, then, that Miss Lumpkin's *Full Circle* is not a good novel. But in the quietly happy years at King and Queen Court House, rising at 4 A. M. and "working on until around ten o'clock," when after another stint with her manuscript she rested and worked in her garden, Miss Lumpkin recovered her "rhythm." "It is a curious fact," she writes, "that when I have followed a certain routine, what I call getting into my rhythm, a novel or a story is always better. . . . With this novel [*God and a Garden*] I am following the routine exactly . . . I write a chapter or a passage in pencil on one of those yellow pages used in lawyers' offices. Then I copy it on the typewriter, at the same time revising. Then I copy that copy . . . revising it. And sometimes I have to copy it again. I say this because it explains to anyone interested why I am such a slow writer."

She is usually at her best, when "writing about just people." And because she is a born writer and an artist, with two more novels in the typewriter, we may hope that she will turn from the self-enclosed world of private suffering under a mistaken loyalty to a political cult to resume writing about "just people." She has given us to date two novels which deserve to be considered classics, a number of distinguished short stories, and one long one which ranks with the finest examples of American short story literature. For these Grace Lumpkin should be studied in college literature courses, along with her Southern compeers: Eudora Welty, Katherine Anne Porter, Carson McCullers, Flannery O'Connor, and the too-long neglected Marjorie Kinnan Rawlings. I would hope that republication of *The Wedding* might see the beginning of a Grace Lumpkin revival.

NOTES

1. Grace Lumpkin's letters to me, here quoted from, are from King and Queen Court House, Va., 3 August and 11 September 1974.

2. From Stanley J. Kunitz and Howard Haycraft, *Twentieth Century Authors* (New York: H. W. Wilson, 1942), p. 860. Also *First Supplement*, p. 604.

3. To Kenneth Toombs, 22 June 1971.

A Postscript

By Grace Lumpkin

At that time when the title of the novel took hold I was washing dinner dishes in my tiny kitchen located in a small brick house that faced, across a courtyard, a large tenement on East Eleventh Street, in New York City.

My first novel, *To Make My Bread* had been dramatized by Albert Bein and opened in New York at the Broadhurst Theatre. Subsequently transferred to a downtown theater it ran for six months and was later sold to MGM, I believe mainly for its new title *Let Freedom Ring*.

I had promised a novel to a New York publisher, and was distressed because the fountain of inspiration remained dry as a desert. I might go into my workroom where my typewriter sat on the table, hoping for inspiration, but no matter how I tried, the machine continued to sit there: silent, indifferent and dumb. I had reached the place where I was ready to put the blame on the machine instead of on myself.

That evening I had two guests at dinner. As I returned from seeing them across the courtyard and on to Eleventh Street, I found that they had thoughtfully cleared the table and stacked the dishes, all well-scraped, in the kitchen sink.

"Now," I told myself, as I placed the dishes in a pan of hot water, "I am tired of trying to produce inspiration. Let it go. Relax."

Suddenly then, as I accepted defeat and surrendered, without any "hurrah," almost like catching a breath, a certain memory presented itself.

I was twelve years old and my beloved elder sister had just been married in our lovely old church and the guests were crowding our rooms for the reception. My dress was new and beautiful and the full skirt came to my ankles. The wedding guests were exclaiming at my appearance. Yet the anguish remained that had come in me on the preceding day when my mother had explained that my beloved sister would now have another and different life from ours; that she would go away with her husband and belong to him. I had asked her: "Forever?" and my mother had smiled and said: "Yes, forever," and continued to explain.

All this, even a keen breath of the anguish experienced as a twelve year old, came to me as I stood over the dishes in my little kitchen. And suddenly then, as I accepted defeat and surrendered, there came an upsurge of satisfaction that said: "Of course! This is it!"

I wiped my hands and went into my workroom, sat down at the typewriter and typed *The Wedding* at the top of the page.

Columbia, South Carolina
May 15, 1975

Textual Note

The text of "The Wedding" published here is a photo-offset reprint of the first printing (New York: Lee Furman, 1939). No emendations have been made in the text.

M. J. B.

Lost American Fiction Series

published titles, as of March 1976
please write for current list of titles